THE PECULIARITY
OF
Mr. Darcy's Mirror

By

L.L. Diamond

The Peculiarity of Mr. Darcy's Mirror

By L.L. Diamond

Published by L.L. Diamond

Cover and internal design © 2022 L.L. Diamond
Cover design by L.L. Diamond/Diamondback Covers
Cover photos: Big Magic Mirror by Mia Stendal, Regency Woman wearing printed cotton dress and a pink linen spencer by Kathy SG, Surreal Antique Old Clock by Mikhail Leonov courtesy of Shutterstock

ISBN-13: 978-1-7373356-8-9

Other works by L.L. Diamond include:

Rain and Retribution

A Matter of Chance

An Unwavering Trust

The Earl's Conquest

Particular Intentions

Particular Attachments

Unwrapping Mr. Darcy

It's Always Been You

It's Always Been Us

It's Always Been You and Me

Undoing

Confined with Mr. Darcy

He's Always Been the One

Agony and Hope

His Perfect Gift

That Perfect Someone

The Peculiarity of Mr. Darcy's Mirror

For Brandon.
Who could've known when we met
that the cute guy who always stole my hair clip
while we worked would turn into a
twenty-six-year romance and the father of my children?
Through basic training, PCSs, and deployments, we've
managed to grow together and most importantly,
love each other through the craziest of times,
even when we were upset with each other.
You still make me laugh, which was why I let you kiss me on
that first night. You were traveling when I thought up Ellie's
crazy journey, and since we are huge sci-fi/fantasy addicts,
I called you and recounted the initial plot in its entirety
while you drove. I never thought I'd write a sci-fi/fantasy story,
but you urged me to give the idea life.
This one is for you.

Chapter 1

29th September 20__

Like an eager child, Ellie Gardiner pressed her face as close as possible to the window in the hopes of catching a glimpse of the great house as soon as it became visible, stopping short of smashing her cheek against the glass. She'd read of Pemberley, of course. Landscape paintings of the great house online and in museums had fascinated her for as long as she could remember. The manor house was as well known as Chatsworth and had been in the news more than ever lately, but this was her first time seeing the place in person. Was it possible to burst from excitement? If so, she just might. After all, the house had been closed for decades. Instead of being lauded for its grandeur, Pemberley was considered a great mystery since it seemed to have been left in the lush Derwent valley to rot.

Except that now everything would change, and she was going to work there! Her entire body trembled with the idea, never mind that she itched to see the artwork contained within those walls, to make it as beautiful as it had been when it was first painted, to give people the opportunity to view those pieces as the artist had originally intended. She'd been dreaming of a job like this for so long. Talk about a dream come true.

As the taxi approached the stone bridge, the trees cleared, allowing the stately old pile to finally come into view—and what an old pile it was! The limestone exterior was weathered and streaked from pollutants in the air and the rain, and one corner of the house was in shambles, with scaffolding erected around the rubble in the hopes of repairing the damage. If the house had possessed shutters, they'd surely be dangling by a single nail.

What an absolute wreck! Reports of its sorry state hadn't been exaggerated, it seemed.

According to the news, a group of Chinese investors had purchased the estate with the intention of making it a tourist attraction, like one of the National Trust or English Heritage sites. They'd need to put a few million pounds, at least, into the restoration before they could open the place to the public. She couldn't wait to see how beautiful the house and grounds would be when all was restored to its former glory.

The long, winding drive brought them to a large entrance along the side of the house where the taxi stopped. "Well, here ya are, miss." The driver heaved himself from his seat and hobbled around to the boot.

Ellie pulled out her rucksack and threw it over her shoulder when she stood, the cool evening air fresh from the high ridges of the adjacent Peak District National Park caressing her skin. A faint hint of smoke tickled her nose. Someone must've lit their fireplace, though it wasn't even October. After she handed the driver the fare, she grabbed the handle of her suitcase and rolled it towards the door as it opened.

"I thought I heard someone out here," said the tall Black man who emerged from the door and stood at the top of the steps. "You must be Ellie?" He had one hand propped on his hip while the other was held up as though he was about to snap his fingers.

"And you must be Oliver."

"That's me. Just never call me Olly, and we'll get along just fine. I know it's all the rage, especially with Olly Alexander and Olly Murs, not to mention the footballers and rugby players using the name, but I just can't abide it for myself." He rushed down and grabbed the handle of her plus-sized suitcase. "Let me help you with that." Between the two of them, they hauled the bag up the steps and through the doors. "Good Lord! I've never seen one so large, and what'd you pack? The kitchen sink?"

Actually, everything she owned was in her bags. The woman who'd hired her said the position was long term, and she'd be living in the house, so what was the point of paying for a fully furnished flat she never used, particularly one in London that was overpriced and the size of a shoebox?

Once they were inside, he let go of her bag and made as if he was dusting off his hands. "Welcome to Pemberley, as it is. The house is in shit shape, but the contractors have been hard at work trying to fix the worst of the problems first. I know you couldn't miss the gaping hole in the east wing, which looks positively dreadful, but the house is in no danger of collapsing, so don't fret for a second about that. Just don't cross the yellow caution tape if you venture into that wing. That's the worst of the damage, so as long as you steer clear, you'll be right as rain." He waved her to follow. "Let's get you settled in, and you can get started first thing tomorrow. I'm nearly done for the day as it is."

He minced gracefully through several small and unremarkable rooms until he ushered her through a door where Ellie came to an abrupt halt, gaping as she took several slow and measured steps into the room. Bloody hell!

"It's incredible, isn't it?"

Her eyes traced over every inch of the black and white marble floors, the stonework, the sculptures, and finally, the frescoes that covered the ceiling and the walls around her. The photos didn't do the enormous hall justice at all. "It looks more like something you'd see in Italy than in a country estate in Derbyshire."

"Doesn't it, though? And there are painted ceilings and walls as well as portraits and landscapes all over this house in need of cleaning and restoration, and I'm chuffed to bits to finally have some help. Girl, I've been begging for you since I started two months ago!" he drawled as he took her by the biceps and gave her a dramatic shake. "I was beginning to think I'd drop dead of old age while still working on this place."

"It's just the two of us then?" She turned in a circle, scanning every inch of the architecture and artwork.

Oliver gave a beleaguered sigh. "Along with a housekeeper, Debbie, who keeps things in shape as best she can and wages a one-woman battle against the dust until everything can be renovated. It's just the three of us for now. I've tried to persuade them to hire my partner Lewis, who specialises in rare books, to catalogue the library, but they're not concerned with that yet, even though he's champing at the bit to get in there and see what treasures are hiding away on those shelves. In the meantime, we have a list of rooms we're to give priority so they can start tours of the house, but the structural work has to be addressed before we tackle the frescoes. If we get a shift of the foundation and something cracks—"

"We'll be back to restoring a work we already restored. I get it." She glanced back up at the ceiling. "As far as the order of the rooms, I suppose they can't keep pouring money into this place without seeing some sort of return."

"And they're already setting dates for that. The gardens open in the spring, and they're pushing to open the house for Christmas of next year. They want to decorate the Great Hall and the dining room for the Christmas holidays and give Chatsworth a run for their money. A little birdy also spilled the tea that the BBC wants to film a period drama here in a couple of months, but no one has confirmed or denied the report. Maybe we'd get more help if they did. Wouldn't that be fab!" He grabbed the handle of her suitcase and helped her pull it towards the staircase. "Come on. I'm sure you're knackered from your trip. I don't want you falling asleep standing up, now, do I?"

"I doubt I'll do that. More like I need to stretch my legs after the train ride from London. Are we restricted from any part of the house or the grounds? I'd love to go for a ramble around and explore."

"As I said before, the only parts of the house that are closed are in the east wing because of the damage. As long as you don't cross the yellow caution tape, you'll be okay. The gardeners ask that everyone stick to the pathways unless we're heading into the forest. There's a footpath up to the old folly on the hill, and I've heard there are several more paths that extend from there, but I'm not much for nature. The minute bugs or mud are involved, I'm out."

Ellie checked out her surroundings while she followed him down a long corridor. This place was a maze! What was she going to do when she had to figure her way around all on her own?

"We're in what used to be the family wing, the part of the house that's still liveable and where the fireplaces and radiators have been cleaned and repaired."

"So we don't freeze at night."

"It's draughty, as most of these old homes are, but you should be comfortable enough." He opened the next door along the hallway and held out a hand. "This is yours."

She lifted her eyebrows. The room was bigger than the tiny studio flat she'd had in Lambeth. "They don't care if we use the furniture?" That four-poster bed surely dated back to the 18th century and the bed curtains tied back at each corner had to be a hundred years old.

"Don't ask me. I was told to give you the room next to mine, which is the old mistress's chambers. This room was the master's, and as far as I'm aware, there hasn't been a master since the 1930s when the house was sold upon the last Darcy's death to a man who'd made his fortune in diamonds. When he died, his son inherited, but between the death taxes and his spending habits, he lost the house to the bank before he passed on, although as I understand it, he lived in London and never set foot in here. Even before the foreclosure, it was rotting away empty."

"I understand they had a difficult time finding a buyer."

"True, though some of the artwork could've been sold to recoup their money. Wait until you see the Canova sculptures."

"Canovas? As in multiple? There was nothing about that online."

"I don't think anyone knew they were here until I found them a few weeks ago. They were packed away in a storeroom downstairs. I was sceptical crates that large were used for household items, so I opened one or two. When I saw what was inside, I had some of the workers help me shift the rest so I could open them all. I'm guessing they've been hidden down there since World War II. They'll require a cleaning, but I haven't noticed any damage."

Her eyebrows lifted. "These houses were often used by the government. I suppose the household staff moved them to protect them."

"And to free up space for whatever they needed. One of the locals said the house was used as a hospital." He sighed and gave a dismissive wave of his hand. "Anyway, when we heard you were coming, Debbie ran out and bought some new bed linens and such, or you'd have been sleeping on a bare mattress."

"Is she here?" A woman poked her head through the door with a large grin before she entered the room and held out her hand. "You must be Ellie. I'm Debbie Fortin, the housekeeper."

"Then shouldn't you be Mrs. Fortin?" asked Ellie with a raised eyebrow.

Debbie waved her hand dismissively. "Only if you want me to look around for my mother-in-law, so please, call me Debbie. Has Oliver shown you around yet?" She opened the door closest to them. "This is the old sitting room for the master and mistress."

"I brought a telly so we have something to do with our free time." Oliver opened another door. "And this is your ensuite."

"You have a couple of towels on the shelf if you didn't bring any," said Debbie.

She poked her head inside and gave the sizeable room a glance. A door led from the ensuite into a large walk-in closet. "When were the dressing rooms updated?"

The housekeeper shrugged. "I believe one of the architects said these were first updated in the late 19th century. I'd wager they were renovated again before or after one of the world wars since people were still using the house."

Ellie shook her head. "Can you imagine deserting a place like this?"

With a chuckle, Oliver patted her on the shoulder. "If I had to pay the taxes, then yes, love, I can."

A few steps carried her over to the bed, and she ran her hand along the grey floral duvet, a stark contrast to the heavy gold draperies that hung from the ornate canopy on the ceiling and covered the windows.

Debbie stood in an almost prim manner with her hands clasped in front of her. "Waitrose and Sainsbury's are the closest and will deliver, as does the pub down the road and the curry house. You're welcome to anything in the kitchen until you can make your own order. Oliver and I usually plan meals in the evenings and on the weekend that we cook and eat together. Otherwise, we don't stand on ceremony." She peeked out the window through the heavy draperies. "I'll leave you to get settled in and explore. I don't know that I'd venture too far from the house if you decide to head into the gardens. It looks like it's going to rain any minute now."

"Thanks. I can't wait to get started."

"You have my mobile number," said Oliver, holding up his phone. "Ring me if you get lost."

"I'll do that."

Once the door closed, Ellie bit her bottom lip then covered her mouth with her hands, bouncing in place. She finally had a job—a paying job, not an internship, apprenticeship, or volunteer position. Sure, she'd taken those roles for more experience, but this was different. Everything she'd worked and studied toward was finally happening. She danced in place and stifled a squeal.

"Calm down, Ellie. You don't want to appear overeager." She opened the drapery to the window, coughing at the dust shower that followed. "I guess you can't get all of the dust out of something this old." She frowned at the scene outside. "Of course, the weather would be absolutely dreadful by now." The shower wasn't anything heavy, but with the dreary skies and cool temperatures, it was enough to keep her from exploring the gardens.

Once her suitcase was shoved into a corner and her rucksack set beside it, she opened the drawers on the dresser and the bedside table. The furniture was as much artwork as the paintings on the walls, and what about any treasures they contained? An old book was tucked under what appeared to be men's shirts in the bottom of the dresser, so she took the volume out and opened it to somewhere in the middle.

Ellie scrunched her nose and closed it. Ugh! She didn't want to read about someone dying today. No, she was happier than she could remember being since she was a little girl, and she wouldn't read something so depressing. Not right now. She had too much to celebrate. Perhaps she'd check it out later.

A sudden chill made her dig her cardie out of her bag and pull it on. An electrical socket caught her eye so she plugged in her laptop. Hopefully, the wiring wasn't so ancient it'd blow up her only belonging of any value.

As soon as that was settled, she poked her head through the door, then crept down the first staircase she found. At the bottom, she peeked into what appeared to be a storage cupboard. The next door brought her into another corridor, decorated with rich, albeit tattered fabrics on the walls and an occasional chair or dark wood table. She'd obviously passed from the servants' passages to the hallway used by the family and guests.

When she opened the next door, a huge ballroom lay before her. "Stunning," she whispered. She stepped inside, staring at the gilded ceiling, the chandeliers, and the richly covered walls as she crept into the middle of the room. With a girlish giggle, she curtseyed as the actresses did in those period dramas. She was unfamiliar with the dances yet still turned and twirled until her reflection caught her eye. What the hell? Was she hallucinating?

There she was, reflected in an immense mirror on the wall, only she wasn't wearing her checkerboard Vans and green cardie. Instead, she appeared as though she wore one of those Regency period gowns—the ones with the empire waists and long skirts, and rather than her usual ginger bob, dark mahogany curls were pinned atop of her head. The face was also not hers and wore a teasing grin, though the green eyes were eerily similar to Ellie's own.

She glanced down at what she was wearing: an emerald cardigan, jeans, and her black and white shoes. Her eyes shifted back to her reflection while she ran her hand down the front. The soft wool and cotton of her t-shirt rubbed against her palm, when in the mirror, she touched the flesh of her chest and the muslin of her gown. Her arms and the back of her neck prickled and her breathing quickened. What was this? Was she losing her mind?

With a shake of her head, she turned her back on the mirror. She was obviously more tired than she'd thought, or maybe she was coming down with something. No, she couldn't become ill! The last thing she wanted on the first day of a new job was to feel poorly.

Where was the kitchen? Perhaps if she fixed a cuppa and a sandwich then headed off to Bedfordshire, she'd be ready to go in the morning. Yes, a good night's sleep was exactly what she needed.

Chapter 2

"Good morning," said Oliver, lifting his head when she entered. Since she'd started at Pemberley two weeks ago, they'd been using a room near the kitchen, in the old servants' passages, as a workspace. The room was clean and renovated, with a multitude of windows on one side, so the lighting was good, and contained all the supplies needed to clean and restore the paintings that Oliver would bring down from the upper floors before they were catalogued and stored nearby until the upstairs was redone.

"Morning. Who am I working on today?" As much as she would prefer to pick and choose what she spent her time on, Oliver had been bringing her portraits from the gallery. She'd met a Georgiana and an Amelia so far, so when she walked around the easel, she was arrested by the intense gaze of the man in the portrait.

"Isn't he fit? I thought maybe you'd like a gorgeous hunk of a man for a change."

With a laugh, she tilted her head to study the gentleman before her. The men in these old likenesses had never appealed to her in the past, but this one was drop dead gorgeous, even with the overdone sideburns. Haunting, crystal blue eyes popped in contrast to his pale skin and dark, almost black hair. He wore a well-tailored black suit with breeches and the tall, black riding boots she'd once heard called Hessians. "Fitzwilliam Alexander Darcy," she read from the plate at the bottom of the frame, which also listed the artist. "He was quite progressive, wasn't he? He had Emma Crewe paint his portrait. I don't know much about her, but she was a woman. How many men in that day and time would commission a lady to paint their portrait?"

Oliver chuckled and shook his head. "A nice change from the Lawrences and the Gainsborough from last week. I thought you'd like that."

"I do, thanks. I'll have to do some research on the artist. The portrait seems well done, not that I know what the actual Mr. Darcy looked like. The painting itself seems to be in fairly good condition. The frame needs more cleaning than the canvas."

"I agree. I imagine you'll finish quickly, so we can explore and find another painting for you to work your magic on."

"You mean I get to pick?" She couldn't help the higher pitch of her voice. Most of what Oliver had selected so far were simple cleanings. She couldn't wait to get her hands on more of a challenge.

"I confess, I wanted to get to know you before I gave you anything too onerous."

"Didn't the recruiter give you my CV?"

"They did, and it was impressive for someone so young— The School of the Art Institute of Chicago and Northumbria University as well as your internships and apprenticeships, which is why I wanted to make sure you were all you claimed to be. I hope you won't hold it against me." The way he shrugged while he spoke combined with his arms crossed over his chest made her smile.

"No, I'm not upset. You don't know how often I get comments about my age. I should've expected it, really. My birthday is in September, so I started uni just before I turned eighteen and went during every summer session so I could graduate early, and the Northumbria program is two years."

"And now you get to restore this handsome bloke to his former glory."

She grinned. "Yes, well, speaking of that handsome bloke, I should get started, so we can search out a painting that needs some major help. I want to show you what I can do."

"Love, for a twenty-something little thing, you've already impressed me. Don't go biting off more than you want to chew. I'd prefer to get the easier jobs finished first. Then, when they open the house, we can move those in the worst condition down here and display what's finished." Oliver propped his hand on his hip. "I don't know about you, but I'm dying for a cuppa. Can I bring you one?"

"No, thanks."

Ellie sat down on her stool and picked up a soft brush, carefully wiping away any dust or debris before she started a more thorough cleaning. "So, Mr. Darcy. Who were you really? I read online that you were quite the recluse in your day. Were you rejected by your lady fair? Or maybe you were gay and refused to live a lie just to protect yourself?"

"Rumour has it, he grew bitter of society, so after his sister was married and settled, he withdrew from the public and lived a solitary life here."

Her head jerked up to Oliver leaning against the door frame, dunking a tea bag into his cup. "Where'd you hear that?"

"Barbara, the local historian, stops in every once in a while. She likes to see the paintings and talk about what she knows. A couple of her ancestors were housekeepers here. I think one of them even worked for this Darcy."

"How old is this woman?"

"Not sure, older, but a real spry thing, that one." He held up a finger and disappeared for a moment before returning with a steaming cup. "Anyway, the nephew took the name Darcy and inherited the house after Fitzwilliam's death. I'm afraid I only remember bits and pieces. I'll introduce her to you next time she pops by. You can ask her yourself. She loves talking about the history of the Darcys. She'll be tickled pink to share."

"Sounds brilliant. I'd love to hear what she has to say. Cheers."

Oliver sat down and started cleaning the statue he was working on with one hand while he sipped his tea with the other. Without the chit chat, she continued grazing the canvas with a soft brush as she settled in, though those eyes of Fitzwilliam's were certainly distracting. On occasion, she'd catch herself staring at his face and daydreaming, which was an unusual habit for her. She was typically quite focussed. Georgiana and Amelia weren't as unsettling. Why was that? After a shake of her head, she put on her dust mask and continued the job in front of her.

As soon as she completed Fitzwilliam's portrait, she wiped her hands on a damp towel and stood. "I think that's as good as he's going to get."

"Just lovely," said Oliver who stepped over and gazed at the portrait from behind her shoulder. "Let's take a look and see what we can find. So far, I've just been grabbing paintings that I like, but I couldn't resist taking that sculpture since I had you and Debbie to help me get it onto the cart and through the house. I've been itching to work on that masterpiece." He took her hand and pulled her up the closest servants' staircase and through a door into the main part of the house. "Have you seen the Constable yet?"

"There's a Constable?"

He brought her into a room covered in shelves with a huge desk—what had to be the master's study. She turned in a circle as she always did when she first entered a room, stopping at the pastoral landscape with a church to one side of the scene. "It's lovely, though a bit dark. Maybe soot from the fireplace?"

"That's what I was thinking. Can you imagine the colour that's hiding under that grime?"

After moving several small sculptures from the mantel, she reached for the frame. "Can you help me get it down?" She wasn't taking any chances she'd drop it.

With the painting well in hand, they started back down the corridor until they passed a familiar set of doors, and Oliver gasped. "Have you seen the ballroom?" Without warning, he grabbed her arm and tugged her inside. "Here, let's set the painting against the wall for a sec."

"I was in here on my first night. By the time you'd left me, it'd started raining, so I wandered around inside."

He gave an exaggerated bow. "My lady."

"Good, sir," she said, laughing. "You know I curtseyed and twirled the last time I was in here."

"As you should. This room needs someone to give it some love. These walls have been empty for far too long. And take a look at this mirror. I haven't checked, but it's got to be anchored to the wall. The thing is huge, like it belongs in the Hall of Mirrors at Versailles. It also looks new compared to the others in the room, but I'm willing to wager the top of that frame has layer of dust an inch thick. We're going to have to bring our supplies and ladders in here to clean it."

Oliver stood in front of the mirror and gave a graceful bow. He looked the exact same in the glass as he did in real life. Why was she so surprised? That was how mirrors worked, Ellie! She'd clearly been tired and seeing things. After a deep inhale, she stepped beside Oliver and lifted her chin. When her eyes met those in the mirror, she gasped. "What the actual...?"

"What's wrong, love?"

"Why do you appear normal, and I don't? Is this a prank or a trick mirror, like one out of a carnival?"

His brows drew together in the middle. "Ellie, what are you talking about? You look exactly the same. You're wearing that same cute plaid skirt, which I'd totally steal if I had the hips for it, and those white Dr. Martens are to die for."

"That's what I'm wearing, but that's not what I see when I look in there." She pointed to the mirror. "In the reflection I see, I'm wearing an ivory, empire-waisted gown and cerulean blue shawl. I swear I look something out of one of those Regency Mills and Boon novels. My hair isn't even ginger. It's dark brown and curly, and that's not my face. The only similarity is the eyes, which is bizarre. It gives me the heebie-jeebies."

Oliver pressed his palms to her cheeks then her forehead. "Are you ill?"

"I feel fine, but I don't know what's wrong with me." She gave Oliver a side-long stare. "Are you sure you're not playing some awful prank on me?"

"I swear I'm not, love. How would someone play a prank like that anyway?" He watched her as if she might burst at any moment. "Did this happen the last time you visited this room?"

"Yes, but I assumed I was exhausted from cleaning my flat in London and the travel. After a sandwich and a cup of tea, I went to bed and fell asleep the moment my head hit the pillow. I hadn't been back until today."

"Any family history of mental illness?"

"No," she said a little louder. "At least not that I know of, and I'm not stressed. I mean, when I see you in the reflection, you look the same. It's just me that's all wrong." An odd sort of prickle peppered along her neck and down her spine. That had happened last time. Why was she reacting this way?

She shook her head and grabbed Oliver's arm. "Let's go. I don't like it in here. There's something bizarre going on. Maybe the place is haunted."

"So, you think you're seeing a ghost instead of your own reflection?" Yes, his voice held a shedload of doubt, but what else was she to think?

"I don't know, but something is off about that mirror, and it's starting to freak me out. I mean, do you have a better explanation—other than mental illness on my part?"

Oliver sighed. "No, unfortunately."

"Help me with this painting. I want to get it downstairs. Whatever is doing this doesn't follow me to the other mirrors in the house or into my room that I've noticed, so I just won't ever come in here again."

"I suppose you're okay, as long as you don't start holding conversations with yourself or acting even more odd than you are now."

"I'm perfectly fine, Oliver. I'm no different today than the day I arrived. Can we just forget this happened?"

"Yes, of course. I've already erased it from my brain."

If only she could!

Ellie took a bite of her sandwich while she stared at the portrait in front of her. What was it about Fitzwilliam Darcy that fascinated her? Yes, she was taken by his eyes. Eyes that unusual weren't the norm by any means, and though they were unmoving, his gaze held hers and refused to let go. She was riveted. Her chest squeezed at the grim set of his mouth, which didn't appear happy, but wasn't sad either. At the same time, a dullness in his eyes could be sadness or boredom. Somehow, she couldn't quite believe that boredom was the culprit.

From the journal she'd found in his room, he put his people and Pemberley first, so she couldn't understand why he never married. Wasn't one of his most important priorities having an heir to carry on his line? Instead, he'd shuttered himself away at Pemberley and left the heir to his sister. Why? He had a huge estate and, no doubt, the money and influence that accompanied it. His uncle and grandfather had held the title of Lord Fitzwilliam, one of the richest and most influential earldoms in the country during the Georgian era, according to the internet. Ladies were surely lining up in droves for the opportunity to garner his attention.

The first entries in his journal described posh balls and those he encountered while attending. He hated all of it—he hated all of them. Even though he mentioned their exploits, and his objections to each and every lady pushed in his direction, from what she understood of the time, his criticisms didn't seem out of the ordinary. They were common faults.

What could've made him lose his patience with it all?

"Are you in here again?"

She ignored the slightly high-pitched tone of incredulity in Oliver's voice and swallowed her last bite. "It's quiet."

"And you have the portrait of Fitzwilliam." Oliver sat on the floor beside her. "If I moved this painting to another room, would I find you there instead?"

With a shrug, she sipped the last of her juice box. "Maybe."

"Oh, my God. Is that a Ribena? I haven't had one of those since I was like ten."

She snatched the box back from Oliver. "Hey, don't take the piss out of me for my lunch."

"Why shouldn't I? The next thing I know, you're going to pull out a Mr. Kipling's Vanilla Slice or some Hobnobs."

Laughing, she lifted one of the chocolate-covered oaty biscuits from the plate on her opposite side. "What's wrong with Hobnobs? Have you forgotten your inner child?"

"Thankfully, yes. I banished him fifteen years ago along with my Crocs and my low-waisted jeans, and I'm just too posh to go back there. Take me to a bakery or a tearoom for something homemade, but not that processed crap in a box."

"But don't you miss that taste from your childhood?"

"Remind me to take you into Buxton. There's a bakery on High Street that makes the most amazing Bakewell tart, and don't even get me started on their Victoria Sponge. You'll never eat those again." He pointed to her biscuit with his nose scrunched.

She rolled her eyes. "I'll happily go, but don't count on me giving up my guilty pleasures."

He gave an exaggerated sigh. "I suppose that's fair. Are you finished with lunch? Mr. Constable awaits, my love, and I'm more than ready to get back to Napoleon."

"You just find him hot."

He pressed his hand to his chest with an exaggerated sigh. "I do. I love his hair. My partner needs that Caesar hairstyle. He would look delicious. Don't you think?"

"I've only met Lewis the once, but next time he visits Derbyshire, I'll be sure to consider it." Oliver's partner worked in London at the British Museum. It was too bad the company didn't want to catalogue the library yet. Lewis would've taken the job in a heartbeat to be close to Oliver. The way they looked at each other when he visited was proof enough of their commitment. Oliver obviously missed Lewis, and based on their reunion last weekend, Lewis missed Oliver just as much.

"Well, I plan to keep pushing him to sort the library. Hopefully, he'll be up here by Christmas."

"That would be nice. Come on. Let's get back to work. The sooner we get going, the sooner we're done for the day."

Chapter 3

"All right, my lovely! Are you sure you can't be persuaded to join us? With the rain, you won't be able to explore the footpaths or the gardens. You'll be stuck inside all weekend." Oliver stood in the doorway of the sitting room with Lewis's chin on his shoulder. "We're checking out Castle Howard today and spending the night at a B&B in York. We're going to ramble around the Shambles tomorrow. We'll have a grand time."

Ellie set her hands on her hips. "I doubt the B&B has a spare room with so little notice. Besides, you don't want a third wheel trailing you around for the weekend. It's not like you get to spend a lot of quality alone time together. I don't want to crash your weekend together when you should have the time for yourselves."

"Ellie, we don't mind, really," said Lewis. "We both despise the idea of you staying here all by yourself. And the flat we reserved near the Shambles has a sitting room with a sofa. You wouldn't crowd us out if the place is booked up."

She hugged them and kissed their cheeks. "You're both too sweet to insist like this, but I promise that I'm fine. I don't mind my own company at all."

Oliver gave a low growl and took Lewis's hand. "Call us if you change your mind. We can help you arrange a train to meet us, or—"

"I won't change my mind. Besides, Debbie will be around."

"She'll be in and out, visiting her sister in the hospital. I doubt you'll see much of her."

"I'm a big girl. I can manage. So go." She pointed to the corridor.

Oliver exhaled with a growl, then pointed at her. "Okay, I get it, but you're not allowed to work over the weekend. Call a taxi or take the bus into Buxton, Matlock, or Chesterfield for something to do. Get out of this house and away from that portrait of Fitzwilliam. I swear you're obsessed with that thing. I'm going to go hide it before I leave."

She grabbed him by the sleeve and yanked him back. "No, you won't. You're going to go and have a lovely time with Lewis and try not to think about me or Fitzwilliam. Don't even think about the Canovas. Understand?"

With a sigh, his expression turned dreamy. "Now that will be difficult. You know how much I adore those Canovas." He propped a hand on his hip. "You'll call if you need us?"

"Yes," she said, giving him and Lewis a push towards the doors. "If I need you, I'll call, but that's not going to happen, you know. I've been on my own since I was sixteen. While I'm sure I'd have a wonderful time with the two of you, it's no bother for me to be by myself."

Oliver's lip pouted a bit. "You've mentioned that, but it doesn't mean I have to like it."

"Go! Have fun and bring me one of your gourmet sweets from some bakery in York. Okay?"

After one last kiss to her cheek from each of the men, she gave them a final shove. As soon as she had them through the door, she closed it behind them and exhaled. "Finally!" Not that she didn't like Oliver. She loved him to death, but he needed a weekend off with Lewis. They'd had too little alone time, and Ellie, who was accustomed to being on her own, hadn't managed enough.

She wandered from the side entrance to the Great Hall, but instead of going to the family wing, she turned at the top of the stairs and headed towards the east wing. On weekdays, the contractors could be heard on that side of the house, so she always steered clear, but since no one was about, she opened doors and peered into rooms. Several paintings caught her eye, so she set them in the hallway. She'd move them into the old kitchens when she had time. They should've been moved before the construction, but Oliver seemed to only grab certain works, leaving others to collect dust and grime or be damaged by humidity. Oliver wasn't to blame. He was one man and couldn't take care of the entire collection alone. The company should've recognised that from the beginning.

She entered a long room with a row of windows down one side and a large portrait of a man who looked a lot like Fitzwilliam but with dark eyes instead of that haunting blue she knew so well. "George Frederick Harold Darcy, Thomas Gainsborough." Oliver left a Gainsborough up here? Once she removed it and set it with the others, she returned and passed several spots where the staining of the wall indicated a painting had already been taken. As she worked, she made a point of avoiding those mirrors along her path. She'd started dodging those after the last foray into the ballroom with Oliver. Why tempt fate?

When she reached the end, she stopped at the last portrait. "Henri Louis Fitzwilliam Darcy, by Léon Coginet." By the dates, he must've inherited Pemberley after Fitzwilliam's death. What was it Oliver had said? Pemberley had been inherited by the first-born son of Fitzwilliam's sister. Had she married a Frenchman? The name Henri was French, and Louis was certainly used more in France. The artist was also French. If left to assume, it would seem he wasn't fully English.

Henri also looked nothing like Fitzwilliam unless one took into account that they both had dark curly hair. The nephew's complexion was darker with fuller eyebrows and poutier lips, and he wore a bright red cravat. Had she ever seen a red cravat in a portrait? She couldn't remember one. Was Henri more interested in his appearances and the social whirl of London or Paris than Fitzwilliam? Was he why the house eventually fell into disrepair, and the family couldn't pay their death taxes?

"If you were the reason, maybe I should leave you here to rot."

She shook herself. Where had that come from? Maybe it was time to go outside or watch the telly. She took the painting, then moved the ones she'd collected down to the old servants' hall, but on her way to her rooms, she stopped at the family wing and gazed up the staircase that led to places unknown. Before she could think too much about it, she continued until she reached the top where a door prevented her from going further. With a click, the latch gave easily, and she stepped inside, meeting a cobweb directly in the face. "Brilliant. Looks like I've found the attics."

After wiping her face clean, she turned, taking stock of her surroundings. More artwork: paintings, sculptures, and other bits and bobs were scattered around the large space, along with a few trunks and—Crap! How many mirrors were in this house? A tattered, old quilt was in a pile on the floor. She grabbed it and tossed it over the mirror that leaned against the wall before her reflection became visible in the glass. When she reached the other side of the room, she opened the first trunk and lifted the fabric at the top, revealing a dress that appeared Victorian with its high neckline and plethora of fabric on the voluminous skirt.

She moved onto the next, which contained what appeared to be British military uniforms. Likely they were left behind from whatever function the house served during WWI or II.

The last contained several books similar to Fitzwilliam's journal that she'd found in her room, as well as some small wooden boxes. When she opened the first, a pocket watch was nestled in a nest of velvet with "Fitzwilliam 1805" engraved into the back.

The next contained the most incredible and unusual necklace she'd ever seen. Silver was entwined and twisted into an almost choker style and wrapped around emeralds appearing like a vine with clusters of ivory pearls made to look like white grapes. "Beautiful," she breathed. With a gentle touch, she ran her finger along the emeralds. "I'd wear this if I had the occasion."

She tucked the boxes under her arm and brought them to her room. Oliver would probably roll his eyes at Fitzwilliam's pocket watch, but without a doubt, he'd be gobsmacked by the necklace. That needed to go in a display case somewhere when the house finally opened.

When she pulled back the draperies, she growled at the rain that continued to fall. Perhaps she should call the local pub for some takeaway. Some bangers and mash on such a cold and dreary day would do nicely, and with the pub's delivery service, she wouldn't have to find a way to pick it up in this weather. Perhaps she'd order something to put in the fridge for tomorrow since the rain didn't look like it was going to let up anytime soon. Debbie's sister was still in the hospital after her car accident the week before. They wouldn't be cooking.

Ellie pulled on her cardie and opened her laptop. After dinner, she'd open that bottle of wine she'd bought at Waitrose earlier in the week and sit in front of the fire in her room. Settling in for a lazy evening sounded perfect right about now.

Ellie took a sip of her Malbec and fingered the cover of Fitzwilliam's journal. While she'd tossed it aside when she'd first found it, she'd soon picked the book back up and given it a second chance, starting at the beginning rather than flipping to the middle as she had initially. Her biggest question was, why was it still in this room after two hundred years when the others appeared to be in a trunk in the attics?

This particular volume started at the beginning of the 1811 Season and covered each and every ball and theatre performance. The way he described his feelings and interactions were painfully awkward since he seemed to do all in his power to avoid conversation and any contact with most of the guests at each event. Before the Season had ended, he fled to Pemberley, escaping the last of his invitations for the peace and tranquillity of home. She couldn't blame him. If she found the Season and elite of London as insufferable as he did, she'd do the same.

She'd just finished an entry, dated in June, which told of his plans to visit his sister who was summering in Ramsgate. The portrait of Georgiana was one of the first paintings she'd cleaned and had been completed a few days before she'd started Fitzwilliam's. His sister had resembled him with the same dark hair, except Georgiana had the dark eyes Ellie now knew were inherited from their father. By the dates on the portraits, Georgiana was quite a bit younger than Fitzwilliam, but they seemed to be close by the way he referred to her in his writings, perhaps due to his becoming her guardian after their parents' deaths. Ellie hadn't checked the journals in the attics to see if they were dated earlier than this one, but she would at some point.

Discarding the book on the duvet, she rose and flinched at the mirror as she passed. "This is ridiculous." Ever since she'd visited the ballroom with Oliver, she'd balked even at the mirror she used every day to brush her hair and put on her mascara. Why? That reflection had always been her own. At this point, the only mirrors she could bring herself to use were in her ensuite and her room. She was too freaked out to look in the others.

She set her wine glass on the dresser and grabbed her phone. When she left the family wing, she turned on the torch she kept in her room as she started down the corridor. Not all of the lights and electrical fixtures in the house worked as they should, and she didn't want to drain her mobile battery with how much she used the light in the evenings.

In only a few minutes, she reached the ballroom. With a flip of the switch, the chandeliers flared to life, illuminating the huge room and glittering against the darkness of the windows. The room really was stunning, like something out of a fairy tale, as though at any moment, Cinderella would waltz by with her Prince Charming.

Her feet carried her directly in front of the enormous mirror. She half-expected to see her grey joggers and bare toes, but the reflection hadn't changed—it was the same ivory muslin gown, blue shawl, and dark mahogany curls. How was this possible?

With a slight tremble to her hand, she pulled out her mobile and aimed it at the mirror, but when the picture popped up on the screen, she wore her grey joggers in the reflection. What the...? The hand holding her phone dropped to her side while she continued to stare, leaning closer and inspecting her face...the lady in the mirror's face more closely. How was this possible, and why could she not let it go? Was she losing her mind?

She raised a shaky hand and stepped closer. What would happen if she touched the image? Would it feel like someone else or would her fingers merely graze the cold glass of the surface? The reflection moved just as she did, and when she stepped forward, so did her counterpart. She held her breath as her fingers drew ever so close. The moment her fingertips made contact with those of the reflection, a freezing shiver travelled through her body and pulled, then there was darkness.

Chapter 4

Ellie groaned and stretched under the warm covers. Why was her head pounding as though a hammer was trying to pummel a gaping hole into her skull? She hadn't been out in the wet and cold yesterday, but somehow, had she become ill? How much wine had she drunk? Certainly not enough to give her this bad of a head. With a palm pressed to her forehead, she paused. Wait! How had she gotten back to her bed? Ugh! Hopefully, Oliver hadn't found her passed out in front of that stupid mirror and been forced to drag her up to her room. He should've thrown a duvet over her and left her to sleep on the floor.

"Lizzy, thank God!"

She froze. Whose voice was that, and what were they doing in her room? And who was Lizzy? She cracked one eyelid. Bright, almost white light flooded her line of vision with the pale skin and blonde hair of a young woman hovering over her. Both eyes flew open, and she gasped. What the—? Who—? Her head darted in all directions. This wasn't her room! The walls were covered with a white fabric decorated with a muted green foliage. The sole window was covered in flimsy cotton draperies that allowed a fair amount of light to filter into the bedchamber. When her gaze returned to the blonde, the young lady stared at her with a creased forehead.

"Lizzy?"

She flinched as the bed dipped, then squeezed her eyes closed and breathed. Flinching had been a horrible idea. It only made the throbbing in her temples worsen! One eye opened for a peek. The same beautiful young woman still sat beside her, making Ellie squeeze her eyelids as tightly closed as possible once again. She was losing it! Had she any separation between reality and the fiction her mind was creating? This was all too bizarre for words.

A cool hand pressed against her forehead, just as Oliver's had a mere two days ago. She shifted away and gave the woman what was hopefully her fiercest glare. "Who are you?"

The lady frowned and moved her hands to Ellie's cheeks. "Why, Lizzy, it's me, Jane. Do you not remember?"

"Who?" Once again, she ducked back from the lady's— Jane's hands. When she jerked further away, Jane cried out and grabbed her just as she began to slip from the edge of the mattress.

"You truly do not remember, do you?"

"Sorry, but no." She wrenched her arms from the woman's grasp and crossed them over her chest, huddling against the headboard.

Jane's eyebrows drew together a bit. "Perhaps I should fetch you some water."

"Water sounds good." While Jane turned to a tray on a table against the wall, Ellie scanned the room once more. Where was she? Her gaze crossed back to Jane, who was wearing a dress similar to the one she'd seen in the mirror, complete with an empire waist and a long, flowing skirt.

When Jane returned, she handed Ellie a cup that she brought to her lips to take a large mouthful, but the moment the liquid touched her tongue, she spewed the contents all over the duvet. "Bloody hell? Did you put wine in the water?"

The lady's eyes bugged, and her mouth opened and closed several times. "Perhaps you would prefer tea," she said hoarsely. She hurried out, and Ellie glanced down into the cup before she set it on the bedside table. What was going on? She was in a strange room with a strange woman giving her wine mixed with water instead of a simple glass of water. Had Oliver sent her to some hospital? Good Lord, could he have had her committed? No, wait, that was a ridiculous notion. No hospital would give her wine. They'd be medicating her within an inch of her life. The nurses also wouldn't be in Regency Period gowns but wearing uniforms typical of the NHS.

She lifted the covers. They had a sheet and a duvet covering her, or was that a quilt? No one in Europe used a top sheet anymore. In fact, she hadn't seen a top sheet since she'd lived in America for university. She sat straight up and pinched the fabric covering her chest, rubbing the thin material. A white cotton nightgown? Who wore those except little girls with plaits and ringlets?

With frantic movements, she shoved off the covers and swung around, setting her feet on the cold wood floor. Mirror! She needed a mirror! Her legs were a bit wobbly when she stood, but she rushed over to the dressing table where she leaned close to her reflection, her fingers touching her cheek, then her nose, then her lips. She was dreaming! She had to be! Just like at Pemberley, the reflection wasn't hers. In fact, it was the same reflection as in the Pemberley ballroom: the same dark mahogany hair, except plaited down her back with a few curls escaping for fringe, the same pixie nose, the same vivid green eyes staring back at her. She reached back and found the long plait, pulling it around so she could see it with her own eyes. At Pemberley, the reflection may have been brown, but her hair was still its usual ginger. This time, the image that stared back at her was actually there—the image *was* her. Her fingers traced over the mahogany plait. She gulped and shook her head, hard, but when she lifted her gaze to the mirror, the image was the same.

"What's going on?" she said softly. She straightened and walked over to the window. The view that greeted her made her cover her mouth with her hand to stifle a cry. She may as well have been looking at a Constable landscape, one of his idyllic views of pastoral life. Directly outside the window was an apple tree, laden with fruit, while beyond, a hedgerow separated the garden from the property further afield where a man unloaded straw from a cart near the doors to the stable. Meanwhile, sheep grazed peacefully in a field further away. Where was she? Scratch that! When was she?

Her mind spun, her knees wobbled, and everything went dark.

"Miss Elizabeth?"

Ellie blinked and pressed her palm to her forehead. Why wouldn't that infernal pounding stop? Lord, it was miserable. Her head had never ached this badly before. "Paracetamol. Please, can I have some paracetamol?"

"I beg your pardon?"

That wasn't Oliver's voice. Her eyes shot open once again. That wasn't Oliver's face! She stared for a moment at the tall man who stood beside the bed. He wore a brown coat, and dear Lord, was that a cravat? This had to be a prank. Oliver was playing the worst joke ever on her, and she was falling for it hook, line, and sinker. "Where's Oliver?"

"Who? I am afraid I am not acquainted with an Oliver here in Hertfordshire."

"Hertfordshire?" She sat straight up, then pressed her hands to her head again. "How'd I get to Hertfordshire?"

"Miss Elizabeth, where else would you be?" The man's head tilted a little to one side.

She blinked and stared at him. Her brain was so muddled, she couldn't think. "Huh?"

The young woman from before, Jane, sat on her other side. "Lizzy, listen to me. You took a fall while on one of your rambles and hit your head on a stone. We have quite despaired for you. Mama has shut herself in her bedchamber with an attack of nerves that surprised even Papa in its severity."

"Miss Elizabeth," said the man. "Do you remember your sister, Jane?"

"Who are you?" she asked. Her fingers went to the back of her head where a lump the size of a cricket ball protruded from her scalp. Bollocks, simply touching it hurt!

"I am Mr. Jones, the apothecary. Miss Elizabeth?—"

Ellie started and looked up. "Ellie. My name is Ellie."

The man's eyebrows shot up onto his forehead. "Very well, Miss Ellie. Do you remember your sister, Jane?"

Her head hitched back some. Sister? She had no sister. What was she supposed to do? Whenever she was awake, she was living whatever life this was. Had whatever controlled space and time experienced a malfunction? Had the Matrix rebooted, and her file inadvertently sent to the wrong time and place? She looked at the blonde woman who had tears flooding her eyes. "Jane?"

"Yes, dearest. It's me." Those sea green eyes seemed to be pleading with her, but what was she supposed to say? She wasn't this "Lizzy." She was Ellie Gardiner. The problem was what would happen if she insisted upon her identity. If this was a dream, she'd eventually wake up and everything would be back to normal, but if it wasn't a dream…How was she supposed to go along with what people expected of her? She couldn't simply pretend to remember a load of memories she'd never experienced. Simple. She'd need to stick with what was simple for now. "How long was I asleep?"

"Three days." The man gave a gentle smile. "You gave your family a fright, though you seem to be no worse for wear now, except for the pain in your head and your memory loss. I have treated similar maladies due to this sort of injury. They seem to resolve themselves more often than not."

"My head aches."

"Some willow bark tea would be beneficial, I think," he said to Jane. "If that's not sufficient, send word, and I shall bring some laudanum for her."

Ellie waved her hand. "I'm still here, you know."

Jane took her hand. "Of course you are, dearest."

With a sigh, Ellie made to throw back the covers. Headache or not, she needed to get out of here. "I'd like to get dressed and go for a walk."

"Lizzy!" Jane shoved the quilt back around Ellie's waist. "You have been unconscious for almost three days, and you just complained of your head paining you. You have been exceedingly ill, and you must rest. Pray, understand we all thought you would die."

"And I'll be bored to tears if I stay in this bed for any length of time."

Mr. Jones chuckled. "See, she sounds more and more like the Miss Elizabeth we are accustomed to. Perhaps, once I have departed, you can help her to the chair by the window. The view may help settle her restless spirits."

The chair by the window? Um, no. She wanted to get outside and wear herself out so she would hopefully wake up back in her own time and her own body.

"I must be going." The man picked up a bag from the chair. "I promised Mr. Goulding some of my tonic for his gout."

"My family is very appreciative of all you have done for Lizzy, Mr. Jones."

"For now, if she insists on being addressed as Miss Ellie, I see no harm in it," he said as he stepped through the door. "Further agitation could only..." Jane held up a finger to her before she followed the man from the room.

Further agitation could only what? With a huff, Ellie jumped from the bed as soon as the door closed and teetered for a moment, pausing until the room stopped spinning. She turned with one hand pressed to her forehead. Why did that seem to help a little with the throbbing? "Clothes. Where would clothes be?" She lunged towards a wardrobe nestled in the corner and pulled the door open wide. One gown looked suspiciously similar to the ivory one in the mirror. Nope! She wasn't touching that one. The last thing she needed was confirmation that she was mad or that something not just improbable but impossible was happening. Besides, she had no interest in wearing that. It would be too odd to see her reflection in that again, so she opted for a floral-patterned thing hanging on a peg to the opposite side. When she held it up, the light shone through the fabric. She glanced down at the nightgown she was wearing. "Crap! Where are the underclothes?" The fabric was too thin to wear without a foundation of some sort. "Sod it!" Without further ado, she pulled the dress over what she was wearing but couldn't reach to fasten the back. Oh well! She had to get out of here before Jane returned, or she'd never go anywhere. At least this way, she was covered.

She put on a pair of what appeared to be tan ballet flats then peeked through the door. Voices travelled up from the foot of the staircase, so she crept in the opposite direction. Wouldn't there be a servants' passage somewhere? Pemberley had entrances in each of the bedrooms, but this house seemed a lot smaller. Perhaps they didn't have those extra corridors upstairs. When she turned the corner, she threw her arms in the air and mouthed, "Yes!" at the sight of a back staircase.

At the ground floor, a woman hummed in the kitchen as she stepped into the next room, giving Ellie the chance to dart across and through a nearby door, which thankfully, led outside. No one was behind the house, so she walked as fast as her legs could carry her to the hedgerow and ducked behind it. She took in a great breath and let it out. Her head still ached dreadfully, and she was somewhat dizzy, but she'd made it outside. Now which way to go?

In one direction, the stable was tucked back away from the house. In the opposite, a well-worn dirt path headed into the trees, so she opted to follow it away from the house and those who surely believed she was having a breakdown of some sort. When the pathway took her up a gradual slope, she continued on until the trees broke, and she stood at the top of a hill, looking out over the surrounding fields, some of which were still green. A stream flowed along to one side until it disappeared into a small wood dotted with some autumn colour. "Just lovely."

"Miss Elizabeth?"

Chapter 5

No, no, no! She pivoted around and almost fell on her bum at the sight of the tall man standing at the edge of the trees. How was this possible? It was him! It was actually Fitzwilliam Darcy—the one and the same Fitzwilliam from the portrait—the portrait Oliver had given her to clean. He was even more fit in person, his muscular thighs highlighted by those tight breeches.

"Fitz..." No, people didn't speak to each other that way. She needed to start being more careful before they locked her up in hospital here. They could lock her up, couldn't they? "I mean, good afternoon, Mr. Darcy?" Her eyes darted around. It was afternoon, wasn't it?

He gave a shallow bow and stepped forward. "We had heard you were grievously injured. I must say I am relieved to find you well enough to enjoy the countryside so soon after your accident."

Her head still pounding, she attempted a curtsey, but the dizziness became worse, making her wobble. "Reports of my possible demise have been greatly exaggerated." She gave an awkward laugh. Perhaps a modified Mark Twain quote would sound more normal to him than her own words.

His eyes narrowed ever so slightly and dropped down to her clothes before shifting back to her face. "May I be of aid to you? I would be pleased to see you back to Longbourn."

She shook her head, which made her squeeze her eyes closed for a moment. Why did she keep forgetting how much that hurt? "Thank you, but I'm fine here. I don't want to go home yet." Was Longbourn home? Never mind. She'd go with it and hope for the best.

Her head throbbed, so she pressed the heels of both hands to her temples and closed her eyes again. "Good Lord, I'd give my right kidney for some paracetamol." She stumbled and strong hands grasped her by the elbows.

"You are unwell. Allow me to help you."

"I don't want to go back. Please, just let me close my eyes for a moment. I'll be fine."

"Here, pray, sit. Perhaps resting will do much to remedy the pain." He steered her back and guided her to sit upon a cold surface. She opened her eyes and touched the boulder before clutching her head again.

"Sip this," he said.

When she cracked an eye, he was on one knee before her and held a silver flask. She had no paracetamol, so what could it hurt? She wasn't bleeding—not that she knew of, anyway. With shaky fingers, she opened the cap and tilted the container so the contents spilled into her mouth. After two large swallows, she paused and took a small breath before she downed the last in two more gulps. "Thank you."

Fitzwilliam gaped at the flask for a second before he tucked it into his boot. "Do you often drink brandy?"

Her chest had warmed from the strong liquor, making her cough. "My father would allow me a sip at Christmas, but that was a long time ago."

His eyebrows drew together. "You no longer continue your tradition?"

"No." She shook her head gently for fear of increasing the ache. "Mr. Darcy?"

"Yes?"

"What is today?"

"'Tis Monday."

"No." Why was she becoming dizzier? "The date? What is today's date?"

"Oh, today is the 21st of October."

She huffed. "You didn't say the year."

He blinked and watched her for a moment, his head slightly tilted. Why? Had she truly said something so shocking? Since she'd woken up, everyone was staring at her as though she were a bomb primed to explode. If she was going to survive this dream, shouldn't she know more of when she was? Not that she knew a great deal about day-to-day history. If it was art she needed to know, she'd be much better off.

"'Tis 1811. Do you not remember?"

"No. My memory is foggy, I suppose."

Those amazing crystal blue eyes she'd admired in his portrait softened. "You are not well. Allow me to return you to Longbourn."

She shook her head. What she needed was to get up and walk again. If she couldn't wear herself out, nothing would go back to normal. "Up." With a hand to the stone under her, she pushed herself to stand but teetered to the side, almost rolling off her perch.

"Miss Elizabeth!"

With a slight snort, she covered her mouth with her hand as she giggled. "I might be a tad pissed." Fitzwilliam hauled her back to her seat and kept his hands on her arms, steadying her. "And why does everyone keep calling me Miss Elizabeth?"

"Is that not your name?" His voice was low and oozed like warm chocolate. She'd imagined he had a lovely, low voice. She could listen to him for hours, especially when he spoke all soft as he was.

"Ellie." She meant to press her hand to her chest but ended up hitting her breastbone with a thud. "I like to be called Ellie. What was the alcohol content of that brandy? I swear, it's the strongest I've ever drunk."

He took her arm and wrapped it around his neck. "Forgive me for behaving so improperly, but I should ensure you arrive home without incident."

"Please don't make me go back. I don't want to spend all my time here in bed, and that lady...Jane, she keeps looking at me as though I've sprouted a third eye."

He chuckled as he lifted her into his strong arms, making her gasp and grab as much of the wool of his coat as she could manage. He glanced at her with a slight curve to his lips. "Miss...Ellie, pray, forgive me. I fear by trying to alleviate your megrim, I have put you in your cups. You cannot possibly be expected to return to Longbourn on foot in your present condition."

"Why do I have to go back?"

"Why must you return?" His tone was similar to a teacher's correcting grammar.

She gave a sort of growl. "Yes, why must I return?"

"Because Longbourn is your home."

Ellie scrunched up her face. "I don't have a home. Not really."

"Do not despair. What memories you have forgotten are due to the injury and will surely come back to you with time."

"The way you speak is lovely," she said on a sigh, leaning her head on his shoulder.

Another deep chuckle rumbled through his chest. "I am pleased you think so. Since you seem in a happier mood, I must apologise for what I said at the ball."

"The ball?"

"Yes. The evening before your accident, you attended the assembly in Meryton with your family, and I joined my friend Bingley and his family. I was of a poor disposition and insulted you within your hearing. Since your mishap, I have felt terrible for what I said. I should not have been so rude."

She blinked and lifted her head. "So you feel guilty because I almost died and you were mean to me."

"When you say it in such a way, I sound rather selfish, first insulting you then seeking forgiveness for nothing more than to alleviate my own suffering."

"Don't worry about it. I don't remember what you said anyway."

"But should you recall, do keep in mind I have begged your forgiveness."

"What did you say?" She rested her temple back on his shoulder. The throbbing improved when she wasn't supporting the weight.

"'Tis not important, I suppose. Has your head improved at all?"

"The brandy helped a lot, and as long as I rest against your shoulder, it doesn't hurt much."

"Well, that is excellent, is it not?"

At a loud squeal, Ellie squeezed her eyes tight. "Who is screeching like that?"

"Your mother is at the door with whom I believe is Mrs. Philips. Is that not her sister?"

"You're asking me?" She laughed, then groaned and pressed her hand to her forehead.

"Lizzy!" She'd heard that softer voice before. Poor Jane must've been searching everywhere for her. "Mr. Darcy, I cannot tell you enough how much we appreciate you returning my sister. I do not know what she was thinking, wandering off as she did, but at least she seems to have come to no harm."

"Mr. Darcy," said a masculine voice. Ellie opened an eye and shifted just enough to make out an older balding man with white tufts over his ears and a sort of crooked curve to his lips. "Perhaps you should bring my Lizzy into the drawing room so you both can tell us how you came to find each other."

"Oh! That wilful child! She has no compassion for my poor nerves! First, she takes a dreadful fall, making us all think she was going to die, then she runs off only to turn up in the arms of Mr. Darcy. What if word gets around that she is feeble-minded? What shall we do then, Mr. Bennet? I always told you she would ruin us."

"Blimey, stop that horrible yelling, will ya?" said Ellie in a moan. "The pitch is like a knife through my skull, and I can't take much more of it." Even though she wavered when Fitzwilliam set her on the sofa, she pointed at the loud woman. "And I'm not feeble-minded. *Mark but this flea, and mark in this, How little that which thou deniest me is; It sucked me first, and now sucks thee, And in this flea our two bloods mingled be; Thou know'st that this cannot be said, A sin, nor shame, nor loss of maidenhead—*"[1]

"We must thank you again for bringing Lizzy back to us." Why had Jane cut her off? There was still more of the poem she could recite. Not to mention, Jane had spoken so loudly it'd

---

[1] Donne, John. "The Flea." 1633. Poetry Foundation. https://www.poetryfoundation.org/poems/46467/the-flea. Accessed: January 11, 2022.

rattled her brain. That wasn't like Jane at all. Not that she really knew Jane well, but she'd seemed so soft spoken before now.

Two of the girls in the room burst into peals of laughter. "La! Lizzy, what are you wearing?" asked one while the other guffawed.

"Quiet, Lydia." The older man's eyes twinkled, and his slight smile had grown.

Fitzwilliam cleared his throat. "I found Miss Ellie at the top of Oakham Mount. She complained of her head paining her, so I gave her my flask for a sip of brandy. I had hoped the liquor would be of aid, but I fear she drank the whole of it before I could stop her."

The older gentleman chuckled. He was Mr. Bennet if the loud woman was to be believed. "She is not herself since the accident, but apparently, she is not so addled or in her cups since she is capable of reciting Donne. We beg your forgiveness and would be pleased to fill your flask before you depart."

"That is not necessary, but I thank you for your kind offer. I was simply happy to be of service to your daughter. She is not yet sure-footed, and I would not see her fall from the north face of Oakham Mount when I could ensure her well-being. 'Tis quite steep on that side."

Why was everyone else in the room so quiet? Ellie had leaned her head against the back of the sofa, but now she turned to see the loud woman staring at her with bulging eyes and an open mouth. Jane's expression was similar, the two girls in the corner covered the lower part of their faces with their hands while their shoulders shook, and a serious-looking girl with glasses watched her with her eyebrows raised. If Ellie had wanted to go incognito, she'd cocked it up somehow. She'd noticed worn volumes of Donne in the Pemberley library on one

49

of her forays around the house. Hadn't Donne lived long before 1811? Something in her brain niggled at her that he was 17th or 18th century. What else could it be?

"I have no wish to importune your family at such a time, so I shall leave you to situate Miss Ellie." Fitzwilliam bowed to everyone, then to her. "Miss Ellie, I hope you continue to improve and remember what you have lost. Good day."

As soon as Fitzwilliam departed, the older gentleman stepped around the sofa. "Come, my dear, let us get you settled. Jane has fretted for long enough; do you not think?" Without further comment, he lifted her, carried her to the same bedroom she'd fled a short time ago, and set her on the bed.

"Thank you, Papa," said Jane, who first removed the ballet flats and tossed them into the corner. "House slippers, Liz...Ellie? Could you not lace up your boots?"

"I found the slippers first."

"I brought you the willow bark tea. 'Tis likely cold by now."

Ellie took a sip and recoiled. "This is some foul shit. Will this truly work?"

When she looked up, Jane's eyes were bulging. "Ellie, ladies do not use that word."

"What word?" Ellie couldn't help herself. "Shit?"

Jane winced. "Yes, that one as well as the other vulgar expression you used not long after you woke. I cannot even imagine where you heard them."

"Okay, I'll try not to say them. How's that?" She tipped back the cup, downing the willow bark tea as fast as she could. "Vile stuff."

Once Jane helped her remove the dress, she tucked Ellie into the covers. "Rest, dearest. Maybe on the morrow you will feel and sound more like yourself."

Ellie's eyes fluttered. Perhaps on the morrow, she'd be back in her own time. She could hope, couldn't she?

Chapter 6

The light penetrating Ellie's eyelids told her she was still in 1811 before she so much as attempted to crack a single eyelid. The master's bedchamber at Pemberley wasn't this bright, even when the draperies were pulled back. Those heavy gold panels also had a musty, dusty odour that tickled her nose when shifted, but as worn and ugly as they were, a part of her missed the ragged old things.

She pushed herself up to sit and rubbed her neck as she sighed. Was she simply stuck here until whatever powers that be decided she needed to return to the future? What about her own life? What about poor Lizzy? Was she stuck in limbo somewhere, or had she moved forward in time, existing in Ellie's own time and place? Not that she had much of a life—a handful of friends in London and Chicago, though none of them much more than casual, and her job, of course. The problem was she loved that job. Sure, she'd only been at Pemberley for three weeks before touching that mirror, but she'd been in heaven. Art had been her passion since she was a little girl, first drawing then exploring museums in Europe and America. What if this Elizabeth Bennet tried to restore an important work of art and failed? Or worse, was committed for insanity? After all, if she travelled forward in time and insisted she was Elizabeth Bennet of 1811, people would question whether she'd had a mental break. This was a nightmare!

So, why was Ellie stuck in 1811? Could this have to do with cleaning Fitzwilliam Darcy's portrait? He had been one of the first people she'd encountered, other than Jane, at least. The only problem with that theory was Ellie first saw the odd reflection of herself on her first evening at Pemberley, which was two weeks before she ever set eyes on Fitzwilliam and his smouldering stare in that painting. So why was she here, at this time, with Fitzwilliam Darcy. That couldn't be a coincidence, could it?

"You are awake." She turned to Jane, who stepped through the door, closing it behind her. She set a tray on the table then sat down on the edge of the mattress, a wary gaze on Ellie. "How do you feel this morning?"

"My headache is still there, but it's a little better."

"Do you know who I am?" She handed Ellie a cup. "This is willow bark tea to help with the ache in your head."

After Ellie drank the bitter liquid down, she scraped her teeth along her bottom lip. "Jane? You are Jane." Was that what she was looking for or was there something else?

"Yes, dearest, but do you remember anything more?"

Ellie shook her head. "I'm sorry, but no." She remembered her own life but knew nothing of Lizzy's, so she wasn't exactly lying.

Jane exhaled with a groan. "I have worried of this since you fell asleep last night." She stood and poured two cups from the tea pot, added milk, then paused. "I feel I should enquire if you take milk and sugar in your tea."

"Milk but no sugar, please."

After Jane handed her a cup, she sat once more and took a sip from her own. "Your predicament has turned over and over in my mind. I am uncertain this is the correct course, but as much as it pains me to say it, we must concern ourselves with Mama's tongue."

"I don't understand." She, of course, had no idea who Mama was, but what could be wrong with her tongue? Had it swollen? Had she burnt it on tea?

With a sigh, Jane's shoulders slumped a bit. "I should start at the beginning, I suppose. My name is Jane Eloise Bennet, and I am your elder sister."

"So, I am Lizzy Bennet?"

"Elizabeth Elinora Bennet, born the 31st of May 1791. The older gentleman who carried you upstairs yesterday is your father, Mr. Thomas Bennet, and the lady you scolded for her loud tone was your Mama, Francis Bennet."

"Wouldn't they be *our* mother and father then?"

Jane nodded. "Yes, but that is not what we say."

"Why are you explaining all of this?" The question was reasonable. After all, wouldn't they expect her to remember on her own or something? That was what happened in books and movies.

"You heard Mama's mention your being of feeble mind. Do you want her gossiping of that to the neighbourhood? Forgive me if I am blunt, but we have always been the closest of sisters and in the past, have shared every confidence. I cannot imagine any of our neighbourhood being so cruel, but Papa scolded Mama at dinner last night, saying you and even our entire family could be ridiculed due to Mama's lack of discretion. While I do not want to believe Mama or our neighbours would do as Papa says, I admit I am worried."

Ellie hoped she wouldn't be here that long, but what if she was? Jane could be right. Weren't people with disabilities treated poorly during this time? "No, I don't want anyone mistreated, but what do you want me to do about it? I can't suddenly conjure up memories that don't exist."

"To prevent whatever possibility exists, I propose to teach you what you need to know so you may appear to remember—

until you actually remember, that is. Once your memories return, all will return to how it was."

This could work. It needed to work. The last thing Ellie wanted was to be confined to this room for the rest of whatever this dream was, or the rest of Elizabeth Bennet's life if she was truly in her place, however long that was. "Okay, deal, but I'm not sure about being called Lizzy. I've never been called that in my life. What if I don't answer to it?"

Jane tapped her lip with her finger. "We may be able to get that by, but I can promise you naught."

"Naught?"

"Nothing. In public, you may still be called Miss Elizabeth. I fear that shall be more difficult to arrange, but within our family party, I believe we can persuade even Lydia."

Ellie relaxed back into the pillows. "I suppose we should start with who I should know, so other than Fitzwilliam Darcy, Mama, and our father, who else was downstairs yesterday?" She took a sip of her tea and glanced into the cup. "This is good."

"I am pleased you like it," said Jane. "You should address Mr. Darcy as Mr. Darcy. Do not use his Christian name. We call father 'Papa.' The two laughing girls in the corner were our sisters, Kitty and Lydia. Lydia was the lady who mentioned that you were wearing your gown over your nightgown."

"And the one with the glasses?"

"That is Mary. I am the eldest, then you, then Mary, followed by Kitty and Lydia."

Ellie's stomach growled and she put a hand over it. "I don't think I've eaten much since I hit my head."

"No, you mostly had broth and bread yesterday. I am certain you must be famished. I shall ring the bell and have Smith bring up a tray."

"Can't I go downstairs? I don't want to stay here all day. My bum will be flat if I do nothing but sit in bed."

Jane looked at her oddly and set her cup on the saucer. "If your head worsens—"

"I will tell you straightaway. I promise."

"I *shall* tell you," said Jane.

"Sorry?"

"You have spoken in an odd fashion since you awakened. You must say 'I shall' or 'we shall' unless you are determined, then you may use 'will.' He, she, you, and they all take will."

"That's confusing. I've always despised grammar."

"Nevertheless, you must make an effort to speak as others do. People will take notice if you speak so." Jane took Ellie's cup and placed it on the tray. "Come, I shall help you dress. The less Smith hears of our discourse the better."

"Who is Smith, and why does it matter if he hears?"

"Smith is our abigail, or ladies' maid, who assists us when we dress. We know she will gossip of what occurs in the household, so we never speak freely in front of her. If she hears of any of this, she will tell servants from the other households." Jane pulled a dress from the wardrobe. "What would you call this?"

"A dress." Did Jane think her daft?

"A gown, a morning gown." She tossed it on the bed and pulled another gown from the wardrobe along with a few more items from the dresser. "Your stockings."

Ellie sat on the bed and drew up the nightgown. What the!—Had Elizabeth Bennet never shaved her legs? How had she not noticed before? Most of the time she couldn't tolerate letting it get to this point. Were Jane's legs just as hairy? How could she wear stockings without the thin fabric catching and pulling? Ellie started to check her armpits until Jane crossed her arms over her chest, waiting for her. With a start, she pulled the stockings up her legs, but when she stood, they slid down and made granny ankles. "How do you make them stay. There's no elastic."

"Your garters." Jane held up a pair of pale blue ribbons. "You tie them around the top."

She then helped Ellie put on a chemise, stays, and what turned out not to be another gown, but petticoats. After all that, she helped her slip the actual dress...gown over her head.

"Do you know what kind of fabric this is?"

"It feels like cotton, so muslin?"

"Yes, it's a sprigged muslin because of the leaf pattern embroidered into it," said Jane with a nod. "You are fond of green and nature, which is why you picked these wallcoverings from our uncle's warehouse, as well as this fabric."

Once the back was fastened, Jane steered her to sit at the dressing table while she removed the plait from Ellie's hair, brushed it, and wound it up so the curls were displayed just so on top of her head. The entire time, she spoke of the servants at Longbourn and the different rooms. She tossed Ellie a pair of slippers similar to the ones from the day before. "Wear these. When we are downstairs, consider each and every word you say and try to mimic me. Can you do that?"

"I'll do my best. If I fail, you won't lock me up like Mrs. Rochester, will you?"

"Who?"

"It's from a novel, Jane Eyre."

"I have never heard of Jane Eyre." She took Ellie by the arm and tugged her towards the stairs. Why was she so nervous all of a sudden? This wasn't her family. If everything worked out, she wouldn't be staying. If only she could somehow go to Pemberley and touch that mirror. She'd probably zip right back to the future without any problems.

When they stepped into the dining room, Jane steered her to the chair closest to Mr. Bennet, so she sat. "Good morning, Papa."

"Good morning, Lizzy, or are you still insisting upon Ellie?"

"I prefer Ellie."

He watched her for a moment, then nodded. "You were always getting some odd notion into your head. I suppose I should not be surprised by this. I hope you will give an old man some time to adjust."

"Of course." She looked to Jane, who smiled and gave a subtle dip of her chin. Okay, she could do this.

Jane poured her a cup of tea from the pot on the table and held a plate in front of her. "Muffin?"

"Thank you." She took it carefully with her fingers, waiting for someone to object, but no one seemed to notice anything odd. Her neck and back muscles, which had been twisting and squeezing, ceased their torture and let her relax for a moment. While everyone ate, the two youngest, Kitty and Lydia, giggled and whispered. The name John Lucas was said loud enough to be heard at one point, but they clapped their hands over their mouths, tittered, and continued. Mary, the one with the glasses, read from a book while she picked at her own muffin.

"Likely Fordyce's sermons," whispered Jane from beside her. Sermons? Ellie'd never heard of Fordyce but reading sermons sounded dull as dirt.

Mrs. Bennet, meanwhile, began to rant about whatever gossip a woman named Mrs. Philips had told her the day before, prior to the arrival of the "disagreeable" Mr. Darcy in her drawing room. Mr. Darcy disagreeable? "He was very kind." Ellie almost swallowed her tongue when Mrs. Bennet's head swung to her, her lips tight and her face pinched.

"Kind?"

"You must admit, Mama, he returned Ellie to us and prevented her from being injured further. We owe him a great debt." Jane looked at her and gave a slight one-shouldered shrug.

The lady scoffed and rolled her eyes while chewing loudly. "He carries you from Oakham, and you forget all about his insult at the assembly, then, do you?"

"He apologised for his behaviour."

Mrs. Bennet rolled her eyes. "Did he now? Well, I still think him ill-mannered indeed. You do remember that he sat by Mrs. Long for a half an hour at the assembly and never spoke one word. No, he will need to do more than apologise to make up for his slight to you. A daughter of mine, merely tolerable." She huffed. "I still believe it would be quite a misfortune to be liked by him."

"Mama, do not forget he has ten-thousand a year." Jane nudged Ellie with her elbow.

"For such a great sum, I suppose I could tolerate him for one of you, though I still say Mr. Bingley suits you best, Jane. He is so amiable." Mrs. Bennet said the last as if the man had flirted with her and not Jane.

"I would not want such a proud man," said Lydia, "I should prefer any man wearing a red coat." She and Kitty tittered. "The uniform serves to make any gentleman a great deal more handsome and agreeable, does it not, Mama?"

"Oh, it does! It does!"

When they finished their breakfast, Jane led Ellie into the drawing room and handed her fabric secured in a hoop with a needle.

"What is this?"

"Your needlework. You were embroidering your initials and a sprig of lavender on this handkerchief." Ellie studied the evenness of the stitches and the overall effect. She'd known a girl at uni who'd loved embroidery. While Ellie despised it and found it mind-numbing, she'd still learnt a bit about the art, and if she had to guess, she'd assume Elizabeth Bennet wasn't overly fond of needlework either. Some stitches were tighter than others or larger, and the back was messier than it should've been. Ellie set the fabric beside her. "I'm not sure my headache will allow it."

"Do you need to rest?"

"No, I just don't want to do this." She stood and walked to the window. Behind the hedgerow, the trees were full of autumn colour, and their branches swayed with a light breeze. She'd much prefer to be outdoors, but after yesterday, she couldn't imagine Jane allowing her out of her sight.

With a drawn-out sigh, she stepped behind Kitty, who sat at a small table with paper, sketching a pear that sat on the surface beside her, the light from window giving great depth and shadow to the subject. Ellie frowned as she glanced back and forth from the fruit to her sketch.

"Try making the shadow a little darker as well as increase the contrast where the pear meets the wood. This area here is much darker than what you have." She showed Kitty with a finger next to the shadow.

Kitty stared up at her with wide eyes.

"The proportions and the shape are good. You're missing some shading is all."

"If you know so much, why do you not draw something, Lizzy?" Lydia's tone held a note of challenge, making Ellie's spine stiffen. She'd never backed down from a reasonable dare.

"May I have a piece of paper?" She pointed to Kitty's supplies as she sat to the opposite side so she didn't interfere with the light for Kitty's practice. The girl passed over a sheet of paper, and Ellie touched the different implements. There was what appeared to be charcoal, chalk, and was that graphite wrapped in twine? An art history teacher had once mentioned what graphite was called before the invention of the modern pencil, but she couldn't remember. "What do you call this?"

"Black lead," said Kitty. Yes! That was it!

"May I use it?"

Kitty nodded. "Of course, I have another I can fetch from my bedchamber. I also have a board if I want to tilt the paper to better see my subject. Mr. Hill made it for me. You may use it if you wish."

"Thank you." Ellie accepted the board and situated the edge in her lap with it propped against the table. Now, what to draw? She peered around the room, passing over the paintings on the wall, a small sculpture on a dais, and a vase or two before she was distracted by Lydia laughing at her.

"Lydia, hush," said Jane.

When Jane settled back with her sewing, she held still and steady, which was always preferable in a model. Without searching further, Ellie set the graphite to the paper and made the first light marks. Just like always, she zoned out while she sketched, letting the lines and shading of her subject rule the strokes of her pencil until a gasp came from near her ear, making her jump. "Lizzy! That is incredible!"

Lydia scoffed. "Lizzy has never drawn before. It cannot be *so* brilliant?"

Mary came to her shoulder and gave a swift gasp. "'Tis Jane. How did you capture her likeness so perfectly?"

With a crinkled forehead, Jane stood and walked around behind her. "How...?" She looked at Ellie as though she were a stranger.

"What has Lizz...Ellie done that has you all so entranced?" asked Mr. Bennet as he entered. When he stepped behind her, he set his hand upon her shoulder and squeezed. "'Tis a remarkable likeness. How have you never shown us this talent before, my child?"

"I don't know." This wasn't good. Maybe she shouldn't have taken up a pencil. The last thing she needed was for this to give herself away. Everyone seemed more shocked than she would've expected for a simple drawing.

He shook his head and patted her shoulder this time. "Do not fret about remembering. Since you show the inclination now, I shall pen a letter to your Uncle Gardiner to procure you your own supplies. Would that be acceptable?"

Her shoulders relaxed, and she breathed a bit easier. "I would like that. I would like that very much."

Chapter 7

Fitzwilliam Darcy steered Lysander through the trees. This morning, he had set out determined to gallop unfettered across the fields in order to clear his mind, but instead, he found himself in this wood at the base of Oakham Mount, picking his way up the path to the top. Why was he here? What a foolish question! He knew exactly why he had steered Lysander in this direction. The reason was the same as yesterday, and the day before, as well as every day for the past week. He hoped to see Elizabeth Bennet, or should he still call her Ellie Bennet?

He had been compelled by some mysterious desire to visit the well-known hilltop the day he had found her, alone, and in such a peculiar state. His story of wishing to beg her forgiveness for what had occurred at the assembly had been true, though not a tale he had ever planned to tell a living soul, including her. After the whispers in the assembly room of "ten-thousand pounds per annum" and "a great estate in Derbyshire," he had meant to put the first lady who showed even the slightest hope in her place. Why would he not? He had always despised the attention his income and estate brought him; however, he had not counted on the flare of her emerald green eyes and the way she had appeared to mock him after. When word reached him of her accident, the remembrance of his words and haughty behaviour had plagued him. He had been intemperate and cruel to call her 'tolerable but not handsome enough to tempt me.'"

When he met her again upon the crest of this very hill, he had wished to be of aid to her, but he had not counted on what had occurred next. Those same green eyes looked directly into his, but in some eerie way they were different—they were somehow altered since the ball. He could not explain the difference except that some inherent quality they had previously held had disappeared and another distinctive quality had taken its place.

The way she spoke intrigued him as well. Could her sudden want of pretentions and polish be a result of her lack of memory or have the same cause as the change in her eyes? Whatever the reason, he had been fascinated by the differences, not to mention her lack of artifice and her earnestness that existed without the silliness of her younger sisters or the haughty vanity of his aunt. Had anyone ever been so free with their thoughts and feelings while in his company? Georgiana never exhibited such little restraint, particularly since her heartbreak at Wickham's hands during the summer. His young sister was even more guarded than before, and her severe reserve pained him.

Since the incident at Ramsgate, he was exhausted—tired of the pleasant behaviour he was forced to assume every moment he was in company. He was weary of the Season and all that accompanied it. To tell the truth, he had been weary for the past few years. He was not a prize bull up for auction but a human being with thoughts and feelings, and the longer he endured, the more embittered he became. How did those of his circle cope with a marriage of convenience? He could not imagine such an arrangement. He never could.

Lysander nickered, so he stopped. Was that humming? He dismounted and led his horse through the last of the trees, emerging at the small clearing at the top where Elizabeth Bennet sat on a large rock, scribbling in a book upon her lap. He paused and admired the curve of her neck and the sunlight bringing out the copper highlights in her hair. Was she writing in a journal? No, she had no ink well, and what she held was not a pen.

When she looked up, she gasped and jumped to her feet. "Mr. Darcy!"

A part of him wanted to sag at her formal tone. "Miss Elizabeth." He draped Lysander's reins across a low tree limb and stepped forward to bow. She gave a slight flinch, made to curtsey, but not with the same grace she had managed while dancing at the assembly. "Forgive me if I startled you."

"Not at all." Her lips curved in an alluring manner. "I don't own the view, so anyone who wants may...partake of it."

He stepped forward. "I hope your head has improved since last we met."

"Yes, the willow bark tea has helped with the ache, and the dizziness mostly comes when I overdo."

The manner in which she spoke was similar to their last meeting, yet improved in some ways. With narrowed eyes, he stopped a foot or two in front of her and held her gaze. At first glance, her irises were the same rich green as before, but as he took a moment more and delved a bit deeper, his heart leapt in his chest. The change was still present, concealed just below the surface. "You have not regained your memories as yet."

Her chin hitched back. "How could you...?"

"I cannot explain fully, but your speech—"

"Yes, Jane is attempting to correct that, but we have only a certain amount of time each day where we are alone."

He frowned. "May I ask why?"

"Why we are only alone for such a short period of time each day, or why we are correcting my speech?"

"The latter," he said.

"Jane fears Mrs. Bennet...Mama may harm the family by telling all in the village and beyond that I'm feeble-minded. Our mother is a huge gossip, it seems."

With a nod, he clasped his hands behind his back. "Miss Bennet has good reason to be concerned, though I hope she does not alter you too severely. I must admit, I enjoyed our conversation when last we met."

Miss Elizabeth spluttered out a laugh. "Are you serious? I was a bit gormless until you got me pissed, and according to Jane, I speak as though I live in the worst parts of London."

He shook his head. "I meant nothing more than I enjoyed your honesty. Few in our world speak what they mean or feel with any truth behind the words, and I do not appreciate the manner of many for that reason. Our discourse now is far too open and improper by the standards of most, yet I find I wish to continue. Keeping myself under such strict regulation has become tiresome. I have come to despise London and those whose company I am supposed to seek, even those who aspire to travel in those circles. My friend, Bingley, is more open with his behaviour than most, which is why I enjoy his company."

"Well, I must pass for a lady of standing, whatever that means. I don't want to do anything to hurt Jane. She's been brilliant since I woke up here. I could not have done without her."

Woke up here? Had she added the "here" as part of the recent oddity to her speech? He had to assume so. "May I?" He pointed to the book on the rock beside her gloves and bonnet.

"Um, sure," she said with a shrug of her shoulders.

With careful hands, he removed the stick of black lead from the top and lifted the book by the edges to keep from smearing her efforts. "This is good—extremely good. Have you ever studied under a master?"

"In a manner of speaking." She spoke hesitantly but did not elaborate.

He glanced back and forth at the view from the top of Oakham Mount to its impression on the paper: the fields and stream, and the shadow of Netherfield in the distance rendered with great skill upon the page. The details and shading of the trees and the shadows of the clouds upon the ground brought the sketch to life despite the monochromatic colour palette. She was talented—talented indeed. "Perhaps I should commission you to paint Pemberley. I believe you would have done my home more justice than the artist my father commissioned in his lifetime.

Her cheeks turned pink, and she scraped her teeth over her bottom lip. "I am not terrible at landscapes, but I prefer a different type of subject." She shifted closer and turned back to the beginning, pulling out a paper she unfolded with care.

A sharp inhale escaped before he could prevent it. "You have done a remarkable job of capturing Miss Bennet."

"If you turn the page, I also have one of Mr. Ben...Papa. I also started a sketch of Kitty this morning, but I haven't finished yet."

When he turned the page, the completed drawing of Mr. Bennet, though smaller, was as incredible as the likeness of Miss Bennet, from the crinkling around his eyes when he smiled to the individual hairs in the tufts over his ears.

"After I sketched Jane, Mr. Bennet sent what he called an express to London for supplies, which arrived the next evening. I don't believe I've ever received a parcel so quickly."

He passed the sketchbook to her. "I hope to see more of your efforts in the future. You are quite accomplished."

"Thank you," she said softly.

"Have you ever been to an exhibition in London at the Royal Academy or the British Institution?" He could just imagine her viewing the works with an eager eye. Her opinions would be decided on which were her favourites as well as what she could not like. He would relish hearing her thoughts on each and every one.

"Not recently. I should love to go, but I doubt Jane will let me out of her sight until I can behave as a proper lady."

He closed the book. "Then perhaps I could be of aid."

Miss Elizabeth—or did she still wish to be called Ellie?—lifted an eyebrow as she set the sketchbook he returned to her on the rock. "How would you do that?"

"Well, your curtsey."

She groaned and covered her face with her hands. "Is it really so bad?"

"No, but you are thinking too much about what is expected of you, so the movement fails to be unaffected." He backed from her. "When we greet each other, our formal names are used. Your 'good day, Mr. Darcy' was appropriate, but you hesitated on your curtsey and your foot did not slide back with so little effort as it should."

"So, I would say, 'Good day, Mr. Darcy,' then..."

"You allow me to greet you. Good day, Miss Elizabeth."

"Please, I am Miss Ellie. I am afraid I won't...shall not respond to Miss Elizabeth. Mr. Bennet and Jane believe my preference has changed from taking such a severe blow to the head."

"Do you say 'please' because you wish me to address you as such?"

"Yes, is that wrong?"

"Use 'pray' instead. Pray, address me as Miss Ellie. That will *please* Miss Bennet." He dipped his chin. "Do you understand?"

"Please has only the one meaning? Jane never mentioned that. She has said to try to speak more like her, which I am attempting. The adjustments are more difficult when I do not have her to follow."

"I am certain it is."

Lysander neighed, and Miss Ellie gasped. "Oh, he is lovely. I assume it's a 'he' isn't it? Forgive me. I don't know much about horses."

He chuckled and glanced over his shoulder at the great black stallion. "Yes, he is a 'he.' Would you care to pet him?"

Her head shook rather vehemently. "I've seen horses, of course, but I've never ridden or been close enough to touch one. I find them intimidating."

"For a stallion, Lysander is very even-tempered. Come, you should make his acquaintance. The introduction may be of aid when you are near a horse in the future."

She took slow steps down to where his horse awaited him but lagged behind, stopping four feet behind him with her hands clasped together. "Give me your hand." When he reached back for her, his palm met hers, and a jolt shot through his glove, travelling through his wrist and into his shoulder.

With a gasp, she snatched her bare hand back. "This may be a bad idea."

Ignoring the shock, he carefully wrapped his fingers around hers and tugged her forward until he could place her palm upon

Lysander's nose. After a swift inhale, she stroked the horse's muzzle gently. "The skin here is soft. Why did you name him Lysander?"

"*A Midsummer Night's Dream* is my favourite of Shakespeare's comedies. Most of the horses at Pemberley are named for characters in Shakespeare's plays, Greek gods, or creatures from mythology."

"I do not enjoy most of Shakespeare's tragedies, but I do like *Twelfth Night* and *Much Ado About Nothing*."

He could not help but smile. "Then you should have a mare named Viola."

"Oh, I don't ride though," she said.

"You could learn."

"Maybe, some day." She moved her hand between the stallion's eyes and stroked down to the nose, but Fitzwilliam caught her hand before she reached Lysander's lips. "Always take care around his mouth. If you flatten your hand like so..." He brushed her fingers so they were extended and together. "He will nuzzle it." Her breathing quickened, her chest rising and falling at a faster rate than before while her hand trembled.

"It tickles."

"Hmm?"

She glanced back at him over her shoulder. "His lip. It tickles when it brushes my palm.

He straightened her fingers. "Never curl them, or you give the horse an easy method to bite them."

"Couldn't he bite me like this?"

"He could, but 'tis more difficult for him."

"*And indeed, a horse who bears himself proudly is a thing of such beauty and astonishment that he attracts the eyes of all beholders. No one will tire of looking at him as long as he will display himself in his splendour."*

"I am unfamiliar with that verse."

She scratched Lysander's cheek as she tilted her head so she looked in his direction. "That was by the Greek philosopher and historian, Xenophon of Athens."

"You are an intriguing lady, Miss Ellie. First you quote Donne and now a Greek philosopher—"

She squeezed her eyes closed. "Do not remind me of the Donne. Papa laughed and laughed at my expense over the subject of that poem. I had not realised it would be considered scandalous for me to say."

He grinned and patted Lysander on the neck. "I believe you can be forgiven, considering the sizeable amount of brandy you enjoyed when combined with your lack of memory before I carried you home. Your accuracy was most impressive given your state. Your father's wide eyes were rather humorous as well. I believe no one ever expected you to know much less quote such a poem."

"Would *you* want your sister to recite that poem in public?"

"How do you know about Georgiana?"

Her mouth opened and closed two or three times. "I was speaking in hypotheticals, of course." He watched her for a moment. At times, she spoke as though she could remember the entirety of her life, though her memories were not Miss Elizabeth's, and now, she avoided his eye when he questioned her about Georgiana. Was she telling him a falsehood? If so, why?

"No, I would not wish for Georgiana to speak so in company, but you, Miss Ellie, are not my sister." Thank God for that!

L.L. Diamond

Chapter 8

Ellie gripped the ribbons of her reticule, as Jane called it, as she stepped down from the carriage, a new experience she couldn't imagine repeating. How did people travel that way? The thumping and bumping down the road were enough to rattle her brain without a fall, and the ride was only six or seven minutes at the most. Her bum! Her poor bum would never be the same. The last thing she could imagine was a road trip. She'd be sore for weeks. "I'm nervous. What if I cock it up?"

"What if you make a mistake?"

She gave a slight growl under her breath. "Yes, what if I make a mistake."

"Then do not fret and continue on as if naught is amiss. If you are unsure, a second's delay may be beneficial in remembering the information you require or to overhear what is necessary for your purpose. I promise I shall not go far."

"Jane!" Mrs. Bennet grabbed her eldest daughter by the arm and dragged her back. "You must find some way to be in Mr. Bingley's society tonight. Do not forget!"

"Mama, I promised Ellie to remain with her."

"Then how will you capture Mr. Bingley? He showed you preference at the assembly, but you must keep him interested, particularly since we have been unable to return his sisters' call thus far."

"Come, Mrs. Bennet," said Mr. Bennet as he dragged her ahead of them.

"She has not stopped talking about Mr. Bingley for the past two days. Why is she so determined you marry him?"

Jane sighed. "Since Mama never bore a son, Longbourn is entailed to a male cousin, so when Papa dies, we shall be forced

73

to survive on no more than Mama's settlement and the generosity of our relations. She only wants us to wed for our own security, and Mr. Bingley is a very eligible prospect. We do not have many of those visit our small neighbourhood." Jane spoke in low tones next to Ellie's ear as they approached the door, which was opened by a servant. A heavy-set man stood in the entry and pressed a hand to his stomach with a wide grin.

"Mr. Bennet, Mrs. Bennet, so good of you to come. With the accident, my wife and I thought you may remain at Longbourn. How is Miss Eliza faring?"

"You may see with your own eyes, Sir William," said Mr. Bennet, gesturing behind him.

"Ah! Miss Eliza! You certainly appear hale." He bowed, and her stomach flipped. Now to perform that dreaded curtsey she'd been practicing.

"I am much improved, Sir William. I thank you for your concern." As soon as her curtsey was completed and the last word left her lips, she exhaled long and slow in an effort to relax.

Sir William nodded. "Miss Bennet, I am pleased to see you as well."

"Thank you, sir." He greeted the younger Bennet girls after they passed. Jane's arm pressed against hers. "You performed well." When they arrived inside, a number of people stared and whispered. "Do not let them disturb you. We shall prove you are the same as you always were."

"Even though I am not."

"No one need know but those we can trust. Your curtsey has improved greatly, yet I have not seen you practice it."

"Mr. Darcy helped with that."

"Mr. Darcy? When would he have had the opportunity to be of aid to us?"

"He happened upon me at Oakham Mount while I was drawing."

"And you told him the truth?"

Ellie shrugged, lifting her arms some, then letting them drop back to her sides. "He guessed. What was I supposed to say? It was the strangest thing. He stared at me for a minute or two, then just declared that I still didn't remember. I don't know how he could tell from looking at me, but he could."

Jane gave a quick glance around them. "Will he tell our secret?"

"I don't think so."

"What do you mean you do not think so?"

"He said he enjoyed our conversation when he found me on Oakham Mount and appreciated my honesty."

"It is very good of him to come to your aid, but if he appreciates honesty so much, why is he willing to deceive our neighbours?"

"I'm not certain, but I thought asking would be rude." Ellie fidgeted with her reticule while she watched those around them. Some still stared as if they expected her to start screaming and slapping herself, but others had returned to whatever they'd been doing before she entered the room.

"You must take great care not to be discovered with him. If you are found together and your reputation is harmed, Papa may have no choice but to force the two of you to marry." Jane gave a pointed look across the room that Ellie followed. "The lady to the left in the corner with her mother is Charlotte Lucas. The two of you have been friends since Sir William was knighted and moved from Meryton to Lucas Lodge."

"I was five years of age, correct?"

Jane gave a single nod of her head. "Yes, Charlotte would call with her mother and help us with our letters."

They both turned in the direction of a commotion at the door. Mr. Darcy entered, walking beside a shorter blond man with a wide, cheerful grin. "The man at Mr. Darcy's side is Mr. Bingley. Mr. and Mrs. Hurst and Miss Bingley are behind them."

"Miss Bingley and Mrs. Hurst believe they are better than everyone here."

"No," said Jane without a second's pause. "They are terribly kind. They called the day you went missing, condoling with us until you were found. We truly should return their call soon. I would not want to overlook their charity to our family."

Mrs. Hurst glanced over at them, then leaned towards her sister. The two of them smiled with their lips pressed tightly together before Sir William spoke to one of them, and they turned to listen to whatever he was saying. "Think what you wish, Jane, but ladies who want to be your friend do not peer down their nose as those two do."

"You made a similar comment after the assembly, though stated in a different manner. I suppose it is reassuring your first impression of them has not altered."

"Miss Bennet!" Mr. Bingley stepped up to join them with Mr. Darcy at his side.

"Mr. Bingley," said Jane while they curtseyed. "I hope you are well this evening."

"I am pleased to be in such genial society once again." He tilted his head to look past them. "I see your parents by the window. Would you accompany me while I greet them?" Jane glanced at her.

Ellie peered over her shoulder at Mr. and Mrs. Bennet then back to Jane. "I will be well." Jane's eyes darted to Mr. Darcy before she departed with Mr. Bingley.

"She seems wary of me," he said.

"I had not told her of your help until a few moments ago. She questioned your motive for assisting us. You said you appreciate my honesty, yet you are helping us deceive those around us."

"Disguise of any sort is my abhorrence, yet I understand the necessity of your deception. In our world, people can be unnecessarily cruel to those who, through no fault of their own, are different. My grandfather's youngest sister was blind, and she ceased even going into the villages and market towns around Pemberley for fear of what someone might say or do."

"How sad. She wasn't lonely?"

"She had a companion, the widow of a cleric, who was good to her. Between her companion and the family, I believe she was content. She lived a long life. I remember reading to her once I learnt. We would read to her, and her companion would pen her letters when we left her at Pemberley to stay in London for the Season."

"She was lucky to have the lot of you."

"I thank you. We were fortunate to have her; I assure you. She possessed an irreverent sort of humour and could restore my good humour with little effort. I wish Georgiana remembered her, but she passed when my sister was young."

"Eliza!" When Ellie turned, Charlotte rushed up to her with her arms outstretched. "I am relieved to find you here and looking so well."

"I am pleased to see you as well, Charlotte."

Before she could curtsey, Charlotte took her hands and kissed her cheek. "You had us quite worried, but I am satisfied that you seem to have pulled through without permanent injury."

"I am much improved."

The corner of Mr. Darcy's lips twitched, and he cleared his throat. "I am certain all your neighbours are pleased to find you so recovered."

"We are indeed. Eliza is quite beloved in Meryton." Charlotte clasped her hands. "Do you know what I shall do? I shall open the instrument. I am certain we should all enjoy hearing you perform. All our guests will see your good health with their own eyes."

Ellie's eyes bulged. What was she supposed to do? Sing or play the instrument? This was a huge problem. No one would want to hear her warble out whatever emerged when she attempted to sing, not if they wanted to survive with their eardrums intact, and she couldn't play. "Charlotte, I beg you, don't make me sing. My head does not ache as it once did, but I don't want to tempt fate. The accident wasn't so long ago."

"Then you must play."

"I am certain Mr. Darcy and his friends are used to hearing better musicians than me. The last thing I wish to do is frighten them with my lack of skill."

Charlotte's eyebrows drew together a little. "Well, Eliza, I enjoy your efforts, so I must insist."

Ellie started to tremble before Charlotte so much as crossed the room.

"You do not remember how to play?" asked Mr. Darcy.

"I can manage chopsticks, but no one here wants to hear that."

"Chopsticks?"

"Yes, Chopsticks." She pressed her hand to her stomach. "What am I supposed to do?"

Charlotte waved her over, and Fitzwilliam's arm appeared in front of her. "If you will place your hand upon my arm, I shall tell you as we approach the pianoforte." Once she did as he requested, he took the first step toward her impending doom. "The instrument's position in the corner and surrounded by chairs may work to our advantage." As they approached the instrument, her stomach began to flip and roll. "May I turn the pages for you, Miss Elizabeth?" asked Mr. Darcy in a loud tone.

"Yes, thank you." How would him turning the pages help her? She needed to learn to play a piano in the next few seconds or the jig would be up!

He led her to a table where he flipped through some pages, then held out an arm so she could squeeze into the corner, looking out over everyone in the room. She was screwed! When Fitzwilliam sat beside her, he set a piece of music on the stand in front of them. How was that supposed to help? She couldn't read music! "The sheet is for show and to hide us further. Place your fingers upon the keys but do not press. Keep your gaze on the music." He sat closer than she would've expected, stretched his fingers, then began playing the most beautiful melody. Despite the emotion of the music, he sat rigid as he performed. His technicality wasn't perfect; he fumbled a couple of times by the end of the song, and even turned a page when he had a one-handed passage, but she couldn't have done any better if she'd tried. Thankfully, no one approached, and all seemed content to listen from where they stood.

When Mr. Darcy released the last note, he reached for the music in front of them. "Make your curtsey and return to your parents and Jane. I should speak to a few people lest we offend the room by not mingling with the other guests."

"Thank you." She did her best to match his low, soft tones.

"You are most welcome."

Ellie stood, moved around the instrument, curtseyed to those who applauded, and hurried over to where Mr. Bennet stood against the far wall. Where had Jane disappeared to?

"You played well," said Mr. Bennet. "I do not believe I have ever heard you practicing that particular piece."

She froze and bit her cheek. What was she supposed to say?

"Mr. Darcy also sat rather close to you for someone he found merely tolerable." Mr. Bennet leaned closer. "At times, I could have sworn he was performing instead of you."

Her eyes hurt they bulged so.

"I think we need to have a talk tomorrow, Ellie. You are dissembling, and I want to know why as well as why Mr. Darcy is aiding you in the endeavour."

"Yes, sir."

"I do wish to know if Jane is aware."

"She is."

An ungodly racket came from the piano, making her wince. "Who is that playing?"

He stared at her for a moment. "Do you not recognise Mary's feeble attempts?"

Ellie scanned the room one more time and found Jane, who lifted her eyebrows at her as she curtseyed to Mr. Bingley. After Ellie shrugged in return, Jane took Mr. Bingley's hand and began to dance to Mary's performance. What a relief no one had cornered her to dance! She'd never have been able to follow along much less keep from tripping over herself or crushing someone's toes. In the meantime, Mr. Bennet had been more observant than she and Jane had anticipated. What would he ask her when they talked? With any luck, she would instead wake in her own time and bed tomorrow and worrying now would be nothing more than a colossal waste of time. If only!

Mr. Darcy stood against the wall on the opposite side of the room with Miss Bingley at his side, fluttering her eyelashes while she spoke to him. Mrs. Hurst set a hand to Miss Bingley's arm, which made the lady turn away from Mr. Darcy for a moment. He appeared bored and hacked off, his mouth screwed into a frown, but when Miss Bingley turned back to him, he changed to a more neutral expression and stared at the dancers. Lydia shrieked and guffawed at the top of her lungs, and he pressed his lips together and turned away.

"I would say Mr. Darcy is annoyed by Miss Bingley. What do you think?"

She turned to Mr. Bennet. "I'd have to agree with you. She needs to be careful. If she bends any farther forward, she may fall on him chest first."

Mr. Bennet startled but chuckled. "I believe Mr. Darcy would move too swiftly, and her tumble would be wasted."

"You're probably right."

"What else about our company amuses you?"

She laughed. Where should she start?

Chapter 9

As had become routine, Ellie sat beside Jane at breakfast the next morning, with Mr. Bennet to her right and at the head of the table, while Mrs. Bennet crowed at Jane's success the evening before.

"Mr. Bingley was so attentive to our dear Jane."

All the while, Lydia and Kitty giggled and sometimes even guffawed at whatever they whispered into each other's ears.

Lydia had flirted with John Lucas all evening, leaning forward to give him glimpses down the low neckline of her dress, fluttering her eyelashes, and even touching his arm when she laughed at whatever nonsense he uttered. Even in the 21st century, she would've been over the top and obvious. Why did Mr. and Mrs. Bennet let her behave like such a shameless flirt? Wasn't it a poor reflection on the family during this day and age? She still couldn't believe Mrs. Bennet had purchased Lydia those low-cut gowns. All evening, Ellie held her breath, waiting for Lydia to attempt such a deep enough breath, her nipples would burst from her stays for all to see—not that she mentioned the possibility to Mr. Bennet. Talk about awkward!

Without warning, Mr. Bennet rose. "Well, Ellie, if you would join me in my book room, I should like to have our talk."

When Jane made to stand, Mr. Bennet patted her shoulder. "Finish your breakfast, my dear. We shall do well enough on our own. Besides, I believe your mother wishes to return that call from Mrs. Hurst and Miss Bingley this morning."

"I do," said Mrs. Bennet while chewing, "and you *must* come. What if Mr. Bingley is there? He must see you if he is to ever propose."

Jane's eyes darted between them, so Ellie gave her a small wave as she rose and followed Mr. Bennet. Hopefully, the gesture would reassure Jane, even though Ellie was anything but assured. When Mr. Bennet entered the room, he waited for her to enter behind him before he closed the door. "I was going to ring for coffee. Would you like some?"

Coffee? Like real coffee? Tea was nice, but a cuppa was her afternoon or evening go to. She'd always preferred coffee in the mornings. "Yes, I'd love some."

He rang for a servant, and when Mrs. Hill knocked, he requested a tray. "Why do you not sit? Unless I have unsettled you to such an extent that you wish to pace."

"I am...well. May I look at your print?" She pointed to an etching of London over the mantel.

"Yes, of course."

She stepped forward and studied the lines and colours of the aquatint and glanced at the artist's signature. The view of St. Paul's Cathedral from Ludgate Hill was striking, though William Marlow was more known for his landscapes and sea view subject matter.

"Your uncle took me to an exhibit where I purchased that almost fifteen years ago."

"Do you like London?" He rarely left this room. The idea of him walking about a city as large as London seemed at odds with his personality—what she knew of him anyway.

"I cannot abide it, but the work is well done."

After a quick knock, Mrs. Hill hurried in and set the tray on Mr. Bennet's desk.

"Thank you," he said. After Mr. Bennet poured them each a cup, he sat in his well-worn chair and reclined into the leather, making it creak, while she stopped at a small portrait propped between books. "I have never known you to take such an interest in art."

With a shrug, she took her cup from the tray and sat down. "I admire the skill and time involved in making something so detailed and perfect. I also find the perspectives of others fascinating."

He nodded while he peered at her over his glasses. "I must admit that you have become quite the puzzle of late."

A sharp sensation shot through her chest. "How's that?"

He stared at her for another moment. "Well, you look just like my Lizzy, and the tone of your voice sounds just like my Lizzy, but nothing else resembles my daughter in the slightest."

"Perhaps when I remember—"

"Where did you first read that poem by Donne?"

She blinked and frowned. "I am sure I probably read it in a book in here, but I don't remember, of course."

"I do not have a collection of Donne containing that poem," said Mr. Bennet, lifting a single eyebrow. "I happened to read that piece while searching for a particular volume at Hatchard's when I was last in London. You were not with me and had instead gone shopping with your aunt. When I sent an express to your uncle for the art supplies, I enquired if maybe he had that particular book of poetry, which he does, but it was only purchased three months ago. You have not visited Gracechurch Street in that time."

"Then I do not know."

He took a sip of his coffee and swallowed, his eyes watching her in a way that made her insides twist and roll. What did he want her to say? "What confounds me even more is your sudden ability to draw while you seem to have forgotten how to play the pianoforte. I had your uncle bring us a drawing master when Kitty was young for a few lessons. Kitty, though her ability is limited, showed some promise and has continued practicing and improving over the years. The master had told me you showed little talent and no interest. You escaped every lesson as soon as you could, taking refuge out of doors. I found you more than once atop Oakham Mount, and you would shed bitter tears at even being made to try. Now, you are drawing with the skill of someone who has studied under a master for most of her life.

"Between your quotation of Donne and your drawings, I cannot reconcile who you are now with my daughter. You speak differently, your deportment is nothing like my Lizzy, and your accomplishments and tastes are the exact opposite of my daughter. I knew you were dissembling at the Lucas's by your acceptance of Mr. Darcy's aid. Lizzy was insulted by his comment that she was 'merely tolerable' and would not have forgiven him so readily."

Her foot began tapping in a quick rhythm upon the floor, a bad habit of hers when she was nervous. "So, what is your explanation? What do you think happened? Why am I so changed?"

"I was hoping you would tell me." He lifted his bushy eyebrows. "My Lizzy despised coffee, yet you seem to have no difficulty with the flavour."

"I hope you will forgive me, but I'm not sure I can tell you what you want to hear. Jane is afraid Mama will continue to tell people I'm feeble-minded, which is why we began faking that my memory had returned. I'd also prefer not to be locked up somewhere."

"Locked up? As in…"

"Like the attics or in a hospital." She waved her free hand while she spoke.

"I assure you. I have no intention of sending you to Bedlam."

"Bedlam?"

"Royal Bethlehem Hospital in London is where people are taken for their mental infirmities, but many call it Bedlam."

"Yes, that would be what I'm talking about."

He chuckled and resituated himself in his chair, leaning against the arm. "You hardly seem dangerous to us or to others. I have no intention of taking you anywhere, much less Bedlam. Mrs. Bennet spends enough on triflings and gowns that I do not have the funds. I also do not desire the scandal that would bring, even had I the inclination."

"If Mrs. Bennet spends too much, why don't you stop her?"

"Because I've never desired the upheaval such a demand would cause—but we need to return to your situation."

"My situation?" Unfortunately, Mr. Bennet wasn't as easily distracted as she'd hoped.

"Now that you know I shall not be confining you to your rooms or in Bedlam, will you not answer my questions?" He glanced at her as though she would flee the room while he poured himself more coffee.

What was she supposed to do? He wasn't daft, by any means, and he knew something was up. "I can hardly explain something to you I don't understand myself."

He shrugged and held his cup close to his chin. "You sound as though you could use another opinion."

She pressed her lips together, set her cup on the desk, and rose. "And if you second-guess your opinion about Bedlam?"

"Second-guess?"

"Reconsider."

"Ah, I doubt that will happen. I would have reservations about putting a mangy dog in that pit, much less a person."

Ellie exhaled and crossed her arms over her chest. "My name is Ellie Gardiner. I am an art restorer, and on the 29th of September 202_, I started a job at Pemberley—"

Instead of gasping or some other gesture of surprise, Mr. Bennet's head only tilted a hair more to one side. "Is that not Mr. Darcy's estate?"

"It is, but much of the land had been sold off after this Mr. Darcy's death, and the house is in poor condition. It was purchased by a group of businessmen who wanted to restore the house and property and make it a tourist attraction. People would pay to tour the house, returned to its former glory, and wander through the gardens. I was one of two art restorers hired to help clean and repair the artwork around the estate."

"So, you have an occupation?"

"Yes. In the future, some ladies stay at home, but many women are employed in all sorts of professions. We've even had female prime ministers."

His eyes gave a slight flare. "How fascinating. Pray, forgive my interruption and continue."

Ellie nodded. "On my first night at Pemberley, I wandered around the house and found a huge floor to ceiling mirror in the ballroom. I was being silly and dancing around, but when I stopped and looked at myself in the mirror, the reflection wasn't mine."

His eyebrows drew down a little in the middle. "I do not understand. Who else could it be?"

"Your daughter." Mr. Bennet's chin hitched back. "I am well aware how mad this sounds, but I returned with my colleague a couple of weeks later, and the same thing happened.

Oliver, my colleague, saw *my* reflection, but I still saw your Lizzy's. After, the only mirrors I didn't avoid were in my bedchamber. Whenever we explored the house to remove paintings and bring them downstairs for restoration, I would stare straight ahead rather than look into any mirror, even though I'd never noticed your daughter's reflection in those before.

"By the weekend, I was fed up with it all, drank a couple of glasses of wine, and somehow got it into my head that touching the blasted thing was a good idea. I ran down to the ballroom and stood in front of the mirror for a few moments, then touched the tips of my fingers to the glass. The next thing I knew, I woke up here in 1811, and everyone was calling me Lizzy."

"Then, if you are here, where is my daughter?"

She shrugged and blinked. Why was she teary? How bizarre! She never cried. "I'm terribly sorry, but I have no idea where your daughter is—or when in time she could be for that matter. I found that Donne poem while writing a paper for an art history class. I thought it funny and read it a great deal. Unfortunately, I have a talent for remembering anything I don't need to know, and since I didn't need to remember the Donne, I memorised it of course."

"Do you know the artist who painted my view of St. Paul's?"

"William Marlow. He's known for his landscapes, marine scenes, and etchings. He began with the Incorporated Society of Artists, but eventually began exhibiting with the Royal Academy. I don't remember the exact date, but he dies sometime in the next few years."

Mr. Bennet started to gasp but swallowed it.

Ellie wrapped her arms tighter around herself. "Have you changed your mind about Bedlam?"

He studied her, making her fidget and squirm. "No, I do not think you are fit for Bedlam. Believe it or not, I find your explanation more plausible than the notion that you are my daughter. Have you told my Jane your tale?"

"No, I didn't think she would handle it well." Jane would faint dead away.

"I agree, and I would be grateful if you would not mention it to her any time soon. Have you told Mr. Darcy?"

"No, he knows nothing more than my memory still hasn't returned. He has said there's something in my eyes that's different than at the assembly. That's how he has recognised that I haven't remembered." Speaking of Mr. Darcy, was he waiting for her at the top of Oakham Mount?

Mr. Bennet sat forward and leaned upon his desk. "I would wager he recognises the different soul within you as I do. Since I am unsure if we can trust him, pray, do not speak further of this to him. Thus far, he seems to be an ally, but I would prefer to be certain."

"When I go to Oakham Mount for peace to draw, he comes, and we speak of what I should know so I can fit in better."

"I am unsure of the customs between the sexes in your time, but you must take great care. If your meetings become known—"

"My reputation would be in tatters. Yes, Jane mentioned that again last night after our return."

His forehead furrowed, and he tilted his head. "You said your name is Gardiner. I do wonder if you are related to my brother's family in London."

His brother? Their surnames were different. "Is he your half-brother?"

"No, he is my wife's brother?"

"Ah, okay. Um, I don't know. I have my family's genealogy in my belongings at Pemberley—in the future—but I've never studied it." Good Lord, she could be related to Mrs. Bennet if she was related to those Gardiners. Perhaps she could erase Mrs. Bennet from the family tree. The woman's shrill tone and excitability could give Ellie a headache, even without the head trauma.

"I can see the prospect does not thrill you," he said with a chuckle. "Do not fret. My brother is not as ridiculous and unguarded as my wife, and do sit down. You have hopefully told me the worst of this. While I am worried for my daughter, I shall not treat you as any less than her. Aside from your story of journeying here from the future, you seem a sensible sort and, from what you have said, educated."

"I have a university degree in art and a graduate degree in art restoration."

"So, you have taken classes for drawing? Ladies are truly allowed to study?"

"Yes, women are allowed to be educated, go to university, and even vote. While at uni, I took drawing classes as well as painting, and other forms of art, and art history."

"That explains why you are not as silly as my youngest daughters. You have been required to use your mind. I should be pleased to speak with you. You can entertain me in Lizzy's stead."

"How would I do that?"

"We oft times read the paper together and discuss the happenings." He shoved the morning's broadsheet across the dark oak. "Pray, do skip the gossip columns. I hear enough of those from my wife."

Ellie glanced down at the first page and lifted an eyebrow. "Are you sure? Perhaps the Prince Regent has done something worthy of a mention."

"Bite your tongue, Ellie." The words were said in a sort of growl, but one side of his lips curved. His eyes, however, held a different quality. A light had dimmed. Ellie wished she could help him—that she could bring his Lizzy back, but how? It seemed for the moment, both she and Lizzy were stuck wherever and whenever they happened to be, and she had no clue how to fix the situation.

Chapter 10

"Can you imagine, Mama?" Lydia clasped her hands together. "An entire regiment of militia? I would much prefer a man in a red coat to any other gentleman. Perhaps one will take a liking to me, fancy themselves very much in love, and propose. Would that not be perfect?"

"Very much so," said Kitty with a dreamy expression. "Did Aunt Philips truly say they were to remain the whole of winter?"

"That she did." Mrs. Bennet couldn't stop smiling and giving little squeals of delight. After Mrs. Philips's early morning call and the fifteen minutes of excited chatter since, Ellie wanted to squeeze her head between two cushions, blocking out their insipid conversation until they were over and done with the subject. God, she missed her noise-cancelling headphones right now! How much had she taken for granted before she found herself here? The list was growing daily.

Mr. Bennet rolled his eyes. "I must say I am convinced three of the silliest girls in the country reside under this roof."

"Oh, Mr. Bennet!" His wife's voice rose in pitch, making Ellie wince. "They are indeed not silly at all. Besides, you cannot claim Lizzy so clever anymore. She is quite altered since her fall. I am certain she is not even half as clever as well."

Ellie stiffened and let her gaze shift to Mr. Bennet, who glanced at her before he returned to his wife. "I believe in essentials Ellie is much the same. She has always been quick-witted, lively, and intelligent. Naught has changed in that regard. We enjoyed ourselves immensely at Lucas Lodge, observing those around us, and you must admit she performed well on the pianoforte."

"She performed very well indeed," said Jane.

Mrs. Bennet huffed, obviously about to continue when a footman entered and held a note in front of Jane. "Well, Jane, who is it from? What does he say? Make haste and tell us; make haste!"

"It is from Netherfield."

"Netherfield!" Mrs. Bennet jumped from her seat, snatched the letter from her daughter, and ripped it open. Poor Jane hadn't even broken the seal. "'Tis from Miss Bingley! She and Mrs. Hurst request you dine with them today. The gentlemen are to be dining with the officers. Dining out? That is very unlucky."

"They are dining with the officers? Why did our aunt not speak of it?" Lydia pouted and slouched in her chair. Now, why was she so put out? Did she think she could have joined them? Lydia was an annoying and self-centred child. Mr. Bennet needed to get her under control, or she'd be even more horrible one day.

Jane pressed a hand to the table in her father's direction. "Papa, can I have the carriage?"

In the quickest move Ellie had ever seen her make, Mrs. Bennet's head whipped around to the window and peered outside. "No, the carriage will not do! It will not do at all. My dear, you had better go on horseback, because it seems likely to rain; and then you must stay all night." She clapped her hands and giggled. "Yes, that will do well." The lady bustled to her chair and plopped back down.

"Mama!" said Jane on a gasp.

Ellie rolled her eyes. "I would think them more apt to send her home, wet through and ill."

"Nonsense! Besides, the horses are surely wanted on the farm. Are they not, Mr. Bennet?"

"I had much prefer to take the carriage." Jane spoke to her father while Mrs. Bennet huffed behind her.

"It is late to call the horses back from the fields," said Mr. Bennet, "but I am certain we can spare old Bertie."

"Bertie!" Lydia dissolved into peals of laughter. "Can he make it the three miles to Netherfield? I think he is more apt to drop dead before the trail forks at Oakham Mount."

Mr. Bennet frowned. "Hush, child."

"Well, Jane, what are you doing sitting there still?" said Mrs. Bennet. "Call for Smith, for you will require her aid to dress. You must look your best."

Ellie crossed her arms over her chest. "Yes, riding on horseback will certainly help the state of her hair and the wrinkles in her gown. I am certain Miss Bingley and Mrs. Hurst are just dying to smell horse during their dinner as well."

Mr. Bennet chuckled while Mrs. Bennet reddened. "But she must stay, which serves my purpose."

When Jane left the room, Ellie followed. "Let me help you." She had learnt a little of how the different garments worked, but not long after she helped Jane remove her morning gown, Smith arrived, courtesy of Mrs. Bennet, to complete the task.

As soon as Jane departed, Ellie hurried into Mr. Bennet's library and closed the door behind her. "How could you let Mrs. Bennet bully Jane into riding to Netherfield?"

"Why must I argue with her when I can let her do as she pleases and have my peace?"

With a huff, Ellie strode forward and set her hands on her hips. "Because as you said, she spends more than she should, and she has spoilt Lydia. If I'd had that girl for a sister, I might have had to slap her a few times. Her infatuation with grown men screams knocked up by sixteen."

"I beg your pardon?"

"If she lived in my time, I'd expect her to be unmarried and pregnant at sixteen. When I entered the parlour this morning, she was making a comment to Kitty about the tightness of John Lucas's breeches. I refuse to elaborate on that."

Mr. Bennet paled. "What could she know what is contained within a gentleman's breeches?"

"I am unsure of who taught her, but from what I've heard her loudly whisper, she's rather well versed." With Lydia's knowledge and a regiment of soldiers, the combination could prove a disaster.

He swallowed and took a sip of his coffee. "Very well. I shall attempt to do something, though I am not certain what to do."

"Should she be going to parties and meeting men?"

"Her mother declared her out when she turned fifteen just as she did with the others."

"What is out?"

"She is eligible to meet appropriate gentlemen and marry."

Ellie swallowed what had risen into the back of her throat. "Then take that back. Take away some of that money your wife overspends and hire someone to keep track of your youngest daughter."

"I hope you know I would never allow Lizzy to lecture me as you have."

With lifted eyebrows, Ellie poured herself a cup of coffee. "But would she disagree with what I've said?"

"No, I believe she would agree with you, quite emphatically, I am certain."

At a sound at the window, Ellie turned. The first heavy drops of rain slapped against the glass. "Jane will be wet through by the time she arrives at Netherfield."

Mr. Bennet rapped upon his desktop. "Come sit. We cannot but wait for Jane's return now."

Ellie's shoulders dropped. As much as she hated to admit it, he was right.

The steady rain continued into the night with the morning dawning bright and sunny despite cooler temperatures. A letter from Jane arrived as they were finishing breakfast. The poor dear had woken up with a headache and a sore throat. "I knew it," said Ellie with a sigh.

Mrs. Bennet, who had been crowing of her success, slapped the letter onto the table. "She will be well. People do not die of little, trifling colds!"

With a heavy exhale, Ellie turned to Mr. Bennet. "I want to go to Netherfield to see Jane."

"Do not be ridiculous!" cried Mrs. Bennet. "What can you do for her that Miss Bingley and Mrs. Hurst cannot? No, you will remain right here where you belong. We do not need you displaying your oddities around Mr. Bingley and frightening him away from Jane."

"That is enough, Mrs. Bennet," said her husband.

His wife straightened. "What do you mean?"

With a quick glance in Ellie's direction, Mr. Bennet cleared his throat. "I believe the time has come for a change at Longbourn. Mrs. Bennet, you have household funds and pin money. You are to keep to those sums from this day forward. Should you overspend, I shall sell your jewels to pay your debts and notify the dressmaker that I shall not pay for her services unless I give my permission ahead of your visit. Am I understood?"

"Mr. Bennet—?"

"I will brook no opposition to my scheme. I merely wish to know if you require it explained once again."

Mrs. Bennet's jaw clamped shut with an audible click, and Ellie pressed her lips together to keep from laughing. For the first time since she'd arrived in this house, Mrs. Bennet was silent. That feat alone was an accomplishment!

"But Papa—" began Lydia.

"As for you, Lydia, some of your recent comments have been brought to my attention. You seem to have no concept of what is appropriate or inappropriate for a young lady of your age, so you will no longer be out."

The ear-piercing whinging and exclamations from Mrs. Bennet and Lydia made Ellie close off one ear to protect her hearing. Dear Lord, that tone was painful!

"Enough!" Mr. Bennet stood and leaned upon the table. "I have yet to decide what I shall do with you. I penned a letter to your Uncle Gardiner, enquiring of the cost of a governess who could teach you what you have not learnt from your mother." Mrs. Bennet gave a gasp with her hand to her chest. "You are not allowed to walk to Meryton without Jane or Ellie along to mind your behaviour. Mary and Kitty are not adequate substitutes. You would ignore whatever Mary says, and Kitty would follow you without question. This is my final word on these matters. Do not disturb my equanimity by coming to my library and begging for me to change my mind. I shall only make my instructions stricter." Without another word, he left.

Lydia narrowed her eyes at Ellie. "This is your doing."

"I do not know what you mean." Yesterday afternoon, she and Mr. Bennet had discussed what would need to happen as well as what he'd say. She couldn't believe he'd actually pulled it off. It was all she could do not to grin like the Cheshire cat.

Mrs. Bennet narrowed her eyes. "You seem very pleased by it all and were almost smiling while your father spoke so to us. What has Lydia ever done to you? What have I done, for that matter, to make you so ungrateful?"

"Are you ready for Lydia to make you a grandmother?" asked Ellie without any drama. Why complicate the question and give Mrs. Bennet more reason to complain?

The lady furrowed her eyebrows and sat silent for a moment. "I think it far more likely Jane will be the first of my daughters to give me a grandchild—once she is wed to Mr. Bingley, of course."

Ellie had to struggle not to roll her eyes while she stood. Mrs. Bennet was a bit dim. "Well, I heard that one right there talking about what John Lucas had in his breeches after the party at Lucas Lodge, which is what I explained to my father. Given your youngest daughter's behaviour with men, I think it far more probable that she would be in the family way before Jane."

"But she is not married!" Mrs. Bennet's agape expression and high-pitched response almost made Ellie snort. Somehow, she held it in.

"Exactly my point."

Mrs. Bennet paled with her mouth opening and closing, then turned to stare at Lydia, who had begun to shrink into her seat while Kitty looked everywhere but at her mother or Mary. Well, she wasn't going to wait for this explosion! After grabbing Jane's letter, Ellie rushed out and joined Mr. Bennet in his book room.

"What of me going to Netherfield?"

"Do you really think it a good idea?"

She moved to close the door. "I want to help Jane as she did me."

"Which is laudable, but you invite scrutiny from the Bingleys, and you will be thrown into company with Mr. Darcy. Have you seen him since the party?"

"No, but with the colder weather and the rain, I haven't been able to walk to Oakham Mount as often."

His mouth was pressed into a fine line while he watched her in a way that made her want to squirm. Why? She'd already been honest with him—to a fault. What else could he discover? "You will need to be careful to avoid questions and to prevent Mr. Darcy from learning more than he already knows. While he has been more understanding than most, we are unaware of how his views may change when confronted with the prospect of time travel and body switches."

"You believed me."

"For lack of a more plausible reason, yes. You must understand, at a glance, you resemble my daughter, but upon further study, you are not her. Mr. Darcy has no such history with my Lizzy with which to form a basis for acceptance, and I do not wish to see either you or my daughter condemned for witchcraft."

"I understand. I do. But I know I can help Jane, even if I only sit with her."

He sighed. "Very well. I have sent a servant to fetch Bertie. He should return with the horse—"

"I don't ride, sir." Her hands were out before her, palms facing Mr. Bennet.

"Then I am afraid you must walk. The quickest route is through Meryton, but perhaps it would be best if you avoid the town. Should Mr. or Mrs. Philips detain you, you would be forced to feign memories you do not possess, which could give you away without Jane or my aid. A path exists that crosses through the fields, but do you know the way?"

"Netherfield is the estate visible from the top of Oakham Mount?"

"It is."

"Then I believe I can find it."

Mr. Bennet nodded. "I would avoid Mrs. Bennet. She will object most strenuously to your going."

"I'll sneak out of the kitchens, then." She started to leave, but he called her name. "Yes?"

"Do take great care with your every word."

"Got it," she said, and walked out the door.

Chapter 11

Ellie passed the turn that she usually took when she walked to the top of Oakham Mount and instead, followed the pathway through the wood until it emerged from the last of the trees into a verdant green pasture. Her father had called the grass that remained green in the autumn and throughout the winter rye, but whether it was in truth, she wasn't sure. Mr. Bennet would know, not that she'd thought to ask.

The galloping hoofbeats of an approaching horse made her whirl around as Mr. Darcy slowed and dismounted a metre or so away. "Good morning, Miss Ellie."

"Good morning, Mr. Darcy." Blimey, he was handsome, all smartly dressed while he led Lysander towards her.

"You have ventured farther than normal this morning."

"I am going to Netherfield to see Jane."

"Ah," he said, nodding. "I had heard at breakfast she had taken ill." He glanced in the direction of Netherfield. "If you would not object to my company, I shall walk with you."

Her stomach fluttered, and her cheeks heated. "I do not object at all." What was she doing? No! She needed to find some polite way to say no. This was a terrible idea.

As he fell into step beside her, he fidgeted with the reins in his hands. "Just to forewarn you, it would be best if we part ways before we reach the house since Miss Bingley and Mrs. Hurst will talk if we arrive together. I can ride ahead and return my horse to the stables while you approach the house." As she nodded, he gestured to her sketchbook. "You brought your drawing materials."

"Yes, I thought it would give me something to pass the time if Jane is sleeping."

"Did you have a pleasant evening at Lucas Lodge? I regret I was unable to speak to you and your father after your performance." He gave a crooked grin that made her knees almost buckle.

"I did. I must thank you again for coming to my rescue on the pianoforte. Where did you learn to play?"

"My mother taught both me and my sister, though Georgiana is more proficient than I. I have less time to practice with my estate duties, and I never had the benefit of the masters I have acquired for her. Since I arrived at Netherfield, Miss Bingley and Mrs. Hurst spend a prodigious amount of time practicing, preventing me from playing. I cannot force them from the instrument so I may have my turn."

Ellie grinned at him. "If you ever feel the need to do so, pray, let me know. I would love to watch."

He chuckled all low, sending a shiver through her. Stop it, Ellie! She'd been too overwhelmed at Lucas Lodge to react to how close he sat at the pianoforte, but at every other meeting, he had a way of making her insides go all topsy-turvy. She needed to slam closed that can of worms. The last thing she wanted was a broken heart.

"What have you against those ladies?" he asked.

"I have never spoken to them, but when I saw them enter at Lucas Lodge, they appeared to look down on everyone there. Jane has said they are 'amiable ladies,' but she has described nearly the entirety of her acquaintance as 'kind.' Papa has claimed her faking that my memory has returned is against her character. Apparently, she sees the world through rose-coloured glasses."

His brow furrowed. "I am not familiar with that saying."

"She sees everything in a positive light, the good in every situation, or in this case, every person."

"Ah. Speaking far too freely, I must say that Miss Bingley and Mrs. Hurst are as you say. They have found little to admire here, and I would wager they invited Miss Bennet to learn what they can use against her."

"Such as using our youngest sisters' behaviour to persuade Mr. Bingley from speaking so much to Jane?"

"Precisely. Since what we have said is not within the bounds of the usual discourse, you must find some way to convince Miss Bennet they are not to be trusted without mentioning my part."

"I thank you for your honesty, and I shall do what I can."

"Your manner of speaking is much improved."

"Mr. Bennet has been helping me. Contractions still slip through."

"As do some unusual phrases—rose-coloured glasses for example."

Crap! How was she supposed to explain that? She couldn't exactly look up certain sayings to know when they originated. "I just speak as it comes to my mind. I shall try to be more careful."

When he looked forward, his expression fell. "Oh, I forgot about the stile. You cross, and I'll mount and jump the fence. We are not far from Netherfield, so continue along the path. I shall meet you in front of the house."

She nodded as he mounted Lysander, doubled back, then took the fence with room to spare. "Shit," she said in a mutter, pressing her hand to her chest. How impressive was that, and again, how hot did he look on top of that horse? She sighed and shook herself. Ugh! She was looking at him *that way* again. She needed to put a stopper in the thoughts and feelings about

Fitzwilliam straightaway. One day—she hoped soon—she'd return to the Pemberley of the future, and Fitzwilliam would remain here. She couldn't become more infatuated with a man who had lived over two hundred years before her. It wasn't realistic, but then what was realistic at the moment?

When he approached her in front of the house, he bowed, and she curtseyed. "Good morning, Miss Elizabeth. I hope you are well." He spoke in a loud tone. A groom was within hearing distance while working with Mr. Darcy's horse. That had to be why.

"I am very well. I have come to see my sister."

"I am certain she will be pleased to have your company. I shall take you to her." When they started towards the house, he tilted his head down a bit. "Forgive me. I know you prefer Ellie, but you should be called Miss Elizabeth before the servants and the Bingleys if possible."

"Don't worry about it. I just hope I answer to it."

When they entered the hall, Miss Bingley hurried up behind the housekeeper, who passed Ellie's pelisse off to a maid. "Miss Elizabeth, have you come all this way on foot?"

She curtseyed. "As you see, Miss Bingley. May I ask how Jane fares?"

Miss Bingley gave a quick curtsey of her own. "Last I checked, she was sleeping. She passed the night quite ill and was feverish this morning. I shall have Mrs. Nichols take you to her."

Ellie glanced over her shoulder at Mr. Darcy as the older woman stepped forward. "Right this way, Miss Elizabeth."

As soon as they were up the stairs, the housekeeper nodded in her direction. "May I say how relieved we were to hear of your recovery. I believe all the servants here prayed for you to awaken. Several of the maids are daughters of Longbourn tenants. You have done so much good for them. They were overwrought when they heard of your accident."

"I thank each and every one for the well wishes." She smiled. "I am pleased to be so well recovered myself."

"The servant who was sent for the apothecary this morning returned a short time ago and indicated Mr. Jones should not be far behind him. We expect him soon."

"I appreciate the concern and attention you have provided my sister. I am certain you have helped her greatly." Mr. Jones? She assumed he was the apothecary. That was who was with Jane the second time she woke up, wasn't it? If only she could ask, but Miss Elizabeth would know Mr. Jones so it would be strange if she did.

"We could do no less. Miss Bennet is a dear, sweet girl." Mrs. Nichols tapped on a door, then opened it with care. Jane was still sleeping when Ellie was shown in, but she thanked Mrs. Nichols and, after checking Jane's forehead for fever, sat near the fire for light to sketch until Mr. Jones arrived soon after.

"Miss Elizabeth," he said brightly. She had been correct. He had been the smiling gentleman that day.

"Good morning, Mr. Jones." She clenched her hands. She'd almost said, "You all right?" as she would've at home. That could've been a nightmare to explain away.

"I am told Miss Bennet has a fever and a sore throat."

Before Ellie could answer, Jane turned her head and blinked. "Ellie? When did you arrive?"

"Only a short time ago. You were sleeping so peacefully; I did not want to wake you."

"Oh, I am so pleased you are here. I could never ask for your presence, so I am relieved you came on your own."

Mr. Jones chatted while he looked over Jane, then rummaged around his bag. "I shall leave you this," he said pulling out a dark bottle and setting it on the table, "and I shall also leave some willow bark with Mrs. Nichols, which should be of aid for the throat as well as the fever."

"Thank you, Mr. Jones," said Jane, her voice raspy and harsh.

Ellie picked up the bottle and looked it over, but other than a generic label that said, "throat linctus" nothing indicated what was in it. "What is this made of?"

"Volatile salt of ammonia, syrup of Balsam, oil of sweet almonds, and water[2]. It should be taken three times in twenty-four hours. Have Mr. Bingley send for me if things worsen, a severe fever develops, or you require more of the tonic."

Ellie stood, still holding the bottle of medicine. "Of course, but would it not be better to return my sister to Longbourn? I am certain she would be more comfortable in her own home."

"I would be hesitant to move Miss Bennet," said Mr. Jones, pressing his lips together for a moment. "The cold may worsen her condition as could the stress of the journey. No, she should remain where she is."

Was he taking the mick out of her? He looked serious, but three miles was not a harrowing journey by any means. Surely Mr. Bingley would return them in his carriage, which would not be difficult other than the jostling on their bums. If not, she was certain Miss Bingley would spare no expense to see them home and out of her hair. Her heart sank. With Mr. Jones's

---

[2] Lloyd, Martha. Martha Lloyd's Household Book. https://janeausten.co.uk/blogs/home-and-hearth/regency-head-colds-and-care. Accessed: January 19, 2022.

recommendation, she'd never persuade Jane to leave, so she plastered what she hoped was a pleasant expression on her face. "We appreciate you coming, sir."

The gentleman nodded. "Good day, Miss Elizabeth." As soon as the door closed, she looked at the bottle. "Ammonia salts? Is he trying to kill you?"

With a hoarse cough, Jane pulled herself into a more seated position, reclined against the pillows. "At least he did not want to bleed me. I despise that."

Bleeding? Ammonia salts? Georgian medicine was known for its backwards theories and use of 'medicines' that were more harmful than beneficial. As a child, she'd loved Horrible Histories and the beauty regimens alone were poisonous as hell. Arsenic, mercury, and now ammonium salts! No wonder people lived such short lives!

With a gulp, Ellie hurried into the dressing room and dumped the contents of the bottle into the chamber pot. "Let them try to figure that out."

Jane relaxed in the pillows with a frown on her face when she returned. "What did you do?"

"Ammonia will not help a sore throat."

"I am certain Mr. Jones knows better what will help and will not. He would never try to harm us. He was of great aid to you after you took that blow to your head."

"You will have to trust me, Jane. I shall ring the bell and request some willow bark tea as you made for me. I am certain it will make you feel much better." The tea arrived quickly along with a small pot of heated water Ellie had requested. While Jane drank down the willow bark, Ellie made some warm lemon water with honey and thyme and swapped out the cups when she finished the first. "Now sip this as you would tea." Ellie then watched while Jane took her first hesitant taste.

"This is lovely. What is it?"

"Nothing more than lemon and honey with a little thyme in water. The mixture is simple but helps with a scratchy throat and sometimes even a cough."

After a few sips, Jane rested the cup on the coverlet. "Mr. Bingley has lemons?"

"The maid said Netherfield has a tree in the orangery."

"How fortunate. Lemons can be quite dear." She cleared her throat. "Has anything of import occurred at Longbourn since yesterday?"

Ellie shrugged while she tidied the tray. "Not much. After Lydia's display at the Lucas's, Papa declared her no longer out."

Jane's mouth was agape. "How unlike him! He can never be bothered much outside of his library. I must not have noticed the worst of her behaviour."

"I suppose not." How could she explain to Jane that as an outsider, her opinion seemed to influence him more than that of Elizabeth's. The circumstances could make Jane question why— and she couldn't question who Ellie was. Jane needed to remain in the dark.

When Jane was finished with her warm drink, she claimed her throat much improved but soon fell asleep, leaving Ellie to once more sit near the fire with her drawing.

"I must say, that fall must have knocked the sense out of Miss Elizabeth," said Miss Bingley as she held her fork, laden with food, over her plate. "What could she be thinking, walking three miles in the mud because her sister has a trifling of a cold?" Darcy stiffened while he chewed. Miss Bingley's criticism was not surprising. On the contrary, he expected it after her eyes darkened the moment Miss Ellie entered the hall.

Bingley's forehead crinkled, and he paused before taking a bite. "I believe her concern for her sister is admirable. What of you, Darcy?"

"I agree. Her care of her sister does indeed do her credit."

Miss Bingley's fork clattered upon the plate, and she clutched her chest with her mouth agape. "But Mr. Darcy! You could not miss her petticoats. They must have carried six inches of mud when she entered the house. I declare she looked quite wild. You would not wish your sister to make such a display, would you?"

"My sister would never find herself in such a situation." Lord! What he would not give to take the meal with Miss Ellie and Miss Bennet! This cloying, self-serving belittling of others was grating.

The lady had puffed herself up until she resembled a peacock, making Darcy clench his fists around his utensils. "See—"

"In similar circumstances, I would provide the carriage or accompany her on horseback if necessary. However, Mr. Bennet once mentioned Miss Elizabeth does not ride, and I am certain if a horse could be spared from the farm, her father would have done so. Miss Elizabeth, no doubt, thought walking her only option." He bit his cheek at the sour expression that overtook Miss Bingley's face, lest he smile and give away his distaste for her. Yes, in this case, dissembling had been worth it. After all, he had said little to Mr. Bennet since arriving in the neighbourhood.

Miss Bingley's cup hit the saucer with enough force that Mrs. Hurst winced. "Perhaps her eyes, which I have heard described as 'fine,' have bewitched everyone in this horrid little town. I have not heard one uncomplimentary word about her since we arrived. A rumour had circulated that she was insensible when she first awakened from her injury, then everyone rejoiced when she returned to herself. What is it about Elizabeth Bennet that enchants this town so? She would be laughed out of London with her connexions and her simple country manners. Could you imagine her or Miss Bennet at St. James's? The daughter of a country squire and his wife, who is the daughter of a solicitor. Oh, not to mention their uncles: Mr. Philips, the solicitor in Meryton, and a Mr. Gardiner, who is a tradesman living in *Cheapside*."

Darcy released a slow exhale in an attempt to release the unbearable tension twisting knots into the muscles of his back. "Yet, they are the daughters of a gentleman. One must not forget that fact. Their connexions may make marrying a gentleman of any consideration in the world more difficult, but it should not preclude such a union if the gentleman is inclined to overlook their relations."

A chuckle came from Bingley. "I would never have imagined you uttering such a thing if I had not heard it with my own ears."

"Forgive me, Bingley. I am intemperate," he said on an exhale. "After the last season in Town, I admit I am fatigued—of it all. If I could shutter myself away at Pemberley forever, I would do so in a trice." Miss Bingley gasped, but he ignored her.

"If you will excuse me." Without another word, he stood and retired to his rooms. He wished more than anything he could remain there in peaceful solitude until dinner. Perhaps, if he was so fortunate, Miss Ellie would join them for the meal.

Chapter 12

By the end of the day, Ellie had managed to avoid the stress of being in company with the Bingleys, the Hursts, and Mr. Darcy other than joining them for dinner. She had spoken little during the meal and allowed Miss Bingley and Mrs. Hurst to dominate the conversation with talk of the balls and routs they had attended during the Season. Wasn't the Season in the spring? They were still speaking of events from March and April over six months later and as though they'd attended yesterday, and Ellie wasn't ignorant as to the why of the matter. They really were the most insufferable women she'd ever met.

After almost fifteen minutes of the same parties hashed and rehashed, Mr. Bingley implored them to change the subject, enquiring why they spoke of events from the past when they had more recent happenings more of interest.

Ellie had remained quiet and concentrated on her plate until she was finished, then excused herself after the meal to sit with Jane. With the help of more willow bark tea as well as the honey and lemon water, Jane seemed to nod off quickly, so once Jane appeared to be sleeping soundly, Ellie returned downstairs, a footman directing her to the drawing room where the rest of Netherfield's occupants were playing cards.

"Would you care to join us?" asked Mr. Hurst when she entered. He swayed in his seat with a large glass of what appeared to be Port, by the colour of the liquor, on the table in front of him. He was still drinking? He had to have downed an entire bottle of wine at dinner, the footman had filled his glass often enough, and now, he lifted another glass to his lips. The man's liver probably resembled a gherkin.

"Thank you, but no. I am not very good at cards and would spoil your game."

When she glanced through some books on a table, she found a copy of *Evelina* by Fanny Burney, which Mr. Bennet had recommended she read to help her better grasp the language differences. After selecting the appropriate volume, she sat in a chair near the fire and flipped to where she'd left off at Longbourn.

"Do you prefer reading to cards? That is rather singular."

She jerked her head up at Mr. Hurst's comment. "I beg your pardon?"

"Miss Eliza Bennet," said Miss Bingley, "despises cards. She is a great reader and has no pleasure in anything else."

Where had that come from? She'd only come downstairs for the light and was trying to stay out of their way while Jane slept. She had no idea what game they were playing and would appear stupid if she attempted to join them. Why couldn't she read without criticism?

Mr. Bingley played a card with a smile in her direction. "I am certain nursing her sister gives her pleasure. Hopefully, Miss Bennet will soon be well."

Her shoulders relaxed a little. "Thank you, Mr. Bingley. I hope so too."

"Are you content with your book?" Mr. Darcy pointed at the volume she held. "I have a number I brought with me. I could send a servant to fetch them."

"Oh no, that will not be necessary. While I appreciate your kind offer, I was reading *Evelina* at Longbourn."

Mr. Bingley grinned. "So, you are able to continue what you already began. Capital indeed!"

Miss Bingley's face was pinched, her nose appearing almost rat-like. "Is Miss Darcy much grown since the spring? Will she be as tall as I am?" The woman gave an annoying titter as she leaned towards Mr. Darcy in a way that reminded Ellie of Lydia flirting. Miss Bingley's gown wasn't as revealing, so she wasn't in the same danger of a breast popping out. Of course, for that to happen, she'd have to have had breasts in the first place. Ellie bit her lip and buried her face in her book.

"Georgiana is about Miss Elizabeth Bennet's height, or rather taller."

"And so accomplished for her age! I never met with anybody who delighted me so much. Such a countenance, such manners! Miss Elizabeth, you should hear her performance on the pianoforte. It is so exquisite I am certain you would beg the name of her piano master for the benefit of your own playing." Ellie let the book drop to her lap and gave a pinched smile.

Mr. Darcy's eyes darted to the lady who still all but batted her eyes in his direction while Ellie pressed her lips together to keep from laughing.

"I thought Miss Elizabeth performed well. We all know she had little time to practice after her accident. I heard a great deal of praise on her playing."

After he set down a card, Mr. Bingley glanced around with a grin. "It is amazing to me how young ladies can have the patience to be so accomplished as they all are."

Miss Bingley scoffed. "All young ladies accomplished! Charles, you do not know what you speak."

Mr. Darcy leaned back in his chair and looked at Ellie. "Yet the most important accomplishment a lady can make is the improvement of her mind by extensive reading." He peered over at Miss Bingley. "Georgiana reads a great deal, and I encourage her in her pursuit."

Ellie's eyes shifted back and forth between them. Obviously, she'd caused a stir by simply walking into the room, and Miss Bingley had already insulted Mr. Darcy—not that the lady understood the implication of the insult she aimed at Ellie.

"Perhaps I should look in on Jane. Pray, excuse me." She made to set the book on the table, but Mr. Bingley's head perked up over his guests.

"Do take that with you if you wish to read while Miss Bennet sleeps. I would be happy for you to keep it during your stay."

"Thank you." A slight smile came from Mr. Darcy before she turned to leave, but since Miss Bingley's narrowed eyes glared at her, Ellie gave him no response before she hurried through the door.

When she reached the stairs, she rolled her eyes. "What a shit show." She spoke under her breath so no servants could hear if they happened to pass. She'd needed to get that out while she could. Miss Bingley was trying everything possible to get Mr. Darcy's attention and failing miserably while Mr. Bingley was trying to be kind and broker peace. Then there were the Hursts! After imbibing a generous amount of wine at dinner and following with a full glass of Port in the drawing room, Mr. Hurst was pissed as a parrot and barely attending his cards. His wife, oblivious to his condition, tittered at the insults flying about, mostly those of her sister's aimed at Ellie, but didn't engage in the conversation. Meanwhile, poor Mr. Darcy was noticeably fed up to his eyeballs with Miss Bingley—not that Ellie could blame him!

When she reached the guest wing, Ellie almost let her laughter loose. "I wonder what Miss Bingley would say if she realised she'd insulted Mr. Darcy's performance on the pianoforte by hinting that I needed a master." She allowed a quiet giggle, then continued on to check on Jane.

Ellie spent the night in Jane's bedchamber. During the times when she was not at her bedside, she settled in for a kip on the sofa until Jane woke or groaned in her sleep, forcing her to rise and care for her. When a young maid entered to replenish the fire, Ellie begged for a tray with coffee and toast to tide her over until the cook made breakfast, and the maid not only brought her coffee, but also muffins, toast, and jam. Bless!

She was sipping her second cup of coffee when a tapping at the servants' entrance made her rise and peek through the door. A sour-faced man stood on the other side. "May I help you?"

"Forgive me for disturbing you, miss. I am Mr. Darcy's valet, Chambers. I heard below stairs that you were awake, and my master wished for me to convey a message without others in the household overhearing."

With a glance back at Jane, she stepped into the hallway and pulled the door closed behind her. "Yes?"

"Mr. Darcy sends word that should you require anything, anything at all, you do not hesitate to request it of him. Word below stairs last night was your sister had worsened. My master indicated he would be pleased to send for a physician from town if one is required."

She scraped her teeth along her bottom lip for a moment. "Pray, thank Mr. Darcy for his kind attentions." That sounded okay, didn't it? "I am uncertain a physician is necessary at the moment, but I require aid to pen a letter to my father."

Chambers's brow furrowed, and he looked at her oddly. "You need him to pen a letter to your father?" Argh! How could she cover this up! She'd seen Mr. Bennet write in his ledger and in what appeared to be his journal. She didn't have the slightest clue how to work a quill and an inkwell! She couldn't give someone a blotted and ink-stained piece of paper to send to Longbourn, and that was if she managed something legible.

"I suppose it sounds peculiar. My hands do not always cooperate the way I would hope since my accident. They have improved a great deal, but not well enough to use a pen." Crap! Should she have said quill? How was she supposed to know?

"My apologies. I had not realised you had such lingering difficulties."

"I beg of you not to mention it to anyone but Mr. Darcy. I have not wanted to call attention to my current inabilities. Your master has been very...solicitous, and I cannot thank him enough for his aid."

"Miss, I assure you, I shall not breathe a word to anyone. Mr. Darcy trusts me implicitly, and you may as well. May I ask what you want the note to say?"

"For my father to send my mother to see Miss Bennet. She may have some instruction on what to do for her."

He gave a slight bow. "Of course, Miss Elizabeth. I shall speak to Mr. Darcy immediately."

"Thank you, Mr. Chambers."

As soon as the valet rushed away, she returned to Jane's side, keeping her company and drawing while she slept until a knock came at the door two hours later. The maid passed Ellie a letter, curtseyed, and hurried away. Ellie quickly broke the seal and unfolded the missive.

Longbourn

13th of November 1811

My dear Ellie,

If it had not been for Mr. Darcy's handwriting when I opened the missive (not to mention his messenger) from Netherfield, I would have thought the message from my Lizzy. Only she would send a note to Longbourn, requesting my wife journey to Netherfield and see Jane for herself. She always hoped her mother was more than she was. That said, since you wrote to me, I shall tell you that nothing good can come of your request. I have no doubt Mrs. Bennet will declare Jane too ill to be moved and insist Mr. Bingley keep her for longer, praising him as though it were his idea all along. Her effusions and flattery would be an embarrassment, and she would bring our three youngest, who would expose themselves and our family to further ridicule. Believe me, child, your judgement is more to be trusted than my wife's. When my girls were ill as children, Mrs. Hill cared for them with the help of a young scullery maid. Mrs. Bennet had no temperament for the sick room.

I sent for Mr. Jones so Mr. Bingley would have no need to do so. He will report to me of her

*condition. If possible, I shall arrange for the
carriage to return you to Longbourn this evening,
but I make no promises until I speak with Mr.
Jones. Should Jane be too ill, she had best stay
where she is.*

Your obedient servant,

Thomas Bennet, Esq.

Ellie crumpled the paper and dropped her face against it.
He was right—of course, he was right—but she hated being
under the microscope of the bitchy Bingley sisters. They had
come to Jane's bedchamber more than once yesterday, declaring
how horrible it was to be ill in a way that reminded Ellie of the
popular girls at school who faked sympathy in front of the
teacher. Their false sincerity did nothing but make her dislike
them more.

With a sigh, she tossed the letter into the fire. If someone
read Mr. Bennet's message and discovered her secret, she would
be in trouble. Nothing was in the letter that she needed to
remember anyway, so it was better destroyed than falling into
the hands of Miss Bingley or Mrs. Hurst.

Mr. Jones appeared around the noon hour and left more
tonic that Ellie once again poured into the chamber pot as soon
as Jane had fallen asleep. The maids delivered teas and broths
most of the day, which helped Jane stay hydrated despite the
fever. The willow bark seemed to lower her temperature a little,

but it was hard to tell for sure. How long did they have before a medical thermometer was invented? Or Paracetamol? What she wouldn't give for either!

When she joined the inhabitants of Netherfield that evening, she sat on one end of the sofa with her sketchbook, keeping an ear attuned to Miss Bingley's ridiculous attempts to engage Mr. Darcy in conversation. She made comment after comment about the letter he was writing to his sister, to which he either made no response or a clipped answer that made Ellie stifle a smile or swallow a bark of laughter.

"I am afraid you do not like your pen." Miss Bingley stepped behind him and looked over his shoulder. "Let me mend it for you. I mend pens remarkably well."

Ellie couldn't hold in her amusement and a snort escaped. She clapped her hand over her nose, but it was too late, and Miss Bingley zeroed in on her. "Miss Elizabeth, are you *drawing?*"

She straightened and held the obnoxious woman's eye. "Why, yes, I am."

"I was unaware you boasted of such an accomplishment."

"Did I not mention it when I submitted my list of abilities and talents to you? How careless of me." One side of Mr. Darcy's lips curved, but he continued writing without looking up.

"May I enquire of Miss Bennet's condition?" Mr. Bingley's expression was open and cheerful. Unlike his sisters, he didn't seem to be fake.

"I believe her fever worsened some today, but she has been comfortable, thanks to you and your household. We appreciate all that has been done to be of aid to her."

"If you require a physician from town, pray, tell, and I shall arrange the matter for you." His eager expression gave her some hope that he liked Jane more than a little.

"Thank you, Mr. Bingley. I shall if she seems to have the need. I do hope she will show signs of improvement soon."

"I am certain Miss Bennet will be well and such drastic measures need not be taken," said Miss Bingley in an impatient tone. "We can send for Mr. Jones again should she worsen. It is not as though you should offer a ball in honour of her recovery."

"A ball!" Mr. Bingley's face perked up. "What a capital idea, Caroline."

Miss Bingley stepped behind her brother with an expression that appeared as though she'd sucked a lemon. "I am certain no one expects such a gesture of you, Charles."

"But I believe a ball would be just the thing. What do you think, Miss Elizabeth?"

Ellie gave a jolt. Why did he feel the need to bring her into the matter? "I am certain no one would hold it against you should you decline to give a ball, but I am also certain the entirety of Meryton would enjoy the occasion should you decide to go through with it."

"Such a decisive recommendation," said Miss Bingley.

Ellie cocked her head a little to one side. "I do all I can."

Mr. Darcy stood and stepped nearer to the fire, holding out his hands to warm them. "Miss Bingley, perchance some music would be of benefit to us all."

At his request, the lady, for lack of a better word, preened. "I should be happy to entertain you, Mr. Darcy. I am certain you have missed the more polished performances of town." The woman then all but sashayed to the pianoforte, selected a music sheet, and began to play.

Ellie continued to sketch while the room filled with a familiar piano sonata. From the recordings Ellie had heard, the piece was meant to be played at a fast pace, though Miss Bingley had obviously put all her time and effort into the technicality of the piece and had not thought to include any emotion, leaving it flat and uninspired, much like her chest.

While Miss Bingley continued to another piece, Mr. Darcy began pacing the room. He stared out the window for a moment before shifting to stand behind Ellie, making goosebumps erupt along the back of her neck. A folded note landed on her sketchbook, and she glanced over her shoulder as he gestured for her to hurry to pick it up. As soon as she tucked the paper into her pocket, the song ended, allowing her to curtsey and excuse herself for the evening.

Chapter 13

The next morning, Jane's fever had broken, and she seemed improved. Her headache had lessened, and her sore throat had subsided some, though she was still fatigued, which wasn't so surprising after a few days of illness.

After ensuring Jane drank her teas and was once again peacefully asleep, Ellie checked the time. How had Jane known the perfect moment to take a nap?

She grabbed her pelisse and shawl, hurried down the stairs, and made it outside without anyone noticing or stopping her. Now, which way? In his note, Fitzwilliam had said the gardens behind the house, and she was in front, so she hurried around until she reached a path between the edge of the rose gardens and a row of lavender. That was when the sound of voices made her search the area. On the opposite side of the house, strolling in the direction of what appeared to be an avenue were three people, two ladies and a gentleman. Was that Miss Bingley?

No, her ears weren't deceiving her. The tall one with the enormous ostrich feather on her bonnet was definitely Miss Bingley. She was the last person Ellie would expect to see outside. She seemed the type to dislike nature in all its forms, but the woman was outside, walking along the avenue with what appeared to be her sister and...Fitzwilliam? Why would he ask Ellie to meet him in the gardens if he was going to be strolling the grounds with those ladies? Of course, he could've been coerced into joining them. Most of the time he was far too polite to say no, and when he threw out the occasional barb, Miss Bingley didn't seem to notice. She'd give one of those insufferable titters and continue on trying to impress him. She was a bit daft, really.

Ellie was so busy watching them, she tripped and scuffled on the walk. Bloody hell! Her heart beat a mile a minute as Miss Bingley's head started to turn. Bollocks! She dropped so she was hidden by the roses and hopefully the lavender on the opposite side. While she was crouched, she glanced back at the exposed root that had possibly given her away. "Traitor," she said in a whisper.

After a few seconds, she took a chance and peeked between two roses. The trio were facing forward again. They took two more steps before Fitzwilliam made a sudden stop, withdrew from their group, and strode back into the house. Miss Bingley and Mrs. Hurst watched him until he entered, then turned and made their way to the avenue. When they disappeared into the trees, Ellie stood and heaved out an exhale. "That was close."

"At least you escaped their notice. I was departing the house when they discovered me."

She whirled around to Fitzwilliam standing behind her. "You startled me. How did you make it around here so fast?"

His lips curved, revealing two swoon-worthy dimples. "Forgive me. I hastened through the front and around the side of the house. I had attempted to meet you here, but Miss Bingley insisted I had no wish to ride this morning and insisted on my company for a walk instead."

"Yet, you managed to escape."

"I claimed I had business that could not be delayed."

"You dissembled again?"

He pointed in the opposite direction of Miss Bingley and Mrs. Hurst. "Perhaps we should walk this way to avoid the notice of Miss Bingley and her sister. As for dissembling, I do have a letter I should be writing."

"Ah, so you stretched the truth."

His forehead creased. "I merely made the matter seem more urgent than it is." When he looked at her, his shoulders dropped. "You are teasing me."

"Sorry. I couldn't resist."

One side of his lips curved. "I am not angry. I find I do not mind you teasing me." He held out his arm, and she set her hand in the crook as she fell into step beside him. "How does your sister fare this morning?"

"Her fever has broken, and her throat is a little better, but she's tired. When I left her, she was sleeping."

"I am certain the rest will do a great deal for her. You do not spend much time with the residents of Netherfield. I believe I have seen you for but an hour each evening after dinner, so I was concerned her condition was more severe than Mr. Jones had indicated. You do know you are welcome to eat with the party for each meal and spend more time in the drawing room when you are not attending your sister. Bingley would insist should he believe you feel unwelcome."

"Oh, I don't feel unwelcome. Mr. Bennet...Papa expressed concern that I may inadvertently give away my lack of memory if I was not careful and spent too much time with everyone. While with the Bingleys and the Hursts, I spend so much time considering every word that comes out of my mouth. The effort is exhausting, which is why I try to entertain myself by reading or drawing. I did not expect to be called out for it. At least with Jane, I do not have to be so careful."

He nodded. "I understand more than you know. I oft times find being in large groups tiring and frustrating. Pemberley is where I find peace. If I could remain there for all of my days, I believe I would be content."

"What of your friends or your sister? Eventually, she will marry, and you would be left all alone. Wouldn't you be lonely?"

He blinked a couple of times and shrugged. "I would not mind visits from friends and certain relations. Bingley would certainly be welcome as would my cousin Richard, who is a colonel in the regulars. If Georgiana has no desire to wed, she may live at Pemberley for as long as she desires. I would never force her from her home."

Why would his sister not want to get married? Wasn't that what a woman's life was supposed to be at this time in history—marriage and children? "You do not believe your sister will want to marry?"

"She is terribly shy, and this summer, she suffered a disappointment. I should hope for her to recover before she makes any life-altering decisions."

"Somehow, when you say 'disappointment,' you make it sound like more than she was rejected by a school or a club she wanted to join."

He frowned and glanced around them. "No, the situation was nothing like that. You see, she despised school and wanted to be removed. My cousin and I, who are her guardians, set up an establishment for her in Ramsgate."

She had read about this in his journal, but the last she'd read was that he was leaving Pemberley to join Georgiana on her holiday. What could have happened?

"After a month, I thought to surprise her and journeyed from Pemberley to Ramsgate where she stayed with a hired companion. When I arrived, I knew immediately something was amiss. Mrs. Younge, her companion, tried to prevent me from speaking to her, and when I ignored her and entered the drawing room, Georgiana was sitting on the sofa with George Wickham, a man I had known since infancy and whom I knew to be a rake and a hopeless blackguard. He had convinced her to elope and keep it a secret from me."

"How old was she?"

"Not yet sixteen."

Ellie looked at him askance. "And how old was this Wickham bloke?"

"Twenty-six."

"Eww," she said, shaking her hands. "She was still a child, and he was an adult." Was this guy a pedo or did he have some other motive?

Fitzwilliam stopped, turned to face her, and leaned in close. "Do remember elopement is a scandal, and without my consent, illegal even in Scotland, which is what Wickham planned to do. No lady should ever wed without a marriage settlement to protect them."

"What happened to your sister?"

"I told Wickham I would never consent, and if they eloped, he would not receive her fortune of thirty-thousand pounds until she turned one and twenty and a legal agreement was signed, placing her fortune into an account for her and any future children. He would never gain access to the money. He became furious and called me a number of names I shall not repeat. Wickham then said, 'I have debts to pay now. Your mouse of a sister would be useless to me for six years unless you pay my debts and take us in.'"

So, his motive was money. "What a wanker," she muttered under her breath.

"I do not know what that means, but by your tone, I am certain I would agree." He sighed. "Georgiana became overwrought and declared she would never marry him after such a declaration. I confess I hoped my statement would goad him into revealing his intentions. While I had no desire to injure my sister, she needed to know Wickham's true character."

Ellie took his hand in both of hers. "You saved her."

"Nothing quite so dramatic, I assure you. I failed her by leaving her vulnerable to his seduction. I am only relieved she escaped with no more than a broken heart. Her situation could have been so much worse."

While he'd spoken, Ellie stared at their joined hands. What had made her do that? She withdrew hers and clasped them in front of her. Perhaps she could control herself better that way. "You could not have known Wickham would go to such lengths. How many brothers would be diligent enough to journey so far to ensure she was well and safe? Because of you, she won't be forced to endure marriage to a man who wanted her for nothing more than the money she could bring him. I can't imagine those situations are happy for either. May I ask where your sister is now?"

"I hired a new companion since we were so misled about the character of Mrs. Younge, her former companion, and she has remained at my home in London while I am residing at Netherfield."

"I am sure home is the perfect place for her. There is always a comfort you can find at home that you can't find anywhere else."

"I agree," he said. One of his dimples peeked through for the first time since speaking of his sister.

"Before I forget, I must thank you for sending the note to my father."

With a nod, he gestured ahead of them, and they continued along the path. "I assumed between Chambers's explanation and that I have seen you reading, that you have forgotten how to use a pen."

She bit her lip for a second. "My lack of memory is rather selective. I know it is, but pray, do not ask me to explain because I can't. I am not even sure what I am going to do if Mr. Bingley throws this ball he mentioned last night. If I am asked to dance, what am I supposed to do? I do not even know the etiquette."

"Until you depart, we can discuss some of what you will need to know and perhaps practice a dance or two. When you return to Longbourn, Miss Bennet may be of more assistance than I on some matters, and we can continue meeting at Oakham Mount unless the weather is poor."

"I also cannot always go in the mornings because Mr. Bennet calls me into his library to talk."

His eyebrows drew down. "You mean your father?"

Crap! "Yes, forgive me. I know who he is, but I have a difficult time calling him Papa. I have no memory of him before I woke up. It's all very strange."

"I suppose that is understandable."

"So, Mr. Darcy, since Miss Bingley believes them so important in a lady, I am wondering, sir, what are *your* accomplishments?" She lifted her eyebrows. "I know you can play the piano, but what else can you do?"

He chuckled and shook his head. "Men are not expected to gain accomplishments."

"That's hypocritical, don't you think?"

"I suppose you are correct. I never considered it before. It is just how ladies are...valued."

She lifted an eyebrow and peered up at him. "Hmm." Valued? Disgusting. "So, these accomplishments of yours?"

"You are in earnest. I am to list what I can do."

With a twirl, she turned and walked backward. "Yes, I must hear how a gentleman of means occupies his time."

He shook his head with a smile. "I ride, of course, and I can fence."

"Like sword fighting?"

"Yes, and I can shoot. I shoot pheasant, grouse, quail, and more. I have studied boxing under John Jackson."

Ellie lifted her eyebrows. "Is Mr. Jackson good at boxing?"

"Is Mr. Jackson good?" he asked in a high-pitched tone. "In 1795, he became the bare-knuckled boxing champion of all England. He is a celebrated pugilist."

She turned back around and fell into step beside him. "Ah, forgive me then. I suppose I have lived under a rock all of these years." She laughed lightly. "Do many gentlemen study pugilism?"

"Mr. Jackson teaches a great many of the peerage. My uncle, who is an earl, and his sons have also taken lessons from him."

She brushed her fingers along the bark of a tree as they passed. "I suppose beating each other is better than dog fighting or cock fighting."

The set of Fitzwilliam's jaw tightened. "I have never enjoyed dog fighting or cock fighting. Setting two animals upon each other to fight to the death in such a brutal fashion is not what I consider entertainment. I also do not care for the type of gentlemen those diversions attract. Wickham takes great pleasure in them."

Which would be another reason he disliked those events. "So we were discussing your accomplishments, sir. Do you have more I should be aware of?"

"I play billiards and can swim...archery, though I am not as proficient as I am with a sabre or a hunting rifle. Must I think of more?"

"No." She tilted her head while she looked at him. "You are quite accomplished for a gentleman, I suppose."

His cheeks reddened a bit, bringing a flutter to her stomach. "I do not believe I am capable of any more than any other gentlemen, but I am glad my talents and preferences meet with your approval."

"Since I am uncertain of what is expected of a gentleman, I suppose they do."

"When do you envisage your return to Longbourn?"

She sighed. "As soon as Jane feels capable of making the trip. I do not want to trespass on Mr. Bingley's generosity one moment more than necessary."

"I should enjoy walking with you again, if weather permits," he said in a softer voice.

"I believe that can be arranged. But for now, I should get back to Jane, so perhaps we should begin our return to the house."

"Of course. Forgive me for keeping you from her for so long." He held out his arm, and she set her hand upon it once more.

"You need not apologise. Jane was asleep, and I truly required the time away and the fresh air this morning. I should thank you for your impromptu invitation."

He grinned and glanced at her with those stunning eyes, once again sending a tremor through her. What was she going to do? She was in trouble. Her heart was leading her towards a man she could not have and should not love. This wasn't your typical bog-standard trouble, it was the worst possible predicament she could imagine. Why did God or fate or whoever was in charge of time and human existence throw her into this mess? What a cock-up!

Chapter 14

The next day dawned with a heavy grey mist that clung to the ground and never seemed to completely clear, lingering in a dreary haze. As had been her habit, a maid brought Ellie a tray for breakfast and luncheon, but by the afternoon, she was dying. She had to get out of the bedchamber or she would go barmy!

Not that the room was unpleasant. On the contrary, the bedroom was sizable and comfortable though still confining. She spent a large portion of her time at the window with the draperies wide open, staring at the unwelcome weather. It was one of those days where the rain never seemed to fall, but fat water droplets would appear out of nowhere as you walked and managed to splash your entire cheek.

"Ellie?"

She turned as Jane pushed herself up to sit. "Are you feeling better?"

"Much. I am less fatigued than yesterday at this time."

"You were slightly warm. I think your fever returned for a few hours, which is why you were so tired." She rang the bell, then sat on a chair she'd moved by the side of the bed. "What do you think of going downstairs after your luncheon? You could visit Mr. Bingley—you know Mama would never forgive me if you didn't speak to that gentleman at least once while we were here."

Jane sighed and settled into the pillows. "I confess it would be agreeable to be out of this bed. Have you fared well with Mr. Bingley and his family?"

"I believe so. Papa's suggestion of reading Fanny Burney has helped, though I did relax a little when Mr. Darcy and I walked yesterday."

"You mentioned walking, but you did not say you were with Mr. Darcy. He has singled you out and shows you considerable attention."

A pang ripped through her chest. Wait, what? "I don't understand. We're friends...I think, nothing more."

"Is he courting you?"

"Courting? As in considering me for marriage?" Was he? She frowned and shook her head. "No, he couldn't be. Who would consider a woman with no memory and who speaks like a common sailor marriage material?"

Jane pulled her knees up and wrapped her arms around them. "Your manner of speaking has improved a great deal, and he seems to seek you out. What if he does not object?"

Ellie stood and started biting her thumbnail. If he was considering her, that wasn't good. What would happen when poor Elizabeth Bennet returned and was stuck with Fitzwilliam for the rest of her life? From what Mr. Bennet and others had said, Elizabeth detested Fitzwilliam. How miserable would that make her to wake up one day and find herself obligated to him. Ellie had to make sure the personal relationships she developed here were similar to those she had in the future. Yes, she had friends, but she'd never been one to get close to anyone, not since her parents died. That couldn't change while she was here. It seemed that she'd let down her guard more than usual. Why she'd done so didn't matter. It simply couldn't continue.

"Ellie, are you well?"

She startled and whirled around. "Yes, thank you. I suppose I shall need to avoid Mr. Darcy in the future."

"You enjoy his company. I know you do. Why would you wish to avoid him?"

"I don't believe I am the best choice he could make. If I knew someone else who would suit, I'd push him in that direction, but Mama insists you are for Mr. Bingley, our younger sisters would drive him mad, and Charlotte doesn't seem his type."

Jane stared at her with wide eyes, and her mouth slightly agape. "I suppose if that is what you wish."

"What's that supposed to mean?"

"Well, I think you like him, despite what he said at the assembly, and I believe you are using your difficulty with your memory as an excuse to keep from becoming attached to him."

"I'm not using it as an excuse."

With her eyebrows raised, Jane situated the coverlet. "I disagree, but I shall not argue with you."

Ellie opened her mouth to respond but was saved by a knock at the servants' entrance. She hurried over and fetched the tray from the maid waiting on the other side of the door. Jane ate the hearty soup slowly, and when she was finished, Ellie helped her select a gown from her trunk.

Jane walked her through helping her dress, which didn't take long, but poor Jane's hair! After a half an hour of laughter and several poor efforts, Ellie finally managed a passable style that the snooty sisters couldn't find fault with—she hoped.

Upon their entrance to the drawing room, Miss Bingley jumped up from the settee. "Miss Bennet! How wonderful to see you so well. You have arrived at the perfect moment. We have had no callers on such a dreary day and have despaired for company." The lady grasped Jane's arm and ushered her to the chair by the fire where she and Mrs. Hurst bombarded the poor girl with questions and spoke relentlessly of how horrible it was to be ill. It was all Ellie could do not to roll her eyes at their overly dramatic tones. Did those ladies have one sincere bone in their bodies?

"Miss Bennet," said Mr. Bingley in a cheerful tone as he entered. "I was attending to some business when Mrs. Nicholls mentioned that you had come down. How lovely to see you well." He joined his sisters and Jane, so Ellie sat on the sofa with her sketchbook. Mr. Darcy stepped into the room, but after a nod in her direction, sat in a chair near the window, reading a book. Ellie opened to a clean page and began laying down the first soft strokes of her next study. As always happened when she drew, she tuned out what was around her, concentrating on the lines and shading upon the page.

"Dear Lord, what an incredible likeness of Darcy!"

Ellie jumped and inhaled, her head turning to Mr. Bingley who stood behind her. She wanted more than anything to slam the book shut, but Miss Bingley had already hurried over, her eyes narrowed. No, no, no! She was not a rival! Ellie had no desire to be in Miss Bingley's way. She was not competition! Really, this was the last thing she wanted or needed!

"What a remarkable likeness indeed," said the lady with a drawl.

Before she could close her sketchbook, Mrs. Hurst and Fitzwilliam joined Mr. Bingley. Mrs. Hurst's eyebrows jumped on her forehead. "You are quite talented, Miss Elizabeth. Miss Bennet, you should see your sister's drawing."

"I shall see it when we return upstairs, I am sure. You should see her other attempts. They are all extraordinary."

"I am flattered, Miss Elizabeth." Mr. Darcy's low tone made her stomach flip. Why did that always happen when he spoke to her or looked at her in a certain way? And why couldn't she make it stop?

"Forgive me for not asking if I could sketch you. You sat across from me and were so still while you read. You made an easy subject."

"You need not apologise," he said. "I am impressed by your skill at portraiture. I wish Georgiana was here so you could take her likeness for me to enjoy."

Miss Bingley's lips pursed, and her nose became pointy again. "It seems you have an eye for portraits, Miss Elizabeth." The words were uttered through her teeth.

"Thank you for your kind words, Miss Bingley." She shouldn't be enjoying the woman's irritation, but she was. Perhaps she should return Jane upstairs. All she needed was to have Miss Bingley more cross with her than she already was. Ellie looked back down at the page as everyone returned to what they were doing before Mr. Bingley's outburst, except Miss Bingley, who was now walking around the room.

After three circuits, she stopped in front of Ellie. "Miss Eliza Bennet, you must follow my example and take a turn about the room with me. I assure you it is very refreshing after sitting so long in one attitude."

Ellie glanced at Jane, speaking in quiet tones to Mr. Bingley. Mr. Darcy had returned to his chair and his book, and Mrs. Hurst had departed at some point, perhaps to find Mr. Hurst, who had been missing since their arrival. "A turn about the room?"

"Yes."

"I am supposed to find walking around a drawing room refreshing?"

The woman huffed. "Yes."

"How?"

"I beg pardon?" Miss Bingley's head turned a little as it shifted forward. "I do not understand."

"Well, you have no scenery, besides the room, which is attractive, but does not change, and no fresh air from the outside. I must admit, I am confused as to how it is refreshing." She shouldn't provoke Miss Bingley, but she had to admit it was entertaining—particularly the part where the lady began to resemble a bird with a large, pointy beak.

"It is merely the change in attitude," said Miss Bingley. "You have been sitting for some time. Standing would be beneficial. I am sure."

"Very well." As she stood, she caught a glimpse of Fitzwilliam's shoulders shaking. He propped his head on his hand, so his mouth was blocked and she couldn't see his expression. Yet, she was certain he was laughing. As she continued around the room, his eyes had to be following them. The prickles on the back of her neck spread down her arms and between her shoulder blades. Only Fitzwilliam had ever caused that reaction. When they turned, his intent gaze was indeed on her. The gormless Miss Bingley preened. Did she actually think that would draw his attention?

"What can you mean by watching us so, Mr. Darcy?" Miss Bingley grinned in a way that was so eager it was almost frightening, and Ellie bit her lip at Mr. Darcy's expression.

"I must admit to being curious of Miss Elizabeth's experience. If she found the turn as refreshing as you promised."

He was wicked to tempt her. "Not so much refreshing as informative. I had not previously noticed the figurine of a shepherd on the mantel or the fine detailing of gold in the draperies. Miss Bingley's ring is unique as well. I do not believe I have seen the like." Was that blue enamel with diamonds? The ring was huge in comparison to the woman's long, bony finger and certainly not something Ellie would choose to wear.

Miss Bingley held out her hand and admired the setting. "I purchased it from a shop on Bond Street in March. The salesman assured me it was one of a kind, and I could not resist."

Ellie could imagine what the man said to sell the ring. He was probably like one of those market vendors that wouldn't stop pushing and pushing, hoping you would finally just buy the piece. She glanced over at Jane who appeared pale. "I should return Jane to her rooms. I do not want her to overexert herself." She grabbed her drawing supplies and hurried Jane back upstairs. Thankfully, Miss Bingley didn't accompany them.

Two days later, Fitzwilliam watched Bingley's carriage drive away from Netherfield with a weight on his chest. Miss Ellie had to return home at some point, but why could they not remain for a day or two longer? Yes, he understood that Miss Bingley was antagonistic and trying; he also wanted to escape her more often than not, but he had never managed that second walk with Miss Ellie. What was it about her that fascinated him so?

She was intelligent. She had awakened from her injury with no memory of who she was and had acquired an odd manner of speaking, yet with the help of Miss Bennet and her father, she was learning proper speech even if she sometimes was not entirely appropriate. Regardless, he could not blame her for her questions when Miss Bingley requested she take that turn about the room. The lady had some ulterior motive for her request, and Miss Ellie was quick enough to have some idea of it, another sign of her superior intelligence.

Then, he had to consider her artistic accomplishments. She had shown him her drawings before, but the portrait she had made of him was exceptional. He wanted to furnish her with paints and a canvas to determine the extent of her talent. Watercolours were considered more of a ladies' pursuit, but Miss Ellie was more accomplished than most. She should be painting in oils, not watercolours.

He was trapped. Every moment spent in her company made him desire more. Perhaps she would walk in the morning or at least go to Oakham Mount to draw. He would take Lysander out for a good gallop through the fields, and hopefully spend more time talking to this lady who had captured his attention.

He did not care if his relations or even Georgiana approved. She was the sole lady who had ever drawn his interest, and he would see if he could perhaps court her into accepting his hand. Something in him said that was the one true way to find happiness in this life. Otherwise, he would remove to Pemberley after Georgiana wed, and one of her sons would inherit Pemberley.

He had done as his uncle had requested and attended a variety of events this past Season. The result had been the same at each and every torturous ball, dinner, and performance—not one lady had stood out from the gaggle and shown herself to be an individual. Was it too much to ask for a lady who possessed more than the average intelligence and could speak without showering him with some inane flattery? He refused to marry a lady he could not abide, and Miss Ellie was the sole lady who had garnered any interest—or tolerance—on his part. She had the intellect and forthright opinions to hold his attention for a lifetime. After becoming further acquainted with her, he could not ignore what his heart and mind were telling him. He had to try.

Chapter 15

Fitzwilliam dismounted from Lysander and led the great horse through the last of the trees before emerging at the top of Oakham Mount, his heart leaping in his chest at the sight of Miss Ellie sitting on the rock. He would never tire of that sensation. The prospect of spending even a moment of time in Ellie's company excited and settled him at the same time. He relished their conversations, and he enjoyed aiding in her pursuit of recovering what she had lost. Not necessarily her memories, though he would be thrilled for her if they returned, but more her quest to observe the necessary proprieties of polite society.

At that moment, she seemed lost in thought as she sketched, so entranced by what she had created upon the page, she did not hear him or Lysander emerge from the path. Her forehead was furrowed, and her teeth were pressing small dimples into her bottom lip. He desired more than anything to tug her lip free and kiss it.

Before he could softly announce his presence, Lysander nickered, and her head jolted around. "Mr. Darcy!" She set her book aside and scrambled to curtsey.

He bowed in return. "Forgive us for startling you. I had not planned to announce our presence so abruptly, but I suppose Lysander had other ideas. He likes you and apparently demands your immediate attention."

She grinned and stepped up to the stallion, holding out her hand out as he had taught her. "I do not mind his interruption. He was being polite. I cannot hold that against him. After all, a gentleman doesn't spy." One eyebrow arched in the most alluring way.

"Does that mean you object to my presence?" Her fingers scratched under his horse's chin. Was it ridiculous to be jealous of a horse?

"Are you looking for an invitation to stay? You seem to be fishing for one."

Where had she learnt such strange language? "Fishing?"

"Hoping?" she said.

"Ah, I merely do not want to interrupt when you may prefer to remain in solitude. I was also admiring the prospect."

She pressed her forehead to Lysander's. She was becoming more comfortable around him. "Prospect?" She blinked and faced him for a moment before she returned her attention to Lysander. She was ignoring his compliment. "I don't mind you being here. Longbourn is too busy for me sometimes, and I need to get away. Mr. Benn...Papa also told me to distance myself from our visitor."

"You have a visitor?"

"A distant cousin, the one who is to inherit Longbourn arrived yesterday, and for some reason, Papa insisted I make myself scarce until dinner. I do not mind since the gentleman is...Well, he's a bit dim."

"I do not know what that means either."

"He is daft, stupid, or in this man's case, simply ridiculous. Take your pick of the adjective. They all fit. Last night after dinner, he attempted to read from Fordyce's sermons to the family and described how he plans compliments that are 'pleasing to the ladies.' For the rest of the evening, he gushed over his patroness, the pompous and patronising Lady Catherine de Bourgh, who must enjoy a parson who grovels since he can speak of nothing but her even when he isn't kissing her ass."

His eyes flared for a moment, and he stiffened while he held in his laughter. "Lady Catherine de Bourgh is my aunt."

Miss Ellie slapped her hand over her mouth. "I am so sorry."

He pretended to be affronted for no more than a minute before allowing himself a chuckle. "Do not worry yourself. She is as you say. My cousin and I jest that her last parson injured his back bowing at her rebukes. Until last year, I have spent every Easter at her estate, ensuring the steward is managing the tenant concerns and the land as he should. My aunt often insists upon her own methods, which are never in the best interest of those involved."

Her head tilted slightly to the side. "You said you spent every Easter until last year. Do you not intend to visit her again?"

He draped Lysander's reins over the nearby tree limb, stepped to the sharp edge of the rise, and turned to face Miss Ellie. "She is insistent I marry her daughter, who is sickly and greatly resembles her mother in temperament—imperious and condescending."

"Ew," she said with a scrunched nose. "Is this your first cousin?"

"Yes. Why do you ask?"

She stepped closer and crossed her arms over her chest. "I know it is common, particularly in the royal family right now, but should there be such a possibility, I could never marry my cousin."

"Well, I shall never wed mine, which I told my aunt in no uncertain terms during my last visit. She was none too pleased and banished me from Rosings. By the by, if anyone ever speaks as I did before about their aunt's steward or a situation equally as personal, compliment the nephew who is guarding his aunt's best interests instead of furthering the discussion."

"Bollocks! I am still becoming accustomed to not talking about whatever I want."

He had no idea what the exclamation meant, but it was interesting. Hopefully, she did not believe he would mind her enquiries. Somehow, he doubted he ever would, even if she regained her memories. "I am not upset and would not have answered so freely had I been offended."

She squinted one eye. "So, I am to say, 'You are a good nephew' and say nothing further."

"Yes."

"This is ridiculous. I can talk about the weather, the state of the roads, or superficial nonsense and that is all."

"Precisely. You cannot make a mistake if you keep to those topics."

She gave a low growl. "I shall never get used to this."

"You are not an addle-pate. I believe you can accomplish any task to which you set your mind." He meant it too.

With a small laugh, she crossed her arms over her chest. "Thank you, I guess, but I am not familiar with the term addle-pate."

"I believe you used the word 'dim.'"

With an impish grin, she returned to the rock and picked up her book of drawings. "Before I forget, I completed the portrait of you I made at Netherfield. If you want the finished piece, you may have it. After all, I should have never started without asking your permission."

He held up a hand. "Pray, do not concern yourself with those formalities. I assure you I was not angry. You must have been hard pressed to find a suitable subject without asking Miss Bingley or Mrs. Hurst, and Mr. Hurst is usually in his cups—"

"And Mr. Bingley was busy talking to Jane. I did not want to interrupt, and his face is very expressive. While he wasn't moving all that much, his expression kept changing while he spoke. Yours remained more even as you read, and the pose was natural. Miss Bingley and Mrs. Hurst would have been stiff."

"I agree." He pointed to her book. "Have you begun a new masterpiece?"

She flipped it open. "I was just laying out a study of that tree. If Papa pushes me out of doors tomorrow, maybe I shall find a hiding spot around Longbourn so I can draw the house. This place has a wonderful view, but nothing ever changes, though I do appreciate the quiet."

He tapped his foot for a moment. Where could she go? The bridge and stream were too close to Meryton so that would not do. She might happen upon someone on the road near Longbourn, which she seemed to want to avoid since she mentioned quiet. Then, he clapped his hands together. "I have just the spot. Come. I shall show you."

"Now?"

Without pause, he pulled out his pocket watch. "It is but nine o'clock. If you are not to return until dinner, Mr. Bennet is not expecting you back soon."

"No, I am only surprised by how excited you are."

"I am certain the place will be to your liking, but the walk is a lengthy one. If I am to show you today, we should depart now."

She shrugged and shoved her black lead into her reticule. "I am not afraid of a little exercise."

He gathered Lysander's reins. "We could also ride, which would hasten our trip."

Her head drew back a little. "Both of us on one horse? Is that proper?"

"No," he said, "but it is doubtful anyone will see us."

She gave a great exhale and stepped beside the large horse. "How do I get up there?"

His heart beat madly in his chest as he stepped closer. "May I?" He held his hands near her waist. At the second bob of her head, he lifted her to sit sideways on the saddle and set his hand on the pommel. "Hold this until I lead him down the hill. I do not want him to lose his footing with both of us upon his back."

She slipped the ribbons of her reticule around her wrist then held her book tightly with one arm while she gripped the front of his saddle until her knuckles whitened. He adjusted the iron on that side so it was near her boot. "Put your foot in this." Once she had done as he asked, he set his hand near the horse's shoulder. "Do not let your nerves get the better of you. Horses can sense fear and will get up to all sorts of mischief."

"Really? Then why did you suggest this?"

He chuckled and set his hand upon hers. "You need not worry."

She startled and began to fidget with her reticule. "I forgot to put my gloves back on."

"You are just going to take them off to draw again."

"You're right." She pulled her reticule closed and again grasped the pommel. "Let's get this over with."

As he started to lead the horse down the path, he glanced back to her rigid bearing and stern expression. "This is not a trip to the gallows, and I am certain you will enjoy the experience."

When they reached the bottom, he passed the reins up to her. "Would you hold those until I can mount?" Then he swung up behind her and sat just behind the saddle on Lysander's rump, reaching around her for the reins. The scent of orange blossoms lingered on her hair. He loved that scent, so light, so feminine. It suited her. Every bit of his restraint was required to keep from burying his nose in her hair and inhaling deeply. He shook himself. "Now hold onto the saddle like I showed you." He clucked and the horse moved forward, walking at a steady pace through the trees. After a few minutes of silence, he looked up at her. "Are you well?"

"Yes, why?"

"I do not believe you have ever been so quiet when it is just the two of us."

They kept to the pathway towards Netherfield, but instead of leaving the shelter of the forest and crossing the fields, he turned and continued through the canopy of the trees until he crossed onto the edge of Netherfield property. Less than five minutes later, he steered Lysander into a small clearing. There, amongst the trees, were the ruins of a small gothic chapel, its walls overrun by nature. The scene was perfect. Between the shadows at different times of the day and the numerous views inside and outside, Miss Ellie could sketch here for weeks and never draw the same picture.

She gasped and looked over her shoulder at him. "This is amazing."

"We were told of this place when Bingley let Netherfield, but I have not ridden here since you were recovering from your fall. I do not believe Bingley has ever ventured this far afield. He would have little interest in such a thing, but I know he will not mind you being here."

"Are you certain?"

He dismounted and helped her down from Lysander's back. "I can tell him if it will make you more comfortable."

"Wouldn't that bring up questions as to how you know I'm here?"

I would merely say I saw you while riding," he said. "Bingley would not think to question me further and would, no doubt, be pleased to know someone has a use for this old chapel."

Miss Ellie opened a rickety and rusted iron gate and stepped through, turning in a circle. She gazed at the ornate window frame, the tree limbs overhanging the walls, and the weeds, which likely produced flowers in the spring, poking out from between the stones.

"Can you remember the paths to come here again?"

She glanced over her shoulder at him. "The route was not complicated. I'm sure I can manage."

He stood in one spot while she peeked around walls and through the remnants of windows at the different prospects. "Will you not draw?"

"What?" Her head hitched back some, and her eyes widened as she turned her gaze upon him. "With you watching me? I couldn't do that. I wouldn't be able to concentrate."

He traced the elegant line of her neck with his eyes as she turned and stepped through a fallen part of the wall. Propriety demanded he depart and leave her, but he was not ready to do so. He would never leave her if afforded the opportunity. "If you do not object to my company, I could teach you a dance for Bingley's ball."

She stepped back inside the chapel and faced him, her countenance full of mischief. "Here? There is no music."

He shrugged. "We do not require music. I can teach you by count to start. Once you have mastered the pattern, we shall worry with the music."

Her book and reticule were placed on the soft grass. "I *should* learn. Are you certain you wish to do this? I can ask Jane. I am sure she will not mind showing me." His heart quickened when her bare hand touched his gloved one.

"I do not object. It is my honour to teach you." Her cheeks became pink while his fingers wrapped around hers. Her hand fit so perfectly in his, as though it belonged there warming his. During the season, when he had been obligated to offer a lady his hand for a dance or some other such nonsense, their touch had been cold. He had grown weary of the cold. He longed for the warmth, and not just any warmth, but that of Ellie's.

His uncle and aunt, no doubt, hoped for a more illustrious union, but they would not make too much of a fuss. Lady Catherine would bluster and fume, but her opinion was neither desired nor a consideration. His heart wanted Ellie—no one but Ellie would do.

Chapter 16

Ellie leaned closer to the carriage window and took in the view of Netherfield as they approached the great house. Bathed in the light of the waxing gibbous moon, the windows glittered from the candles within, and large torches lit the front of the house and the drive to welcome guests. The scene appeared something out of a fairy tale, but would the reality of a real Regency ball live up to the glam or be a colossal disappointment?

"Are you well?" asked Jane near her ear.

"No, this is worse than the party at Lucas Lodge. I am afraid there is too much to remember, and I shall fail at the worst possible moment." She whispered the words as close to Jane's ear as possible to prevent Mrs. Bennet, who sat on the opposite side of the carriage, from hearing.

Jane took her hand and squeezed. "Do not fret. I shall remain nearby as much as possible."

"You most certainly will not," said Mrs. Bennet. Jane had not moderated her voice, attracting her mother's attention. Mr. Bennet winced at his wife's shrill tone. "You must dance with Mr. Bingley and make yourself available to him. He must see you if he is to propose. He is close. I am certain of it."

Mr. Bennet rolled his eyes and tugged at the bottom of his coat as the carriage came to a stop. "I daresay Mr. Bingley will see her whenever he chooses so long as he does not depart to the card rooms or to smoke with the gentlemen. Kitty, I expect you to be on your best behaviour, lest you be relegated to the nursery with your sister upon our return." Ellie clenched her hands to keep from applauding Mr. Bennet's stern warning. Despite Mrs. Bennet's attempts to undermine him, he'd been trying and despite Lydia's and Mrs. Bennet's protests, succeeding. She was proud of him.

"Yes, Papa."

Mrs. Bennet gave a dramatic wail before the servant could open the door, making him pause. "That is enough from you, Mrs. Bennet. I have become startlingly aware how I have failed this family since Ellie's accident."

"But no new gowns, Mr. Bennet!"

Ellie measured her breathing to keep from sighing aloud. Ever since Mr. Bennet forbade a trip to the dressmaker in Meryton, Mrs. Bennet had repeated the same admonishment to him over and over and over.

"You must admit Jane, Mary, and Kitty did an excellent job reworking their gowns as well as helping with Ellie's, do you not think? Due to our newfound economy, I was able to set aside a good portion of the first year's salary for Lydia's governess. Besides, the girls all look exceedingly well tonight while spending a mere portion of what you would have wasted on materials alone, thanks to your sister's aid."

He was correct. Their aunt Gardiner had sent a sizeable package of lace, trim, and ribbons from London, which the Bennet girls had used to make over their gowns. Jane's silver silk gown now boasted of short sleeves of white Brussels lace and tiny silver and white beads on the bodice. Ellie had even helped by sewing on the beads while Jane worked on her gown for the evening. Despite doing what she could to help, Ellie still despised sewing!

Mr. Bennet alighted and helped the ladies down while Mr. Collins almost faceplanted in the mud as he descended from where he rode with the driver. Ellie covered her mouth with her gloved hand and bit her cheek. She would not laugh! The man was an imbecile—and that was not an exaggeration. When he had seen how the Bennets would be packed into the carriage like kippers, he'd insisted upon riding with the driver. Not that Ellie was complaining. The man was not unappealing in terms of looks, but she questioned his bathing habits. Even for this time period, he reeked, and his teeth appeared as though he never brushed. As she'd learnt early on, they did have tooth powder. What she wouldn't give for a tube of real toothpaste, though!

Ellie looped her arm through Jane's before Mr. Collins could swoop in. "Forgive me, but I never thanked you for helping with my gown." Flowers of Brussels lace had been sewn to the front and as accents to the short sleeves of Elizabeth's best gown. After, enough of the lace remained to adorn the front of the skirt as well. With the succession of rain for the past several days, the ladies of Longbourn had little to do but hide away sewing and practicing their dancing with the help of Mary playing the pianoforte. Dancing. That was the part of the evening that was causing Ellie the most anxiety. What would she do if she forgot the steps? All she needed was to flatten Mr. Darcy's or Mr. Bingley's toes—anyone's toes for that matter. Blimey, what if she fell flat on her face?

"I was pleased to do it. You also helped with the beadwork on mine if you recall."

"A trifling when compared with what you and Kitty managed."

"But I enjoy reworking gowns as much as I do drawing," said Kitty, who joined them on Jane's opposite side.

"Come, girls," called Mr. Bennet with a wave of his arm.

When they entered the house, Mr. Bingley's maids and footmen were ready to take the guests' coats and the gentlemen's hats. The tell-tale cacophony of musicians tuning their instruments filtered into the hall as Miss Bingley and Mrs. Hurst gave their usual insincere greetings and flattery, which much to Ellie's dismay, Jane bought hook, line, and sinker. When the sisters turned their attention to her, she gave a tight smile in return. Mr. Bingley wasn't the most forthright individual, and while she was at Netherfield nursing Jane, the sisters tended to walk all over their younger brother. Unlike Mrs. Bennet, Ellie was under no illusion Mr. Bingley would propose marriage to Jane Bennet. Ellie would likely faint if an engagement ever came to pass.

"Miss Bennet!" said Mr. Bingley when he finished greeting Mr. Goulding. "I am pleased you and your family could attend. I hope you will do me the honour of the first set." His sisters' heads swung around, their faces pinched. Ellie pressed her lips together to keep from giving an evil cackle in their direction.

"Yes, Mr. Bingley. I would be delighted." Jane's cheeks held a tinge of pink while she smiled.

"And Miss Elizabeth, I would be remiss if I did not request a set of you. Perhaps the second?"

"I would be pleased to dance with you, Mr. Bingley." Hopefully, without breaking his foot!

"Excellent!" He clapped his hands together, rubbing them while bearing a wide grin. "I do hope you ladies enjoy yourselves this evening."

"I am certain we shall," said Jane as she tugged Ellie away. "Do not start to worry. You danced beautifully when we practiced this morning. I am certain you will manage admirably."

Ellie laughed, but even to her own ears, the sound was forced. "At least I dance with Mr. Bingley after you. If I injure him too severely, Mama cannot hold it against me other than he may have asked you for a second set."

"As the host, I doubt he will have the opportunity for a second set. He would not wish to snub any of his guests. He is too kind for that."

"Indeed."

"Miss Elizabeth." Ellie and Jane both turned at Mr. Darcy's greeting. "Miss Bennet, I hope you are both well this evening."

"Quite," said Jane. "Are we not, Ellie?"

"Yes, thank you, Mr. Darcy. We are all anticipation for tonight."

Mr. Darcy's lip twitched on one side. "You forget that I am aware of the truth of the matter." He dipped his chin a little and spoke in a low tone. "Though if I had not known, I would not have thought you dissembling."

"Cousin Elizabeth!"

Ellie clenched Jane's arm tighter as the cloying Mr. Collins sidled up to them.

"Cousin Elizabeth, they are about to line up for the first set. You agreed—"

"Mr. Collins, I agreed to nothing. You requested my first set, which I indicated was spoken for. You never claimed you desired a different set tonight."

"I thought you attempting to encourage my suit as is with the delicacy—"

No, no, no! The man had been relentless since she had been unable to spend her days outside due to the rain. "Really, Mr. Collins. I have no wish to torment a respectable man. I have a partner for the first set, and my father has indicated he will not approve of an engagement between us, so you had best to set your cap at another lady. You waste your time with me." How many times had Mr. Bennet pulled that man aside and told him to cease his pursuit of her? Too many times if you asked her. Yes, her words were blunt, but her patience had run razor thin.

Mr. Darcy's hand appeared in front of her. "Miss Elizabeth, I believe you promised me the first."

"Yes, I believe I did," said Ellie, swallowing down the frantic twisting of her stomach. She could do this! She would do this! "Thank you, Mr. Darcy."

As soon as they stepped away, he leaned down ever so slightly. "I assume that is the Mr. Collins your father had you avoiding."

"Yes, it seems Mama told him Jane was soon to be wed and offered me up like a lamb for the slaughter. Papa has assured Mr. Collins he will not have his approval, but Mr. Collins has assured my father that he expects me to agree and will persuade my father to relent."

"He feels his self-importance greatly, does he not? I would expect no less from my aunt's parson."

"By how he speaks of Lady Catherine and her daughter, I expect he's half in love with them both. When he learnt you were in the neighbourhood, he had little good to say of you. He feels Miss de Bourgh's rejection acutely; I assure you."

Mr. Darcy burst out laughing, making a few people turn and stare. "I am certain more acutely than Anne. And I have no doubt my aunt and cousin treat his admiration with headstrong officiousness." As they took their places for the dance, he paused before taking his position. "Has Miss Bennet persuaded you to practice your minuet?"

"Yes, she has. Mary played for us this morning, in fact." His shoulders relaxed. With the rain for the past three days, they hadn't been able to discuss the dances at the ball. He couldn't have known Jane taught her a good many. She would be lucky to remember half of them tonight! How did people keep track of them all? The sheer number was mind-boggling.

When the music began, she curtseyed. Well, at least she had that part correct! Her entire body was rigid while Mr. Darcy led her through the first forms. She only relaxed when she curtseyed at the end. When the second dance began, Mr. Darcy whispered cues during the forms to help her through the quadrille, which thankfully, she hadn't seemed to need.

"Do you have a partner for the second set?" he asked as he offered her his arm.

"Mr. Bingley." She glanced over her shoulder. "I do hope Mr. Collins finds another lady to pass the evening pursuing."

"At the moment, he appears to be speaking to Miss Lucas." Miss Lucas? From what Mr. Bennet and Jane had said, the match would be an excellent one for her, but would Mrs. Bennet ever forgive Elizabeth? If the two did marry, Charlotte would become mistress of Longbourn upon Mr. Bennet's death. That would peeve Mrs. Bennet to no end, particularly since she often described Charlotte as plain.

Ellie mis-stepped twice during her set with Mr. Bingley, but when the gentleman led her from the dance floor, Mr. Lucas, Charlotte's brother, requested her hand for the next. When Mr. Darcy claimed her for what he called the supper dance, she let out a huge gush of air. "Does this mean I can sit for a while? My feet are starting to ache."

He laughed as he bowed. "Yes, though you have done well. I have not seen you falter much. I also overheard Mr. Lucas comment that he thought you performed admirably seeing you were so ill such a short time ago."

"I suppose that's a relief." She didn't want Elizabeth to return to the town believing her to have lost any of her wit—she seemed to be quite popular for her sense of humour.

As she turned with Fitzwilliam, Miss Bingley's sour expression caught her attention. "Have you danced with Miss Bingley?"

"No, to be honest, I have done my best to avoid the lady. Since you and Miss Bennet returned to Longbourn, she and Mrs. Hurst have been unbearable. Be warned. She does not want her brother singling out your sister any more than he has already."

"You are telling me nothing I have not already guessed. Their expressions when he requested Jane's first set were obvious." Mrs. Hurst had slapped her sister's arm with her fan, prompting Miss Bingley to take note of Mr. Bingley, who grinned and puffed out his chest like a peacock while dancing with Jane. "They seem to have noticed him dancing the supper set with her too."

"Does Miss Bennet hold tender feelings for my friend?"

Ellie frowned as Jane blushed and dropped her gaze in response to something Mr. Bingley said. "Before my accident, I am certain I could have answered your question with more certainty, but Jane is not the most open person. Based on what she has said and her behaviour when speaking to him, I would say she likes him a great deal. They have not known each other long enough for love, do you not agree?" Love at first sight didn't exist, did it? But, if it didn't, then why did her heart go pitter-patter whenever Fitzwilliam was near?

"I agree. Miss Bingley is certain to imply that Miss Bennet would accept Bingley to please her mother over all other considerations. I wanted to ensure that was not the case."

She glanced to where Mrs. Bennet pressed a palm to her chest and held Lady Lucas's forearm while she appeared to preside over some odd sort of court. "My mother would pressure Jane to accept, but Jane is too kind to feign feelings she doesn't possess."

Fitzwilliam blinked and his eyebrows furrowed. "I had not considered her temperament in such a way. I am certain you are correct. After all, you have known her longer."

With a laugh, Ellie shook her head. "No, sir. I haven't if you consider my memory loss, but I have spent more time with her and spoken more intimately with her than you or Miss Bingley."

"Which is why I shall trust your judgement on the matter." They separated due to the forms of the dance, and Ellie's eyes followed him while he turned with the lady beside her. His head jerked, and he glared towards the windows, but when Ellie peered in that direction, she couldn't imagine what had caused such an angry scowl. He'd been so preoccupied, he almost tripped over his own feet.

"Are you well?" she asked when she stepped forward to take his hands.

"I thought I saw someone I know. I must have been mistaken. I cannot account for why he would be here."

With a shake of his head, he gave her a tight smile. Who could this person have been? With his reaction, they couldn't have been good. His arm was rigid, and he didn't speak as he showed her to the supper room.

"If you give me a description, I may be able to help you."

"Hmm?" He started. "Oh, forgive me, I had not meant to neglect you."

"Not at all." His gaze met hers and made her insides flip. "I merely thought to be an extra set of eyes."

He waved off her answer. "Pray, ignore my preoccupation. I am certain I saw nothing more than a ghost. Let us enjoy the meal and forget it. Shall we?"

Chapter 17

After one last glance to ensure she wasn't seen, Ellie closed the door behind her and stepped to the edge of the balcony overlooking the rose garden. This was mental. She wasn't from this time, yet she was letting Fitzwilliam in—into her heart. Her palms settled on the rough stone of the railing as she closed her eyes and let the cool air wash over her, the scent of dried leaves and grass tickling her nose, a tremendous improvement over the odour of the ballroom. December and winter were coming fast. Would she return to her own time before then? She couldn't remain here forever. She had a life waiting for her. What if time was passing in the future at a similar rate? If so, they'd likely already replaced her at Pemberley...

"I believe you are Miss Elizabeth Bennet."

She whirled around to face a man who stood just outside the door. He wore a red uniform, a militia uniform. When had he approached? He'd done so without making a sound. How? "We have not been introduced. I should return inside."

When she attempted to walk past him, he stepped sideways, blocking her path. "I have yet to make your acquaintance since your accident, though I have heard much of you from the people of Meryton. I only wanted to speak to you. I mean no harm."

A glint in his eye and his crooked smirk made her insides twist and squirm in an uncomfortable way. Something about him was not right, but she couldn't put her finger on it. "Then you should allow me to return to my family."

"For someone kept home for so long, you seem to get on with Darcy well. He was dancing with you. He never dances."

Her head hitched back. Why was he so concerned over her interaction with Fitzwilliam? "I became acquainted with the gentleman while tending to my ill sister at Netherfield. We were in company for no more than a mere portion of my stay, so I cannot claim we are close friends, by any means."

"Yet he stood up with you twice. He would have never done so without some understanding or unless you are allowing him liberties."

Allowing him liberties? What did that—? Ellie gasped. "Why you foul little shit!"

She tried to dart past him, but he grabbed her wrist in a painful grip. Without thought, she covered his hand with her free one and swung the arm he held around in a self-defence move she'd practiced so many times, it came as naturally as breathing. The action twisted his arm and forced him to bend at the waist to protect his shoulder as she locked his arm behind him. "What the hell?" the awful man cried as she pulled the arm further behind him and pushed, forcing him down to one knee. "That bloody well hurts!"

"You grabbed my arm without my consent. I should not have to tell you to never touch a lady without permission."

A door opened and closed, and she looked up in time to find Fitzwilliam standing just outside, his expression turning into an enormous grin. "I knew I saw Wickham in the ballroom, but he disappeared before I could be certain. When a man in regimentals followed you to the terrace, I thought you might require my assistance. I never thought I would discover either of you thus." He laughed and stepped forward. "Well done, Miss Ellie."

"Release me, you...you bunter!"

Ellie frowned. "What's a bunter?"

"You do not want to know," said Fitzwilliam.

"Then I most certainly do want to know."

Fitzwilliam scratched the back of his neck with a wince. "Very well. It means half-whore and half-beggar."

Why that foul—She pulled Wickham's arm further behind him, putting further pressure on the shoulder joint. "Argh! I didn't mean it! I swear!"

At Fitzwilliam's chuckle, she looked up, but he swallowed the sound as quickly as it had come. "Forgive me," he said. "Wickham has never been put in his place by a lady so effectively. I should not take pleasure in his pain, but I have borne witness to his misdeeds for so long, I admit I am enjoying this immensely.

"How do you know Mr. Wickham?"

"His father was my father's steward at Pemberley. I am forever cleaning up his messes, paying his debts. He is a scourge upon my family."

"He was asking about our acquaintance. He accused me of allowing you liberties." She shifted Wickham's arm a bit further behind him, making him cry out. "You were saying, Mr. Wickham?" She let off some of the pressure. She did not want to torture him too badly. "What shall we do with him?"

Fitzwilliam scratched his cheek. "If you release him, he will run like the rat he is, but he will sully your name and mine before he flees his encampment."

The door opened and closed again, and this time Mr. Bennet emerged from the darkness with a raised eyebrow. "When I followed Mr. Darcy, I never thought to discover either of you thus. What have we here?"

"He grabbed my wrist," said Ellie with a shrug. "I thought I'd remind him how improper it is to touch a lady without her consent. Before you came outside, Mr. Darcy and I were debating what to do with him. Mr. Darcy believes releasing him to be a less than prudent idea."

"I have known Wickham all my life. Without sufficient financial remuneration, his tongue will wag out of a thirst for revenge. Deception of any sort is my abhorrence, but I've come to learn, particularly of late, that in some cases it is prudent."

"I see," said Mr. Bennet. "Perhaps turning him over to Colonel Forster would be the best course. Mr. Darcy can claim he followed Mr. Wickham to the terrace, notifying me on his way. When the blackguard attempted to grab your wrist, Mr. Darcy subdued him, and I sent you to retrieve the colonel. We give the colonel our truth of the incident so no one will be able to credit Mr. Wickham's lies, though tongues may still wag at you being alone with two gentlemen, no matter how brief the encounter. We shall have to ensure no time existed for any untoward behaviour."

"I can still speak." Wickham gritted the words through his teeth, and Ellie pulled his arm a bit further behind his back. "Argh! Stop that!"

"What would you have done to me if Mr. Darcy had not arrived?" She despised men who were for all intents and purposes abusers.

"If Miss Elizabeth's reputation should appear to be at risk, I shall be pleased to wed her."

What? Her head shot up at Fitzwilliam's words. No, this couldn't be happening! She couldn't marry him! "Wed?" She didn't belong here.

Mr. Bennet nodded off-handedly. "We shall speak of this, but first, Ellie, go and fetch the colonel."

"I do not know what he looks like."

Mr. Bennet chuckled, his eyes twinkling. "I suppose you do not. Forgive me. He is the elder of the men in a militia uniform. He has been near the refreshment table most of the evening with that silly child he calls a wife."

Carefully, Mr. Darcy took Ellie's place, pinning Wickham in the same position, and she hurried inside. True to Mr. Bennet's description, an older man in regimentals stood near the refreshments with a much younger lady...no, not a lady—a girl on his arm. Blimey! He had to be pushing forty or forty-five and was his wife even eighteen? A shudder wracked her spine, but she continued ahead. "I beg your pardon, Colonel. Forgive me for being so forward, but my father, Mr. Bennet, and Mr. Darcy require your aid on the terrace with one of your men."

"I suppose he has overindulged. I fear they were quite excited at the prospect of a ball. Allow me a few moments, my dear, so I may arrange for his return to camp."

"Of course, Husband." She stepped away and approached Kitty, whispering in her ear and making them both burst into giggles.

"If you would show me where they are," said the colonel with an arm outstretched, urging her to go ahead of him.

When they exited the ballroom, Mr. Wickham was thankfully still in the same position, kneeling upon the ground, while Mr. Bennet leaned against the stone railing, his arms crossed over his chest. "Ah, there you are, Colonel. It seems Mr. Wickham witnessed my daughter depart the ballroom for a breath of cool air, and he followed. Mr. Darcy alerted me as he passed, and we both exited but a moment after Mr. Wickham to find him grabbing my daughter's wrist. Mr. Darcy, as the first through the door, put an end to Mr. Wickham's scheme. We thought you would wish to know the disappointing character of one of your men."

"They lie!" Mr. Wickham panted through the words. "I only wished to speak to Miss Elizabeth. She used some manoeuvre to put me in this position. She did this! Darcy then took her place so she could fetch you. They are lying!"

Colonel Forster's eyebrows drew down as an incredulous smile spread across his face. He looked to a shrugging Mr. Bennet, then a chuckling Fitzwilliam. "You would have me believe a lady did this to you. You must be in your cups indeed if you believe that. That you would admit to being bested by a woman shows how insensible you are. Regardless, you have behaved in an improper manner. You will be confined to the camp until we depart for Brighton. If you show any further nefarious tendencies, I shall be forced to consider further action."

"If I may, Colonel, Mr. Wickham was the son of my father's steward, so I am familiar with his unfortunate lack of respect for the fairer sex as well as his other vile schemes. I recommend enquiring about the village. He accumulated a great many debts around Pemberley after he departed the area last, which I was forced to honour. I fear the local merchants may be put in dire straits if he has continued his usual habits."

The colonel's mouth set in a grim line. "I see." He poked his head in the door, and two of his men emerged shortly thereafter, at which time, the colonel motioned Wickham to stand. "Pray, return Lt. Wickham to camp and have him put under guard. He is not to go anywhere until I have the opportunity to deal with this matter. Do I make myself clear?"

"Yes, sir!" they responded in unison.

As soon as Mr. Wickham was taken around the corner of the house, the colonel gave a slight bow. "Forgive my officer's intrusion on your evening."

"Thank you, Colonel," said Mr. Bennet.

The door to the terrace closed behind the colonel, and Mr. Bennet exhaled heavily. "Now, we wait and hope for the best. Mr. Darcy, regardless of the outcome of our subterfuge, I should like to speak with you in my library tomorrow morning."

"Yes, sir."

Mr. Bennet offered Ellie his arm, and as they returned to the ballroom, Fitzwilliam hurried off, returning with a measure of brandy for each of them. "I took the liberty of bringing you refreshment."

"I thank you," said Mr. Bennet. He smelled the spirit and beamed. "I have not had brandy for some time. My brother gifted me a bottle for Christmas last year, but I have purchased more Port since the war. Despite the problems on the peninsula, Port is not as dear as brandy."

"I do not blame you. Brandy has become costly indeed since Napoleon began causing mischief in France. Port is much more affordable. I drink more Port these days as well."

Ellie took a small sip and savoured the hints of apples and oak. Was it her or did this taste better than the brandy her father would have at Christmas? She blinked and shook off those memories. Dwelling on them was useless.

"Are you well, Miss Elizabeth?"

Her eyes met Fitzwilliam's, and their gazes locked. "Yes, thank you." This was ridiculous. She'd been taken by Fitzwilliam when she'd cleaned his portrait but remaining in his company so often was proving dangerous. She couldn't keep ignoring that jolt of current that travelled through her hand, even through her gloves when they danced.

Despite being surrounded by a room full of strangers, he brought her comfort and gave her a sense of belonging. She was also beginning to care about Mr. Bennet and Jane more than she ought. She had been without a family since her parents were killed in a car accident with a lorry when she was sixteen. Since then, that part of her heart had been walled away, but the time spent at Longbourn was chipping away at that solid barrier piece by piece. Still, she couldn't let her heart forget where and when she belonged.

But how was she supposed to return to the future? So far, she'd given up and hoped it would happen when it happened. Almost a month had passed, and she was still here. No, she needed to be more proactive. It was imperative that she return to the 21st century before she couldn't remember why she'd wanted or needed to return in the first place. Oh, Lord! Would she forget if she remained for much longer? Could she forget? That was another can of worms she simply couldn't open and examine right now.

Chapter 18

After breakfast, Mr. Bennet, as had become the usual morning routine, waved Ellie to follow him to his library for coffee. Once the maid delivered the tray, Ellie poured him a cup then her own as he leaned back and watched her. "You did not appear pleased at the thought of marrying Mr. Darcy."

"I believe I was in shock that he offered." She gave her head a shake and sat back with her cup. "I cannot understand why I'm still here. Last night, the idea that I may forget about the future and simply blend into this time and place occurred to me, but I'm certain I'm meant to go back. How could I forget who I am and when I came from? The problem with marrying Mr. Darcy is so complex. I mean, what happens to your daughter if I marry him? She would return to find herself trapped in a marriage she didn't consent to and to a man she dislikes, particularly since she will not remember what has occurred in her absence. Meanwhile, I'm back in my own time with a shattered heart. Even you must admit the situation would not be ideal."

Mr. Bennet made a sort of hum of agreement as he took a sip of coffee. "But what if you are meant to be here? I am not saying you would forget your past, but what if you never return to your own time? I know it may sound defeating, but do recall that Mr. Collins is set to inherit when I die. If you do not wed, you will be forced to rely on Mrs. Bennet and her five-thousand pounds. She may not take that situation well considering your abject refusal to consider Mr. Collins, and I shall not be here to protect you from her machinations."

"I hardly slept from thinking about the possibility of remaining, but I cannot believe that I am to stay in this time and place. Of all people, I am more surprised that you would consider the possibility. What of your daughter? I am certain you want her back."

He sighed. "As much as it pains me to think it, she may never return. We do not even know when or where she is. I cannot but wonder if this all happened for a reason—that you may have come to live her life?"

She gulped down a lump in her throat. "What a dreadful thought. It's like something out of *Invasion of the Body Snatchers.*"

Mr. Bennet spluttered. "*Invasion of the* what?"

Ellie attempted not to laugh. "Sorry, it's a movie." At his frown, she bit her cheek for a second before holding out a hand, palm forward. "A movie is sort of like theatre. Actors play the different parts, but the performance is preserved and a reflection of sorts can be watched over and over again on a large wall or a box. In this movie, beings from the stars come to Earth and take over people's lives, making copies of their bodies. Except, in the movie, the copies had no emotions."

"That sounds positively dreadful," said Mr. Bennet chuckling, "and people watch such ridiculous and horrific plays?"

"Horror stories are very popular. People of this day enjoy gothic romances, do they not?"

He narrowed his eyes. "Not quite the same. No one steals bodies."

"You don't consider me as having stolen your daughter's body?"

He frowned and let out a sizable exhale. "The circumstances here are different. You saw my daughter's reflection in that mirror for a few weeks before you touched it and awoke in her stead. That alone makes me believe something of this was meant to be. You were supposed to come here, for whatever reason. Maybe you are meant to wed Mr. Darcy, but maybe Elizabeth is supposed to be forced into that union as well, and you have come to facilitate that marriage? I cannot imagine the reason all this has occurred, yet I cannot dispute that more is afoot than what appears to the eye or than falls within reason."

"Do you believe in magic?"

A bark of laughter burst from his chest. "Magic? No, and I do not believe in witchcraft either. They are excuses for matters science cannot explain. Perhaps one day, we may understand those mysteries. For now, people make fanciful explanations and persecute innocent people to assuage their fear."

A knock came from the door, diverting Mr. Bennet's attention. "Yes?"

"Mr. Darcy to see you, sir," said Mrs. Hill.

"Thank you, Hill." As the housekeeper bobbed a curtsey, Mr. Bennet held up his cup. "Pray, bring a cup for Mr. Darcy."

"Will you be needin' more coffee, sir?"

"I am certain we shall. Thank you." Once the door was closed, Mr. Bennet gestured towards an empty chair. "Pray, sit, sir. As you have proven yourself a friend of Ellie, I hope we can dispense with the formalities and have an honest discourse. I fear I am not fond of discussions of the roads or the weather. Conversations on the latest farming techniques are quite a bore as well. I hope you agree."

"I do, Mr. Bennet." Mrs. Hill bustled in for a moment to bring a cup and saucer, then hurried back out.

"Coffee, Mr. Darcy?" said Ellie.

"Yes, thank you."

Those butterflies in her stomach needed to be stamped into oblivion. She had to stop being so caught up with Fitzwilliam. Yes, he was handsome, and yes, he had been kind to her and helped her, but no matter Mr. Bennet's suspicions, she couldn't under any circumstances develop deeper feelings for the man. She was going home. She had to be!

As soon as they were settled, Mr. Bennet set down his cup and cleared his throat. "I have yet to hear any talk of last night's excitement from my wife or the servants, and Mrs. Philips has yet to call with any tittle-tattle. Have you heard any gossip at Netherfield, sir?"

"Not at all," said Mr. Darcy with his eyebrows drawn towards the middle a bit. "If you will forgive my honesty, Miss Bingley crowed of her achievements over breakfast, Mrs. Hurst congratulated her on a successful evening, and Bingley...well, Bingley wore a sizeable grin and spoke little during the meal. His mind seemed occupied elsewhere."

Mr. Bennet laughed and shook his head. "While he stood up with other young ladies as well, I noticed his marked attentions to my daughter. Mrs. Bennet is convinced he is soon to propose. I must admit I find myself wary of a proposal after such a short acquaintance. If he is sincere in his attachment, I should hope he courts her through the Christmastide before any proposal is made."

"I understand. I believe I would feel much the same if the lady in question were my sister. Since my parents' deaths, I have been her guardian. I feel the responsibility keenly."

"I am certain," said Ellie. "Any gentleman in your situation should feel similar." She had been an only child, but her feelings would certainly match his if their positions were the same.

"Indeed." Mr. Bennet leaned forward and rested his forearms upon the desk. "Based on where we find ourselves this morning, I shall not force a betrothal upon you and my daughter." Every muscle in Ellie's body relaxed, even while ensuring her breath didn't leave her in one huge rush.

Mr. Darcy blinked and stared into his coffee for a moment before looking up. "I understand your decision. I do want to be clear that I would never consider marrying Miss Ellie to be a hardship or obligation. She is an intelligent lady, and I enjoy her society immensely."

"As I enjoy yours, Mr. Darcy, yet I do not want to rush into any life altering decisions so soon after my injury." When she glanced at Mr. Bennet, the ends of his lips had turned up a little, and he gave a slight nod. "So, while I would be as honoured as any lady to be Mrs. Darcy, I am not ready to bind myself to such a commitment. I hope you understand."

"Of course," he said. "You still suffer effects from your fall. I believe any person would want to be fully recovered first."

With another clearing of his throat, Mr. Bennet turned his gaze on her. "A relief, indeed. I am pleased my daughter is as recovered as she is, yet while I enjoy her company and care for her as much as before, I do mourn who she was and pray one day, she will return to us. The situation is more complicated than I ever could have anticipated when Ellie was first returned to us."

Mr. Darcy's head swivelled around to her, his expression dark. "Have you suffered further ill effects?"

"No, I am well. My father only means my memories and how markedly altered I am from before."

The gentleman's shoulders dropped back to a more relaxed position. "I am relieved to hear you suffer no further afflictions."

"I can't tell you how much I have appreciated your friendship since you found me atop Oakham Mount. You have done so much to help me."

"How could I do less? You are not at fault for the loss of your memory. You have managed your situation with courage and grace. I greatly admire how you have risen to the challenge."

"Thank you." Her cheeks burned, so she took a sip of coffee in an attempt to hide her reaction.

"You mentioned your sister," said Mr. Bennet without a pause. "She must be much younger if you are her guardian. Has she remained at your estate in your absence?"

"She is almost twelve years my junior, and no, she is with her companion in London where she can benefit from her piano master. Her favourite diversion is the pianoforte and practices quite diligently. I must confess one reason I was glad for your invitation, Mr. Bennet, is I planned to take my leave from both of you today."

The hand holding Ellie's cup lowered, and a sharp pain shot through her chest. "You are leaving?"

"I do not plan to be away for more than a fortnight. I promised Bingley I would help him learn to run an estate, but even though Georgiana has an excellent companion, I prefer not to be away from her for too long. She is but sixteen, and I wish to ensure she is well with my own eyes."

Mr. Bennet nodded as he poured himself more coffee. "That is very sensible of you. Recently, I have been made aware how young ladies of that age require more supervision than I first realized."

"I doubt Mr. Darcy's sister is as unrestrained as Lydia."

"She is reserved and painfully shy," said Mr. Darcy. "Though I confess to learning the truth of your father's observation for myself. I trust Mrs. Annesley implicitly, yet I do need to assure myself of her health and happiness from time to time."

"As I said, quite sensible," said Mr. Bennet with a nod.

Something in Ellie's chest broke open. Fitzwilliam was leaving. Yes, he claimed he would return, yet what if he didn't? As much as she shouldn't have, she had come to rely on him. He was a friendly face who knew she had no recollection of what came before her accident and one of the few people she could trust without question. She needed to ask him about that mirror, the one at Pemberley, but Mr. Bennet had begged her to wait. Why should she wait? That mirror held the answers to why she was here and how she could one day return to her life. What if he held some insight to its power? And what if she couldn't reach Fitzwilliam when Mr. Bennet indicated the time was right? His leaving was worrisome—especially to her.

"We do appreciate the courtesy," said Mr. Bennet. "I am certain our family will be pleased to receive your call when you return to the neighbourhood."

"If you do not object, I should like to correspond with you, sir. I should like to know of Miss Ellie's progress. My offer to send a physician from town is still available to you should you wish it. You need only send word."

Ellie shook her head, blinking to rid her eyes of that ridiculous stinging. "I do appreciate your offer, but I do not believe he can tell me anything more than Mr. Jones has already divulged." She hadn't cried since she was sixteen. Why was she determined to do so now?

Mr. Darcy set his cup upon the desk and stood. "As much as I should like to continue our conversation, I am afraid I must take my leave. I prefer to reach London before supper, and with so much rain this week, the state of the roads is sure to be poor indeed."

"Of course," said Mr. Bennet, rising and giving a brief bow. "As I said earlier, you are always welcome at Longbourn."

Her body was heavy and awkward as she stood and curtseyed. "Safe travels, Mr. Darcy." She sank back into the chair when the door closed behind him.

A chuckle fell from Mr. Bennet's lips. "If you are not planning on remaining in this time, falling in love with that young man was a terrible idea."

"I'm not in love with him."

"You have spent more time with him than Jane has spent with Mr. Bingley and confided more of yourself to him. Besides, the look on your face when he announced he was returning to London was telling. I could see the fall in your countenance. Do not fret, though, my dear, I am willing to wager he is just as taken with you as you are with him." He tilted his head. "You have never mentioned before, but is time travel a commonplace activity in the 21st century?"

Ellie frowned. "No, not at all. Why?"

"As I said before, some reason must exist for this to have occurred. You said Mr. Darcy's family and estate fell into ruin."

"He became disenchanted by society and became a recluse, hiding away at Pemberley for the rest of his life. His sister's eldest son inherited, but the line didn't keep up the estate as Fitzwilliam had." What if she was the reason for that?

"What if you are meant to change the fate of that family?"

"One could as easily suppose I was the cause. But why? Why would God or the fates care so much about one family— one man?"

Mr. Bennet shrugged. "That is a question only they can answer."

"Well, I wish they'd hurry the hell up and do something about it. All this waiting is getting on my nerves."

Chapter 19

After Mr. Darcy departed, Ellie strolled around the garden for some peace and quiet, not to mention some time to think. Her discussion with Mr. Bennet wouldn't stop spinning and turning in her mind. He now questioned whether or not her presence in the here and now was somehow meant to be, but how was Ellie to know? Was her preoccupation with Fitzwilliam Darcy's portrait why she was here, and if so, what was she supposed to do about it? It was not like God or the fates or whoever was responsible for life on Earth was rushing to inform her of their intentions. If only they'd appear and let her know! The entire dilemma was enough to give her a headache of massive proportions. Her head pounded and her neck was wound so tight, the pain travelled down between her shoulders and around the back of her skull.

The most confusing part was her feelings on whether she stayed or returned. The longer she remained in 1811, the more her mind was all over the place. What if Fitzwilliam fell in love with her...or she with him? The last thing she wanted was to take over someone else's body. The idea was creepy and gave her the heebie-jeebies. Her lingering in this timeline prompted an entire new set of problems to consume her: What would happen to Elizabeth if she stayed? Why was she here in the first place? She'd asked that question so many times, she wanted to scream and pull out her hair. There was no other explanation; the fates hated her. They had to. Why else had they given her some mysterious dilemma with no obvious solution?

"Mama sent me to fetch you," said Lydia with her nose slightly lifted and one hip cocked out. She was still furious about being relegated to the nursery with a governess and continued to hold Ellie responsible—not that Ellie cared. As far as she was concerned, she was helping the Bennets, Elizabeth and Lydia included.

Ellie sighed and followed Lydia inside. What could Mrs. Bennet want with her? For the most part, Mrs. Bennet spoke to Ellie for no other reason but to put her down or complain about how wilful she was. The only time the woman was bearable was when Mr. Collins was in the room and that was because she kissed his ass from the very second he appeared for breakfast until he retired each evening.

When they stepped foot into the hall, Lydia flounced into the drawing room as Mrs. Bennet jogged forward and began fiddling with Ellie's gown, tugging on the skirt and finally, adjusting the bodice.

"What. Are. You. Doing?" Ellie punctuated each word with a slap to Mrs. Bennet's hands, shooing them away from her breasts.

"You must look your best. Mr. Collins wishes to have a word with you."

An incredulous bark burst from her. "For what? When Mr. Collins began singling me out, Papa told him he will not sanction a marriage between us. Mr. Collins has nothing to say to me that I want to hear, and if he's intent on proposing, I will never accept him, even with Papa's approval."

Mrs. Bennet straightened and her face hardened. "Your father will agree if *you* insist upon it."

"Which I shall not do," she said, pulling back and shaking her head. "He is grotesque. He sucks his teeth at the dinner table. Have you noticed? It's all I can do not to gag at the sound. Besides, I would never kiss his precious Lady Catherine's ass.

He'd be better off courting someone desperate for a husband. Miss Lucas comes to mind."

While she spoke, that infernal handkerchief Mrs. Bennet favoured emerged from her bodice, and she pressed it to her chest, gasping when Ellie said *ass*. When Miss Lucas's name was mentioned, Mrs. Bennet began fluttering that stupid piece of fabric. "Miss Lucas! What have I done to deserve such an ungrateful child? You, Elizabeth Bennet, have no compassion for my poor nerves. In case you have forgotten, a marriage to Mr. Collins will ensure your sisters and I have a home when your father dies. Otherwise, we shall all be cast out into the hedgerows."

Ellie leaned in. "If you were so concerned about your future, then you should have been pushing him towards one of your other daughters. Mary's interests would be better suited to Mr. Collins than mine, though I am unsure if she *wishes* to wed him. I would never press him towards poor Kitty. She thinks he is as disgusting as I do; however, marrying Lydia to a parson wouldn't be such a bad idea."

The woman scoffed and fanned herself as though she would faint at any moment. "Wishes have naught to do with marriage. Do you think I wanted to wed an older gentleman—an almost forty-year-old widow? No, I was but seventeen and wanted to marry a handsome, young lieutenant out of Colonel Millar's regiment, but Mr. Bennet had lost his wife and child and required an heir. My father insisted upon the match and ensured it took place. I did my duty, and *you*, you will do yours."

Ellie crossed her arms over her chest. "No, I will not. Papa has said he will not give his permission, regardless of the circumstances. Perhaps I should request him speak to you—to ensure you are under no illusions as to his instructions."

"Insolent—"

She dropped her arms. "If you will excuse me."

As she began to walk past Mrs. Bennet, the woman grabbed her by the arm. "I most certainly will not excuse you!"

The tell-tale squeak of the library door caused her to sag just a little. Would Mr. Bennet come to her rescue? "Mrs. Bennet, what are you about?" His eyes darted between her and Mrs. Bennet, his lips in a tight line.

"Mr. Collins desires a private audience with Lizzy. I am attempting to persuade—"

"Well, my dear, you need not persuade her further. I said I would never give my sanction to a marriage between Ellie and Mr. Collins, and I meant every word." He lifted a finger, pointing at his wife. "You will cease your schemes this moment, madam."

"But—"

"Ellie, you may go."

"Thank you," she said before she rushed upstairs. She had been granted freedom from Mrs. Bennet and her schemes and had no reason to refuse. When she reached the room she and Jane shared, the eldest Bennet was sitting on the bed, reading a letter. Her eyes were damp. "Are you well?"

"Oh, yes, thank you." Jane let the hand holding the paper fall to her lap. "I received a note from Miss Bingley. The family has closed Netherfield with the intention of returning to London. She says they have no plans to return."

"That's odd. Mr. Darcy said nothing of the Bingleys leaving." That seemed information he would be likely to share given their conversation that morning. He even indicated that he planned on returning. This made no sense.

Jane held out the letter. "You may read for yourself if you like."

The words upon the page were as empty and meaningless as any of Miss Bingley's compliments. That Fitzwilliam departed to see his sister was true, of course, but Mr. Bingley having an attachment to Miss Darcy? What a load of crap! "While Mr. Darcy did return to London to see his sister, he would never give his permission for her to marry, not yet at least."

"He has spoken to you of his sister?" asked Jane.

Ellie sat on the bed facing Jane. "Yes, he said she is shy, and...Well, I don't know if I can tell you everything, but I am certain she is not wanting to marry anyone at this moment, and he said he would never force her to wed. She can become a spinster if she wishes."

"He has shared confidences about his sister with you?"

"Yes, which is why I am so sure Miss Bingley's words are nothing but lies."

"She does write, 'Am I wrong, my dearest Jane, in indulging the hope of an event which will secure the happiness of so many?' She never acknowledged a betrothal or any indication her brother would propose, so she told no falsehood." Jane stared at the letter, a definite note of longing in her tone.

"Whether she said them outright or implied them is one and the same in my opinion. Besides, I can tell she has upset you. You mustn't give her such power over you. She doesn't deserve your friendship." Given the opportunity, Miss Bingley would chew Jane up and spit her out in pieces. Jane was too kind to hold her own with that woman. Maybe it was a good thing Mr. Bingley had left. If Jane married him, she'd have to deal with Miss Bingley every day for the rest of their lives. That witch would squash Jane like a bug.

"I thought I heard Mama calling for you."

"Ugh, don't remind me," said Ellie with a roll of her eyes. "She thought I'd accept Mr. Collins's marriage proposal and convince Papa that I actually wanted to marry that man. Papa must have heard part of our disagreement since he scolded Mama and let me leave." Jane stood and closed the door before she returned to once again sit next to Ellie.

"You were almost lost to us. He was terribly worried when you were so ill, and with your memory not yet recovered, he would never allow you to wed any gentleman."

Ellie bit her lip. "I suspect he might if the gentleman were Mr. Darcy."

"Mr. Darcy!" Jane's eyes were wide, and her tone high-pitched. "Has Mr. Darcy made you an offer?"

"Not really." The words came out sort of high-pitched and drawn out. That was true, wasn't it? He had suggested proposing but hadn't actually done it.

"Now, you cannot say what you did and leave it at that. Either he did or he did not. You cannot half-propose to someone."

After a quick but forceful exhale, Ellie put her hand to her forehead. Her head still pounded. "Mr. Darcy followed me out to the terrace last night. Papa was right behind him, so we were only alone for a moment, but Mr. Darcy still offered to marry me if Papa wished it. Since there has been no gossip, and no one has seemed to notice, my father hasn't thought it necessary."

"Mr. Darcy's willingness to save your reputation speaks well of him," said Jane.

"Even though he did so out of obligation?"

Jane took her hands and held them between them. "Ellie, if a gentleman is caught alone with a lady, he is not obligated to marry her. He *can* refuse. His reputation might be tarnished, and he may be challenged—"

"Challenged? As in a duel?"

"Yes, a duel, but he is under no obligation to the lady. Do you understand? I warned you about being discovered alone with him."

"And so did Papa. But he joined us a few moments after Mr. Darcy came outside and nothing has come of it, yeah?" She couldn't tell Jane about Wickham. Whatever the dickhead had planned wasn't good, and Jane saw the world in bright rainbows and fluffy, pink unicorns. While Ellie wanted her to see some people as they truly were—adjust those rose-coloured glasses she wore so to speak—she didn't want that outlook stomped into tiny bits.

The door flew open, and Ellie about jumped out of her skin. "I have never been thus treated in my life," said Mrs. Bennet, red-faced and shaking. "First, you refuse to do as I say, you ungrateful girl, but then, your father spoke to Mr. Collins—again! Now, your cousin has departed, walked to Meryton for God only knows what. What if Mrs. Goulding ensnares him for one of her daughters...or Lady Lucas? That artful Charlotte Lucas somehow persuaded him to stand up with her last night; and for the supper set no less! Can you imagine, Charlotte Lucas as the next mistress of Longbourn? I would rather die than see her as mistress of this house."

"Mama, Charlotte is not artful," said Jane. "She is a great friend to Ellie and myself."

Mrs. Bennet gave a ridiculous and over-dramatic wail. "Stop calling her Ellie! She is Elizabeth Bennet, and we have called her Lizzy since she was nothing but a babe. The sole reason for this demand of hers is her feeble-mindedness. Without Mr. Collins, you will never marry. You have ruined everything!"

"I think Charlotte would be a splendid mistress of Longbourn," said Ellie.

Mrs. Bennet narrowed her eyes at Ellie, then swung her arm to point to Jane. "I have had enough of this nonsense! I insist you address your sister as Elizabeth or Lizzy. There will be no more of this Ellie! Do you understand?" Her pitch and volume was like a knife piercing through Ellie's skull.

"What I do not understand is what I must do to keep you from this behaviour, Mrs. Bennet."

When the lady whirled around, Mr. Bennet stood in the doorway, his hands clasped behind his back and his face rigid. "You will come to my library. Jane, Ellie, I shall pen a letter to your aunt and uncle Gardiner. Perhaps a fortnight or so in London with them will give your mother time as well as improve the situation for when you return."

"Yes, Papa," said Jane.

"What is that in your hand?" asked Mrs. Bennet, her gaze locked onto the letter from Miss Bingley.

Ellie snatched the paper and began to refold it. "'Tis a drawing I made of the stables from our bedchamber window."

"Oh." With a sniff, Mrs. Bennet side-stepped past Mr. Bennet before she started down the stairs.

Mr. Bennet's expression softened. "I assume the note is proper and nothing for me to worry over?"

"'Tis from Miss Bingley," said Jane.

He chuckled and nodded. "Well, Ellie, you have certainly learnt how to deal with your mother in an effective manner. Do not concern yourself over the Gardiners. They are sensible people and will be sympathetic to your lack of memory. You have been close to your aunt since you first met her. I am also but a day's journey should either of you have need of me." He peered at Ellie over his glasses. "I expect you to write to me while you are away. I shall require some sense, even if I have to receive it through the post."

Upon her return from Netherfield, Mr. Bennet had taught Ellie to use a quill, which was not all that different from drawing with art pens, but just as much of a pain. She preferred her pencils wrapped with string to the mess of ink. With the quill, she never failed to have ink smudged all over her fingers after she finished, but in this instance, she would make do. "I suppose I could use the practice."

"Indeed" was all he said before he left.

"Come," said Jane as she stood. "We should pack. Papa will want us to leave tomorrow as soon as the sun rises."

"Will you attempt to see Mr. Bingley while we are there?"

Jane shrugged. "I should like to call upon Miss Bingley and Mrs. Hurst. If I do, then maybe I shall see him too." Her face became pink when she said the last.

Poor Jane! She liked Mr. Bingley, that much was obvious, yet there was no way those sisters of his would let him marry Jane without a fight. They mentioned Miss Darcy's connexions in the letter. What connexions could the Bennets have? So far, she hadn't heard of any impressive relation. And wasn't a lady supposed to have money for the husband-to-be? What was that? A dowry? From what Mr. Bennet had said, he hadn't saved for his daughters as he ought. Did Jane have anything to tempt Mr. Bingley's sisters other than herself?

Chapter 20

Ellie straightened in her seat and stared at the letter she was writing to Mr. Bennet. Two large blotches of ink stood out on the page, but for the most part, it was an enormous improvement over her last effort, the note she'd sent to Mr. Bennet upon their arrival at Gracechurch Street.

This morning, she had little to tell him: they'd walked in Hyde Park with the children yesterday, Mrs. Gardiner wanted to purchase a new gown for both her and Jane, and Mrs. Gardiner had given her a kitten from the litter at Mr. Gardiner's warehouse. She stroked the little black and white "tuxedo," or "magpie" as Mrs. Gardiner described him, who slept in her lap. She'd always wanted a cat. It seemed Elizabeth had as well, but the Longbourn barn cat was male, so they'd never had any kittens.

The kitten's paw barely twitched when the parlour door opened, and Mrs. Gardiner entered with Jane right behind her. Despite the noise, the tiny kitten never woke. He slept like the dead.

"How was it?" Jane's wish had finally been fulfilled, and she had called on Miss Bingley and Mrs. Hurst while Ellie had opted to remain behind. Their visit would be more successful without her.

"They were very civil," said Jane with a nod. She stood primly with her hands clutching her reticule in front of her. Something had disturbed her to make her so stiff. "If you will excuse me, I should like to refresh myself before luncheon."

As soon as the door closed behind her, Mrs. Gardiner sighed. "I believe you have the right of those two ladies, Ellie. Their smiles were forced, and their eyes darted to each other throughout the call as well as the door. I am certain they dreaded their brother discovering our presence. Miss Bingley even scolded Jane, in a teasing manner of course, for not sending a note to inform them of her arrival in town." She wagged a finger at Ellie. "If she had, I dare say they would have been conveniently away from home when we knocked."

"I believe you are correct. They have loftier ambitions for their brother than the daughter of a country gentleman."

"Yes. Miss Bingley mentioned several times during the half-hour that they planned to call upon Miss Darcy. They also made mention that the young lady would accompany them to a musical evening next week while her brother attends to some sort of business. Poor Jane paled at the insinuation."

"It would surprise me if Mr. Darcy would allow his sister to join them without his presence." From what Mr. Darcy had said, his sister would balk at going somewhere so public without him. Miss Bingley was a piece of work!

Mrs. Gardiner's brow furrowed. "You believe Miss Bingley to be dissembling?"

"Mr. Darcy mentioned his sister more than once when we were in company together. She is terribly shy, and he is quite protective of her. He told me she stays in London for the benefit of the masters here, but I cannot imagine him permitting her to attend a gathering like that without him."

"Is she not yet out?"

"No, she is sixteen."

Mrs. Gardiner relaxed back into her chair with a shake of her head. "Oh, that does offer some much-needed perspective on Miss Bingley's claims. She spoke of Mr. Darcy a great deal. If I were willing to wager, I would say Miss Bingley has set her cap at him."

Ha! Ellie was willing to bet her meagre life savings, which would be a fortune by this time period's standards. "She flatters him frequently and appeared to seek him out at the Lucas's as well as Mr. Bingley's ball."

Mrs. Gardiner's head tilted just a bit. "How do you feel about her marked attention to him?"

Ellie shrugged. "Why would I have any particular thoughts on it?"

"Jane mentioned he seemed to single you out, and he did attempt to speak to you on the terrace at the ball."

"She told you that?"

"I wish *you* had, but I do understand that your memory loss has caused you to forget how close we have always been."

Ugh! During the past week, she'd grown to admire Mrs. Gardiner. She was pretty, intelligent, and possessed a wonderful sense of humour. She'd never meant to hurt her feelings by leaving her out. "I didn't think it so important."

The lady sat forward and took Ellie's hands. "Do not dismiss him so readily, my dear. He offered to marry you. A man in his position does not offer his hand to a young lady with little to her name. He is connected to the Fitzwilliam earldom; did you know that? They are one of the wealthiest families in England."

Ellie frowned. "How do you know that?"

"I am from Lambton, which is but five miles from Pemberley, his estate. When I was younger, I met his mother when she came into my father's shop. I even saw his father walk through the village once. He was such a handsome man. I would imagine the son favours him."

Had she seen his father's portrait before coming back in time? She couldn't remember. "I do not know if he favours his father, but he is handsome." He was definitely fit!

Mrs. Gardiner tilted her head with a curve to one side of her lips. "Perhaps your father should pen a note to Mr. Darcy informing him of your presence in London."

"What would that accomplish?"

"If he called, we would know for certain of his interest. I know your lack of memories must make you hesitate, but Jane said he knows of your loss and still seems to show you preference. If you like him at all, do not let what has happened stand in the way of your happiness."

Nothing Jane confided in Mrs. Gardiner was a secret, but how much more had Jane told her? "The situation is so much more complicated than that."

She squeezed Ellie's hand. "Then tell me so I may ease your mind."

"Forgive me, but I cannot, and I have to admit that I am not sure I appreciate being discussed."

Mrs. Gardiner frowned and gasped. "Pray, do not hold your sister's need to speak of what happened against her. You terrified her when you had your accident. She is also mourning the person you once were. The longer you go without regaining your memories, the more she loses hope they will ever return. She is thankful you are alive and well, but you are not the same Lizzy she has always known. Can you not understand her despair?"

"Yes, I think so. I'm sorry." This was hard on everyone. She needed to be more thoughtful of Jane's feelings. She hadn't meant to scold Mrs. Gardiner or Jane.

"I do not believe you have reason to apologise. Most people would be put out at the notion of 'being discussed.'" Mrs. Gardiner glanced down to the letter on the small writing table. "Is this another letter to your father?"

"Yes," said Ellie beginning to fold the paper as Jane had taught her. "He requested some words of sense while we were away."

The lady smiled. "That sounds just as he would say. I am certain he will appreciate your thinking of him."

A muffled knock from the front door carried into the parlour, making Mrs. Gardiner jump. "I wonder who that could be? I am not expecting anyone today, and 'tis too soon for Miss Bingley and Mrs. Hurst to return our call."

"It could not be Mr. Bingley." Ellie's eyebrows were raised, and she let one side of her lips tug upward. Would Mrs. Gardiner take the poke at the Bingleys with humour?

"Certainly not," said the lady with a slight chuckle. "Come, we must be prepared to receive whomever this is." Once Ellie shifted to cradle the kitten, Mrs. Gardiner led her from the escritoire in the corner to the sofa while she stood before a nearby chair.

Ellie almost fainted when Mr. Darcy entered with a young lady just behind him. His younger sister perhaps?

They curtseyed, and he bowed. "Miss Elizabeth, I am pleased to see you well. Would you do me the honour of an introduction?"

She opened her mouth twice then cleared her throat. Why couldn't she speak? "Mr. Darcy, this is my aunt Mrs. Edward Gardiner."

"A pleasure to make your acquaintance, Mrs. Gardiner." He held out his hand towards the girl standing beside him. "May I present my sister, Miss Georgiana Darcy?"

Miss Darcy gave a dip of her chin while she curtseyed. "I am happy to make your acquaintance, Mrs. Gardiner, Miss Elizabeth." Her voice was so soft, Ellie had to work to hear her. Mr. Darcy hadn't exaggerated. The poor girl was painfully shy. This was the young lady who bore the heir of Pemberley? How had she drawn herself from her shell long enough for a gentleman to court her?

"Pray, sit, and I shall request refreshments," said Mrs. Gardiner, hurrying to the bell.

Mr. Darcy sat beside Ellie while his sister took the chair to Ellie's opposite side. "I hope we have not come at a poor time. I received a letter from Mr. Bennet this morning, explaining that Miss Bennet and Miss Elizabeth had travelled to town, and I was most eager to introduce my sister to them both." He glanced to Mrs. Gardiner then Ellie. "I do hope Miss Bennet is well."

"She is quite well. She and my aunt had just returned from calling on Miss Bingley and Mrs. Hurst, and my sister wished to refresh herself."

"Today is a good day to pay a call—not a great number of carriages on the roads."

"I agree, Mr. Darcy," said Mrs. Gardiner as she returned to her chair. "Do not make yourself uneasy. We are pleased to receive your call, are we not, Ellie?"

"Yes, of course." She leaned forward a little. "Miss Darcy, I understand you are very talented at the pianoforte. Your brother and Miss Bingley have both spoken well of your skill. I hope to hear it with my own ears some time."

"I believe my brother is partial when he speaks of my playing, and Miss Bingley is too kind. I do love to play, and I spend a prodigious amount of time in the music room. My brother has said you draw exceedingly well, and even drew a portrait of him."

Ellie's cheeks burned while Mrs. Gardiner lifted her eyebrows. "I should not have done so, but your brother sat so still and quiet. He was an ideal model."

"Your sister and your father have spoken of your ability," said Mrs. Gardiner, "but you have yet to share it with me or your uncle. We have been quite curious."

The kitten began to fidget, so she set him in the nearby basket before retrieving her sketchbook from the escritoire. When she returned, she flipped to the page with Mr. Darcy's portrait, pulled out the paper with the first drawing she'd done of Jane, and handed it to Mrs. Gardiner. She passed the book to Miss Darcy, who inhaled sharply. "'Tis a remarkable likeness, Brother."

"You captured Jane's serenity so well in this one." Mrs. Gardiner's eyes held a peculiar quality when they now looked at her. "Your father has not exaggerated your talent." She stood and moved behind Miss Darcy, glancing at the drawing of Mr. Darcy.

"May I look at the rest?" asked the girl.

"Of course." Ellie's eyes met Mr. Darcy's and they held while the butterflies in her stomach flipped and fluttered and she seemed to struggle to breathe.

His gaze shifted to the book. "That is Miss Kitty, Miss Elizabeth's sister."

"She appears so friendly."

"She is an open and happy girl," said Mrs. Gardiner.

Mr. Darcy cleared his throat and tugged at the waist of his topcoat. "Our reason for calling today, aside from introducing Miss Elizabeth to my sister, of course, is to issue an invitation. I thought Miss Elizabeth may care to see the Elgin marbles and other antiquities at the British Museum. I have yet to take Georgiana, and we would enjoy your company if you would like to join us. Mrs. Gardiner, you, your husband, and Miss Bennet are also welcome. Forgive me for not saying so in the first place."

With a nod, Mrs. Gardiner clasped her hands in her lap. "My husband and I have been to the museum several times and enjoyed the sights, but we have yet to take Ellie or Jane. If they should like to attend with you, we would not object. Ellie?"

How much different was the British Museum now compared to the future? With the free admission, Ellie had been many times, sitting in certain rooms and sketching. "I should be happy to join you and Miss Darcy. I shall have to ask Jane—"

"Ask me what, dearest?" said Jane as she entered, curtseying when she saw Mr. Darcy. "Good day, Mr. Darcy."

"Miss Bennet." He stood and bowed. "May I present my sister, Miss Georgiana Darcy? I was just inviting your family to the British Museum. I thought perhaps Friday would be a good day, but if it does not suit..."

Jane glanced at Ellie for no more than a second as she sat beside Mrs. Gardiner. "How generous of you, Mr. Darcy. I thank you for the invitation, but I should prefer to remain behind. I should not be away in the event Miss Bingley returns our call. Ellie? What of you? Would you like to go?" Jane's lips curved ever-so-slightly on one side. She was setting them up!

Ellie put on a smile no one could disapprove of and clasped her hands in her lap. "I should be pleased to see the museum with you and your sister, Mr. Darcy. Thank you for your kind invitation." When she peeked back at Jane, Jane puckered just a bit to keep from smiling wider. Who knew Jane could be so devious? Well, devious for Jane that was. If she hadn't known better, she might have suspected Jane was taking lessons from Mrs. Bennet. God forbid!

Chapter 21

"Did you enjoy the museum, Miss Elizabeth?" asked Miss Darcy as the Darcy carriage rolled through the London streets.

"I did. I thank you both for the invitation. The diversion was most welcome." She enjoyed seeing the antiquities and getting out of the house was definitely a bonus. Since arriving in town, she hadn't had much opportunity to take a tour of Regency London with the dreary December weather. One thing the history books hadn't exaggerated, the smell! No wonder the rich left the city in the summer. The heat and humidity could only worsen matters.

"What time is it, Brother?"

Mr. Darcy pulled out his pocket watch, making Ellie pause and hold in a gasp. It was the very the same one as in the trunk in the attics. "Not yet two. I thought we might stop by Gunter's for some ices before we return Miss Elizabeth to Gracechurch Street."

"But, 'tis too cold for ices," said Miss Darcy. Ellie couldn't argue. Any day that required warm bricks and rugs to travel in the carriage was too cold in her opinion. The day held a damp chill, penetrating the layers of their clothing and prickling their skin. "What if we brought Miss Elizabeth to Darcy House? We could have tea and cake, and I am certain she would enjoy seeing the artwork as well as the library."

Ellie took Miss Darcy's hand and gave it a squeeze. "I have had a lovely time already. Do not think you must entertain me for the entire day. I do not want to impose. Your brother surely has letters to write or business he has neglected for the morning in order to accompany us."

"You could never be an imposition. I have enjoyed the morning, and I was not eager to end the day so soon. I hope you do not object." Mr. Darcy's voice was low and warm. Their eyes held, and Ellie's body shot to life, her palms sweating in her gloves and goose pimples erupting along her forearms. This was ridiculous.

Mr. Darcy rapped his walking stick on the roof of the carriage. After he gave the driver their new destination, they were moving again, turning along the edge of what resembled Hyde Park. The trees were somewhat different, but there was no way they'd be the exact same now as two-hundred years into the future.

"Perhaps if we have a warmer day, we could walk along the Serpentine," said Mr. Darcy.

Her gaze shot to him. "Do you walk in Hyde Park often?" Blimey, that sounded like a pick-up line.

"Fairly often, but never during the fashionable hours. I prefer listening to the birds and catching glimpses of nature in the middle of town."

"Brother often rides Rotten Row early in the mornings."

"Few are out at that time," he said. "Too many race their horses and crowd the row later in the day."

The carriage pulled along the kerb, the step was set, and Mr. Darcy alighted. After he handed them out, Ellie had to hold her jaw closed at the sight before her. He lived on Park Lane. Wasn't that one of the poshest parts of town, that and Berkley Square? At the least, Mayfair, which was where Park Lane was located. She'd walked by this house in her own time. Of course, it wasn't so much a house then, but a business on the ground floor with flats on the floors above and a wide, busy street between it and the park. Few could afford a house this size in present day London. Few could afford to purchase any property in London in the 21st century.

"Miss Elizabeth," said Mr. Darcy with his elbow before her. She took a deep breath and set her hand on his arm. She should've had them return her to Gracechurch Street. She shouldn't be spending any more time with the Darcys than necessary. Why did she seem to lose the will to argue with them?

As they approached the steps, a tall Black man opened the door and stepped to the side, allowing them to enter. "Good afternoon, Mr. Darcy. I hope you had an agreeable time at the museum."

"Yes, thank you, Watson. My sister wished to bring Miss Elizabeth Bennet here for tea rather than Gunter's. Could you ensure Mrs. Newnham is informed?"

"We shall take our refreshments in the music room," said Miss Darcy with a kind, yet firm voice. Watson gave a slight bow and, with long strides, departed while the maids and footmen took their coats and hats.

As they ascended to the first floor, Ellie almost tripped while taking in the beautiful trim and the paintings around her. The chandelier in the hall alone was impressive. If she had to guess based on the façade and width of the house, she'd swear Fitzwilliam's home was larger than Longbourn.

"Are you well?" Mr. Darcy's voice seemed right beside her ear.

Her head whipped around. She had to stop being so startled by him. "Your home is lovely."

"We can give you a tour if you like," said Miss Darcy. "After all, with your talent at drawing, we thought you would wish to view the artwork. My brother has a landscape of

Pemberley in his study, and my father collected several works of art in Italy during his grand tour."

When they entered the library, Ellie paused and clutched her hands together. "Yes, of course. I love art exhibitions and museums. I like to take my sketchpad. I can sit in front of a painting or sculpture and draw for hours." She flinched when Miss Darcy's eyebrows drew together and Fitzwilliam's eyes widened. Bollocks! Elizabeth Bennet could never have sat for hours in one of the museums in London. Now, how to cover for her cock up? She needed a distraction. "This is a sizeable room for town." She spoke quickly.

"Yes, my mother and father preferred a larger library to having a parlour, so they combined the rooms. The house has two drawing rooms downstairs and a mistress's sitting room on the floor above, so we do not lack for space. We do not use those rooms often." Miss Darcy pointed to the right. "Fitzwilliam's study is just through those doors, and the music room is across the hall. We spend most of our days in this part of the house." Thankfully, Miss Darcy seemed to have forgotten Ellie's blunder as she glanced at her surroundings, but what about Fitzwilliam?

With a few steps, Ellie stood in front of the fireplace, a portrait she'd never seen before over the mantel. "Who is this?" She rose on her tiptoes a bit and narrowed her eyes. Whoever the subject was, he had Gainsborough paint him.

"That is our father," said Mr. Darcy. "A portrait was painted of our mother at the same time, which is in Georgiana's sitting room, as well as one of them after my birth together, but that work is at Pemberley."

"Your father was a handsome man." No, she hadn't restored this painting. She hadn't even seen it. Where had it disappeared to?

"Fitzwilliam resembles him so much, does he not?"

Ellie smiled at Miss Darcy's wide eyes and slight smile. The little snot would make Mrs. Bennet proud. "Mr. Darcy does favour his father." She had a hard time holding Fitzwilliam's gaze while his cheeks reddened some. This was embarrassing.

"I wish to refresh myself for a moment. Fitzwilliam, you should show her the landscape of Pemberley in your study until I return." As Miss Darcy hurried out, a maid appeared and began setting a small table near some windows in the room opposite.

Mr. Darcy held out an arm. "I believe I have my orders. Would you care to see the painting, Miss Ellie?"

Something about the way he said "Ellie" as opposed to Elizabeth melted a part of her heart. Between Mrs. Gardiner and his sister, he'd been more formal since they were reacquainted in London, and she'd more or less resigned herself to being called Miss Elizabeth in public.

His study was rather dark, like the study at Pemberley, with large shelves lining the walls and a cheerful fire burning in the grate. The painting was a large one, again over the mantel, but not what she would've expected. She'd seen paintings such as this but had never understood the point other than the notion that they were more to show off the estate's holdings rather than make a beautiful or moving image. The contrast to the last view she had of Pemberley, however, was striking. This was Pemberley at its full glory: the cascade flowing with water, the manicured gardens, the fountain with a spray of water shooting into the air, the orangeries, the hunting lodge on the hill. The folly was missing, but perhaps that had been built later.

"I am not overly enamoured of the work, so pray, do not believe you should praise it."

Her gaze darted in his direction and back to the work before her. "It is rather cold. The artist was attempting to show Pemberley's grandeur as opposed to its natural surroundings or the beauty of the home itself."

He nodded and clasped his hands behind his back. "My thoughts exactly. We do have a good many gardens around the house, but from the time I was a boy, I preferred the wilder parts of the park and the countryside. My mother took out one of the more manicured sections—this one—before she died and replaced it with a large bed of roses and lavender." He'd shifted next to her and pointed to the largest of the formal gardens. The cedar tones of his cologne tickled her nose and that side of her back heated with his proximity.

"You can never go wrong with roses and lavender," said Ellie with an arch of her eyebrow.

"Darcy, my boy," said an unfamiliar voice, making Fitzwilliam step back and clasp his hands behind his back. A second later, an older gentleman stepped through the door leading to the library, startling when he noticed her. "Ah, forgive me. Carson said you, Georgiana, and a guest were to have tea in the music room. When the room was empty, I thought I might find you here."

"Do not trouble yourself, Uncle. Georgiana wished to refresh herself, so I was entertaining Miss Elizabeth during her absence."

The man's eyes darted to her. "If you would introduce me, Nephew."

Fitzwilliam dipped his chin. "My Lord, this is Miss Elizabeth Bennet of Longbourn in Hertfordshire. Her father's estate borders that of Netherfield, the estate Bingley leased for the year. Miss Elizabeth, this gentleman is my uncle, Lord Fitzwilliam, the Earl Fitzwilliam."

Ellie curtsied and made an attempt to shove down the nerves twisting in her stomach. "Lord Fitzwilliam, I am honoured to make your acquaintance."

"My niece has made mention of you to my wife. She was impressed with your drawings. I do not suppose you have them with you?"

"No, sir. Mr. and Miss Darcy wished to show me the antiquities of the British Museum today. I had not thought to bring my drawings with me."

"Of course," he said. "Was my nephew showing you some of his paintings?"

Fitzwilliam stepped slightly forward. "Yes, sir. Miss Elizabeth has shown an interest in Mr. Gainsborough."

"I enjoy many artists: Sir Joshua Reynolds, William Turner, John Constable."

Lord Fitzwilliam's eyebrows drew together. "Constable? I am unfamiliar with him."

Ellie bit her cheek. Shit! She'd forgotten Constable wasn't popular until after his death. "I believe I read of him in the paper. I do not remember his subject matter." Yes, she'd lied, but she'd needed to cover her ass somehow.

"Ah, I see. My wife may know of him. She enjoys art more than me. I simply take note of her favourites for her birthdays, our anniversary, and so on."

"You are a generous husband," said Ellie.

He nodded and tilted his head at Fitzwilliam. "A husband must have more gift possibilities than jewellery for his wife lest he never have the ability to surprise her."

"You have managed well then, sir," said Fitzwilliam. "She still praises last year's birthday gift."

His uncle chuckled. "Yes, well, I am not sure what to purchase this year that will be its equal. Constable, you say?"

"I have heard he is quite talented."

The gentleman gave a half-smile. "Thank you. She adores finding an unknown."

"Miss Elizabeth?" came the timid voice of Miss Darcy from the library.

"I should go to Miss Darcy and leave the two of you to talk. Sir, if you will excuse me." She curtseyed and hurried back out. "I am here, Miss Darcy."

Miss Darcy startled with a hand to her chest. "Oh, did Fitzwilliam show you Pemberley?"

"He did. You have a lovely home. I am certain the painting does not do justice to the beauty of the actual property."

Miss Darcy beamed. "Pemberley is the most beautiful of places, but I am hardly impartial."

"It's your home. I cannot blame you for loving it above anywhere else in the world."

Chapter 22

Fitzwilliam waited for Ellie to depart, the muscles in his shoulders twisted and pulled taut. What had brought his uncle to Darcy House? His uncle made a habit of requesting Fitzwilliam's presence, not making a surprise appearance at his home. This morning's visit was vexing to say the least.

"I am certain you are wondering why I have called," said Lord Fitzwilliam, closing the door behind Ellie.

"I must admit I am. My aunt sometimes calls to spend time with Georgiana, but you do not typically do so on your own."

He studied the books on the shelf for a moment. "I had a letter from Richard yesterday."

"Is he soon to return?"

"He is to remain in Portugal for now. He did make mention of a young lady in Hertfordshire that you seemed to have singled out. By your introduction, I assume the lady he made mention of is Miss Bennet?"

"She is Miss Elizabeth. Her elder sister, Miss Jane Bennet, chose to remain behind in the event Bingley's sisters returned her call. But yes, I mentioned Miss Elizabeth in my last to Richard, however; I had not expected him to blather on about my personal affairs to you or my aunt."

"He is concerned. If he were in England, he would have journeyed to Hertfordshire to assure himself of Miss Elizabeth's character, not to mention her state after a fall such as you described. You must understand, he has witnessed head injuries that render a man to the state of a child. You require a wife, and as he is not present to ensure this lady is what she ought to be, he has requested I do so in his stead."

"Miss Elizabeth is no more a child in mind or body than I am. As a result of her accident, she has a few oddities of speech, which she is endeavouring to correct, and her memories have not been quick to return. Nonetheless, she is intelligent, witty, and will make an excellent sister for Georgiana. Her talent with a piece of black lead rivals any sketches and studies I have viewed at the Royal Academy. I have no reservations making her the offer of my hand, and Richard should trust in my judgement."

His uncle held up a hand, palm out. "Do not be angry. You would likely feel the same should you receive word from him of a similar nature. He shares guardianship of Georgiana with you. Should he not ensure her continued happiness? This lady, should you wed her, would have a great deal of influence over your sister."

"And she has four sisters of her own, being closest to Miss Bennet over the younger three."

"What of Anne?"

Fitzwilliam's chin hitched back. "What of her? I have never planned to wed Anne. She is selfish and shares too many of her mother's less than appealing habits. If my mother planned a union between us, she never made mention of the scheme to me. I have also told Lady Catherine that I have no intention of marrying her daughter. I must admit to being shocked that she has not complained of my recalcitrance to you."

"Relax, son. Yes, Catherine wrote of your declaration, and I would have you know I supported you when I penned my response. I only wish to ensure you are certain of your decision. You give up the possibility of Rosings and Anne's fortune by choosing another—"

"No amount of compensation is worth living with Anne's company for a lifetime. She would gloat over being mistress of Pemberley while I hid away in my study, avoiding her and the near constant intrusion of my aunt. I wish to be happy with my wife. Miss Elizabeth is the first lady I could envision making me content. I will make her the offer of my hand when the moment is right. Nothing can dissuade me from that course. Even if she never regains all of her memories, I could never repine making her my bride."

"As I said, I only wished to ensure you were certain."

"I have never been more certain in my life." At a light knock, Fitzwilliam withheld a growl. "Yes!"

When the door opened, his aunt stood in the opening with lifted eyebrows. "Good afternoon, Fitzwilliam. I trust you have finished your conversation with my husband?"

"Elinor?" said his uncle in a high tone. "When did you arrive?"

"According to Carson, not long after you. Now, Georgiana and that young lady are waiting on Fitzwilliam for tea. You do not wish to be rude, do you?"

Fitzwilliam relaxed and shook his head. "Of course, not. Aunt, would you care to join us? Uncle, you are welcome too."

His aunt laughed as she turned. "I already accepted Georgiana's invitation, but I do appreciate that you would enjoy my company as well."

His uncle's low chuckle followed. "Shall we? Your first lesson in being an attentive suitor: never leave your lady waiting."

Fitzwilliam's insides leapt. "You would support me, then?"

One step before they left the study, his uncle placed a hand on his shoulder and leaned forward, holding Fitzwilliam's gaze.

"I made a promise to your mother before she died that I would do my best to persuade you to marry for love. She never had any agreement with Catherine—"

"But you asked about Anne?"

"You have never seemed inclined towards any young lady. In the absence of any potential wife, I considered whether an alliance between you and Anne would be worth the sacrifice on your part. After all, you have kept Catherine from emptying Rosings' coffers and kept the de Bourgh properties intact. If you wed Anne, you would benefit from your efforts since Lewis's death. The Darcy fortune would rival the wealthiest families in England. That said, as long as the girl will not shame the family, I shall never stand in your way if you have found love."

"Miss Elizabeth could never shame the family."

The earl sighed. "I have long suspected that if you ever wed, you would disappear from the Season altogether."

"I do not desire to take part ever again if I can help it."

"Your aunt and I shall endeavour to change your mind. If for no other reason, then consider your children."

Fitzwilliam groaned and scrubbed his face with his hand. "I doubt we shall prevent them making a good match, but should Miss Elizabeth become Mrs. Darcy, I promise to consider your position."

"Your aunt and I shall not relent."

He sighed and held out a hand in the direction of the library. "I suppose I should expect no less. As you said earlier, we should not keep the ladies waiting."

When they entered the music room, Ellie's eyes brightened and an alluring expression drew him to her side like a moth to a flame. Georgiana set a cup before him as he sat while his aunt's gaze darted back and forth between him and Ellie, who cleared her throat. "Lady Fitzwilliam, your husband mentioned you take pleasure in art."

"I do. I attend a great number of exhibitions. My husband has complained that should I continue to purchase paintings, our walls will never require recovering as they will be covered from floor to ceiling with the works I collect."

"I do not foresee that to be a problem," said Ellie with a teasing lilt.

His aunt grinned and sat back. "Have you had the opportunity to attend any of the London exhibitions?"

"Not lately, but I enjoy viewing great works as often as I am afforded the opportunity."

"Miss Elizabeth is quite talented herself. Hopefully, in the future you will have an opportunity to see the drawings she has made. I hope to persuade her to paint Georgiana one day."

His sister clasped her hands and gasped. "Oh, how delightful! I should dearly love to watch you create, Miss Elizabeth. Your previous efforts are wonderful." She set her hand on her aunt's forearm. "You should see the drawing she made of Fitzwilliam. She is so talented."

Lady Fitzwilliam's eyes darted to him for a second and her lips curved just a little. "You drew Fitzwilliam? I should like to see that, indeed."

Poor Ellie's complexion turned various shades of red that spread from her cheeks down her neck and to her chest. "It's really not *that* good."

"I disagree," said Fitzwilliam. How he wanted to take her in his arms and soothe her! "I still believe you should paint our portraits. After all, mine was painted before I attended Cambridge."

Ellie blinked and stared at him for a moment before she startled. "Forgive me."

"Miss Elizabeth," said his uncle, "do you play the pianoforte?"

The lady bit her lip and glanced at him out of the corner of her eye. "No, My Lord, I do not."

Fitzwilliam bit his lip to keep from laughing and stared into his tea. This would be an interesting afternoon!

Ellie finally relaxed when front door closed and the earl and countess were gone. If she'd known she'd be forced to take tea with a peer of the realm, she may have stayed behind at Gracechurch Street. Hopefully, she hadn't said anything too shocking.

When Fitzwilliam returned, Miss Darcy excused herself to fetch a book she had mentioned. "'Tis in my chambers," she said as she hurried through the door.

Ellie pivoted to face Fitzwilliam. "Your aunt and uncle are friendly people."

"Yes, but they are inclined to like you."

"They like me? They hardly know me." Ellie smiled and looked out of the window as the carriage pulled away from the kerb. When she turned back, Fitzwilliam had stepped closer. He was impossibly close.

"You are correct, of course, but they trust my judgement in the matter." He cleared his throat and gripped and released his hands. What could be the matter? He looked as though he'd gulped down five or six servings of espresso. "Miss Ellie, you must allow me to apologise for the way I offered my hand to you at Netherfield. It was badly done, and you deserved better. You see, I have been captured by you since that day I found you atop Oakham Mount, and our time together has only made my admiration for you grow."

Ellie gulped, and her entire body began to tremble. No! This was not happening! How had he gone from an easy conversation about his aunt and uncle to this?

"You must allow me to tell you how I ardently admire and love you. At Longbourn, I had no hesitation in offering for you because it is what I wish with all my heart. Miss Ellie—"

"It isn't as simple as that." She covered her mouth with her hand and backed two steps from him, her heart in her throat. He couldn't propose. She had to stop him. The last thing she wished to do was break his heart. Even so, she would be breaking hers at the same time.

"If your reservations are due to your injury, I care not about your lack of memories. I want more than anything to return to Pemberley with you and live a life of love and happiness. No one need know of what you remember or do not remember. Of course, should Georgiana desire to come out, we would be forced to endure a Season or two until she decides whether she will wed, but other than an occasional journey for business or the theatre and art events, I would be pleased to leave London behind—to spend the rest of my days with you and you alone. You are all I require to complete my happiness. You are who I have been seeking in the endless litany of London balls and Seasons."

Ellie covered her eyes and shook her head, then held out her hands, palms facing him. "Pray, say no more. My situation is so much more complicated than losing my memories. Mr. Bennet was worried about trusting you with the truth, but I do not know what else to do. I feel as though if I'm ever to live my life, I have to confront what has happened and know whether I will remain or return. How can I do that without confiding in you?"

His brows furrowed with his frown. "I do not understand. Do you not believe the friendship and feelings we have now will last if you regain your past?"

"It's not that." Ellie peered over her shoulder. No one was standing near the doorway, but if she were to be honest with him, she couldn't take the chance of someone overhearing. She closed the door and pressed her back against it. "There's so much more, and I don't know that you will believe me, but I have to try."

"Ellie, if we are discovered thus, you will have no choice but to marry me."

"I know, but should one of your servants or Georgiana hear what I am about to tell you, they will consider me insane."

He was quiet for a second or two, clasping his hands behind his back. "I have thought you were dissembling on certain points and remembrances, but I do not see how any revelation will change what I feel." He stepped forward and grasped her by the hands. "Do you not love me?"

Despite his touch being a major distraction, she didn't remove her hands from his. "As I said before, nothing is that simple. I only wish it were."

"But do you have feelings for me? I have often thought you do. You cannot always hold my eye, and the way you bite your lower lip, and your blushes all tell me you care for me."

"I do, but you must hear the truth. You must know that I am not Elizabeth Bennet."

"No," he said softly, tugging her closer. "You are Ellie Bennet."

Ellie side-stepped and shifted past him. She couldn't have him touching her if she was to think straight. "No, I am Ellie Gardiner. I was born on the 31st of May 199_ in Ipswich. My parents died in a car crash when I was sixteen. I attended the Art Institute of Chicago for university and Northumbria University where I studied art restoration for my post-grad. In late October 202-, I was hired by a group of foreign investors restoring Pemberley, making it a tourist attraction."

His arms had gradually fallen by his sides, and he stumbled backwards. The way he shook his head screamed that he doubted her, that he didn't believe her, yet she had no choice but to plough on. "I'd restored your sister's portrait before yours. In the painting, you appear so similar to how you look now; I was surprised when you said it was painted before you attended Cambridge.

"I can't explain why, but your portrait haunted me. I couldn't get your eyes out of my head. At the same time, I was seeing this odd reflection in the mirror in the ballroom—that huge floor to ceiling mirror across from the doors to the terrace."

His eyes widened. Was she providing enough detail for him to believe her, or would he still freak once she was finished?

"You see, every time I stood in front of that mirror, I didn't look like myself. I saw the reflection of Elizabeth Bennet staring back at me. I am different in the future. I have similar green eyes but my hair is shorter and ginger-coloured. The clothes in the reflection weren't the ones I would wear in my time, but instead, were Elizabeth's ivory gown—the one I wore to Lucas Lodge for the party, the evening you played the pianoforte.

"One night, after exploring the attics and drinking one or two large glasses of wine, I went down to the ballroom and touched the mirror. I don't know why I thought it was a good idea. When my finger met the glass, something pulled from behind my navel and the next thing I knew, I woke up at Longbourn looking like Elizabeth Bennet, and everyone insisting I was her."

Mr. Darcy started shaking his head once more. "This is not possible."

"Then how do I know about the set-up of the ballroom? I was staying in the master's bedchamber. I can tell you the fastest route to the ballroom from your bedchamber through a combination of the family and servants' passages." His jaw worked overtime while she described the path she'd taken on more than one occasion. She described the servants' hallway in detail, as well as the portrait gallery, until he finally waved his hands in front of him.

"Stop. Pray, I beg you. I can take no more."

Chapter 23

Fitzwilliam stared at her. How? How was this possible? None of what she claimed could happen, but if this was a figment of her imagination, then how could she describe Pemberley in such detail? A plausible explanation could be that she had somehow toured the estate, but Mrs. Reynolds never took people into the family wing much less showed them that route from his bedchamber to the ballroom. A guest in servants' passages? His housekeeper would sooner resign her position than show them anything less than Pemberley at its best.

But what Ellie was claiming was impossible, was it not? A mirror in his ballroom had ripped her from the future and put her into Elizabeth Bennet's body in 1811. A fanciful tale, indeed! Could the blow to her head have altered her to such an extent? How could he have not considered such an eventuality?

"I've been in your study as well," she said. "The decoration is similar to here, but you have a Constable over the mantel."

"Who?"

"John Constable, the painter I mentioned to your uncle. He is a landscape painter most known for painting his surroundings near his home in Suffolk. You have a rendering of the Salisbury Cathedral. I put my foot in it when I mentioned him to your uncle, which is why I backpedalled. I remembered Constable wasn't popular until after his death." She pointed to the wall to her right as if she were in the room. "The door is there to the hallway and another door is on that wall to go to the library. The fireplace is there, and you have a large, dark oak desk that in the future is in a similar position to this one."

Her voice had become shaky, and her finger trembled as she pointed. Her description of the room was accurate with the exception of one thing. "I am not familiar with the painting you mentioned nor the artist, although as you said, it is possible I never acquired that work. I have been considering a work of Mr. Turner's for that place but have yet to purchase one."

"I think Constable only sold something like twenty paintings in England during his lifetime. You may have bought it later, or perhaps it may have been Georgiana's son who purchased it after Constable's death."

Something in his chest caved like a blow to his sternum. Georgiana's son? "Should I die or should I never have children, Pemberley is to be held in trust for Georgiana's eldest son."

"Yes, and you spent your life almost as a recluse at Pemberley. I have found several of your journals while exploring the house, but I have not read past you departing for Ramsgate to visit your sister."

He was winded as though someone delivered a second blow to his belly. "You behaved as though you knew nothing of Georgiana at Ramsgate."

Ellie rolled her eyes. "Oh, yes, because I was going to blurt out, 'Hey, I remember that from your journal.' I'm not daft. I know how all of this sounds. You cannot imagine how hard it was to trust Mr. Bennet. He was the one who insisted I tell him the truth. Do you think I want to be locked away in Bedlam or burnt at the stake?"

He rubbed his hand across the back of his neck. Lord, but it was tight. "Mr. Bennet believes this?"

"In the absence of any other explanation, yes. I am too different from Elizabeth for him to believe I am her. Our accomplishments are different, our tastes, not to mention the way I speak—"

"Is markedly different."

"Yes," she said, nodding.

Not that any of her explanations helped. This was simply too fantastical to be true. He covered his mouth with his hand and stared at her. How? How could she know all of what she said of Pemberley? Not even the servants used the mix of passages she described. None of this made sense. He was not one to believe in witchcraft or magic. So many who were accused were like his blind aunt or had some other malady no one could explain. They were persecuted for what they could not control.

Ellie stepped forward. "I know it sounds bizarre and unbelievable, but I beg you to look into my eyes. I am not lying to you. Perhaps you were meant for Elizabeth Bennet, but something happened in the timeline—maybe this happened and it's why you never married. I hope not, but I have no way of knowing. If we fix this, you may get your happy ever after with Elizabeth. What if I'm here for that reason—to bring you together with her?"

He backed against the pianoforte, stopping with a jerk when the edge of the surface met his backside. "You need not say this if you do not want to marry me—"

Ellie's eyes flooded with tears. "If I belonged in this time and place with you, I'd marry you in a heartbeat."

He rushed forward and took her in his arms, his lips brushing against her forehead. "Then how do we prove you belong here? How do we settle your mind?" Could her memories be an elaborate dream she had from the accident? If he proved to her the mirror in his ballroom was nothing more than a mirror, would she accept his hand and forget all of this? Or would these memories she considered real haunt her?

"You don't believe me." She said the words matter of fact and soft.

"The entire story does not make sense to me, Ellie. You must understand."

She pulled away, and his body rebelled at the separation. His arms ached at her absence. "I do. I couldn't understand why I was seeing Elizabeth's reflection when I looked into that mirror, I couldn't understand what was happening when I awoke in her bedchamber at Longbourn, and I certainly cannot understand why I have not yet returned to the 21st century. I have been hoping and praying for an answer since I found myself here. I just keep thinking that if I return to Pemberley and touch that mirror, I'll return and Mr. Bennet can have Elizabeth back. He misses her dreadfully, and I feel like the worst sort of thief."

Her expression was so open. She truly believed what she was saying. He could not imagine why he would consider this, but what if everything she claimed was real? What was he thinking? This could not be the truth. But, what if he took Ellie to Pemberley, she touched that mirror, and she was never the same? He would be devastated. A part of him screamed and shouted not to do it, but she had asked so little of him: merely to keep her confidence. She had never requested anything of great import—until now. He would be cruel to deny her. He loved her too much to tell her no, yet how could he marry her if her mind was so severely addled? His thoughts were leaping in a thousand different directions at once. This was all too much.

"Will your father...forgive me, will Mr. Bennet object to your travelling to Pemberley?" She had just arrived in London after all.

"I do not think so."

He had no choice: he had to do this. She needed the opportunity to prove this to him and to herself whether what she claimed was in fact truth or an elaborate hallucination. "I shall pen a letter to your father and arrange the travel. I would prefer Georgiana not know of this or why I am returning to Pemberley. She would not understand your...truth. Will Miss Bennet be willing to travel with you as far as Longbourn, or should I request the presence of a maid?"

"As far as Longbourn?"

"I plan on requesting your father accompany us to Derbyshire. We do require a chaperon for the journey, and he should be present when you encounter the mirror again, should he not?"

"Yes, I suppose that would be a good idea. I hadn't thought about needing someone to accompany us. It would be best if we tell as few people as possible. Few would understand, really. I haven't even told Jane. Mr. Bennet worried the knowledge would be too much for her. Besides, he will also be needed to explain things to Elizabeth when she returns." Ellie closed the door to the study behind them.

"Do you not require chaperons in the future?"

She gave a tense laugh. "Some cultures, maybe, but no, for the most part, men and women date and marry all of the time without ever needing someone to keep tabs on them."

"Date?"

After a slight shake of her head, she smiled. "Court. They might go to dinner or the cinema or a walk in the park. They spend time together, and eventually either they break up or marry or just become partners."

"Partners?"

"They live together with or without marriage."

He could not help his eyebrows shooting up. "Have you ever had such an arrangement?" How would he feel if she had?

"No, I've never let myself get close enough to someone for that. Something about this entire experience has caused me to let down my guard."

He gestured towards the door. "Let us return to my study so I may pen this letter to your father. Again, I must beg you not to speak of this to Georgiana. The tale is hard for me to accept. Her acceptance and understanding are less likely than mine. She does not know you as I do." He exhaled. "As I thought I knew you, I suppose."

He ignored her stricken expression, sat at his desk, and drew out a pen. "I am unsure how to word this without saying all, and I do not believe that to be prudent."

"Tell him I have told you of my education. That should be enough for him to know what you are saying. You could also tell him that you want me to see the Pemberley ballroom."

Ellie was an enormous distraction while he wrote the short missive. After sanding it, he handed the paper to her. "Will this suffice?"

"Yes, it should."

A rustling of skirts carried into the room before Miss Darcy hurried in. "Did you wish to show her Pemberley again, Brother?" she said with a slight giggle.

Ellie glanced at the painting. "No, your brother needed to write a letter."

His sister turned to him and frowned. "You are conducting business with Miss Elizabeth here? Really, Brother."

"Forgive me. I noticed a missive on my desk that required my immediate attention. It must have come while we were out." He rang the bell. "As soon as this response is sent, we shall return to the music room. I am afraid I am needed at Pemberley for a short time, Georgiana, but I must await a response to my correspondence before I depart so we need not hasten Miss Elizabeth's return to Gracechurch Street. We will enjoy the remainder of our afternoon first." He did not want to disappoint his sister, and rushing Ellie home would cause questions.

Georgiana's eyes dimmed, and she stepped forward. "Is all well at Pemberley?"

"Yes, Sweetling. My steward requested my presence a fortnight ago, and I delayed. I fear he is quite put out with me." It wasn't a complete lie. His steward had been requesting his presence over a tenant dispute, though the two tenants had been at odds for years. He was convinced they enjoyed arguing with each other and had no desire for peace since nothing he said or did satisfied either of the men.

During tea, Fitzwilliam listened to Ellie speak with his sister, noting the cadence of her words and the manner in which she spoke. How was he to credit her claims? He had to admit she did not seem the same Elizabeth Bennet as before the accident. He could tell by her eyes she had not regained her memories, but this was a more shocking explanation than he could have ever dreamt.

He wanted more than anything to dismiss her story. The entire situation was impossible. Yet, how to explain her eyes? How could they be the same vivid green but different when scrutinized? Was it a different soul or nothing more than her lack of memory?

By the time they returned Ellie to Gracechurch Street, poor Georgiana had enquired of his health more than once. He had been too preoccupied with Ellie's claims and had been quiet, even for him. As soon as they returned to Darcy House, he shut himself away in his study and poured a large glass of brandy.

He had done his best to school his features and not let his disquiet peek through when in the presence of the Gardiners and Miss Bennet, but he had been relaxed this morning compared to his last visit. The difference had to be marked.

Ellie had bit her lip when he gave a curt bow and departed. He had not been as rude or short as he could have been, but was it obvious? Her manner indicated it was. Did he care if she noticed?

He rubbed his chest, attempting to soothe the ache that had appeared since Ellie had shattered his hopes for the future. No, he did not care what people said or thought of him, but this was not as simple as he had expected—as he had been led to believe. As much as he loved her, what was he to do? He could not see but one way forward. He had to protect Georgiana. As much as it tore at his soul, he had to let Ellie go. He had thought perhaps he could still marry her and forget this, but how did one simply ignore a belief that may never be resolved? No, after their return from Pemberley, he needed to put Ellie Bennet and her hare-brained stories out of his head and life. The problem was that his traitorous heart wanted Ellie. No one else would do. How was he supposed to convince his heart otherwise?

Chapter 24

The small tuxedo kitten remained curled and sleeping in Ellie's arms, oblivious to her knee bouncing a mile a minute as the carriage plodded along the Derbyshire countryside. They would arrive at Pemberley today, and she was about to jump out of her skin. Would the mirror behave the same way here and now as it did before...or should she say after? Blimey, this was complicated. Her head was throbbing, likely from grinding her teeth. How many times had she caught herself grinding them together during the trip? Too many to count if you asked her. Pets were supposed to reduce stress, weren't they? Little Marlow was adorable and full of kittenish purrs, but at the moment, none of that could quell the turmoil in her gut. Meanwhile, the little ball of fluff had not taken to travelling such a long distance without some complaint, which hadn't helped her current state whatsoever, making her terrified he would injure himself when he jumped down from her lap and searched for places to hide. Then there was Fitzwilliam's silence and the occasional stares he levelled in her direction. Something had certainly changed since they'd left London! He thought she was...how had Mr. Bennet put it? Fit for Bedlam. He hadn't said as much, but he had to. She couldn't blame him either. Some days, she thought she was fit for Bedlam too.

"Good Lord, Ellie, cease that infernal tapping," said Mr. Bennet.

"Sorry, I'm nervous."

With a nod, Mr. Bennet patted her hand. "I understand. I am at sixes and sevens myself. If my daughter is returned to me, I shall be overjoyed, yet I shall miss you terribly. Despite our short acquaintance, you have become as much my daughter as

Elizabeth. Should you return to the future, I shall not have the pleasure of your singular wit."

She covered his hand with hers. "I'll miss you too. I don't know what I'll do without you and Jane. I have kept to myself for so long, and this is why. My parents' deaths were hard enough. This will be like losing a parent all over again."

"You were young and had no other family who could and would take you in. 'Tis no wonder you relied only upon yourself. Do you not agree, Mr. Darcy?"

He started. "I do. I am certain I have done much the same since the deaths of my mother and father."

Mr. Bennet nodded and one side of his lips curved when he turned back to Ellie. "What would be the one thing you would miss most of the future were you to stay?"

"That would be difficult. I have favourite books that will not be written for so long, artists I adore who haven't been born yet—Georgia O'Keeffe for example—and while in some cases women are still fighting to be recognised and treated the same as our male peers, we have made great strides since this time. You and Mr. Darcy have treated me as though I have a rational mind, but how many would dismiss me for my sex alone? I might have to slap a man if he referred to me as 'the weaker sex.' I would also miss the ability to vote, and do not forget my job. I adore taking a painting with layers upon layers of grime accumulated with the ages and restoring it to its former glory. It's exceedingly satisfying."

"Women vote?" Fitzwilliam's eyebrows were high on his forehead until Ellie, unable to cross her arms over her chest with the sleeping kitten, lifted her eyebrows, mirroring his expression.

"Yes, I have voted. Is there a problem with that?"

He cleared his throat and crossed one leg over the other. "No, of course you should vote. I simply cannot imagine a time where that would happen."

A chuckle came from Mr. Bennet. "I agree, yet from what Ellie has said, the world is markedly different. While I would not recommend giving Mrs. Bennet, or Lydia and Mary the right to vote, I do believe Jane, Lizzy, Ellie, and perhaps in the future, Kitty could make a reasonable decision based on facts."

"Kitty has made great strides to improve herself," said Ellie.

"Yes, removing Lydia from the scrutiny of the neighbourhood has helped greatly in that regard. Could you imagine what would have occurred if she were at the Netherfield ball with that militia officer you caught? A few smooth words and she would have been lost to his charming manner."

"As for what I would miss, I have not even mentioned the silly everyday things."

"What would you be pleased to leave behind?" asked Fitzwilliam.

Ellie blew out a breath. "There are devastating issues that affect the Earth as a whole, but we cannot seem to make any headway about fixing the problems. Due to industrialisation, the Earth is warming, but many deny the science and the oil producing companies want to maintain their hold on the energy market. People also have invented horrific weapons that can wipe all life away if used."

"Now, I wish I could keep both you and Lizzy with me," said Mr. Bennet. "Why would people create such things?"

"Initially, to stop a war, but even after witnessing the destruction from just two of the weapons, countries then hurried to make more and better versions. At times, they almost race to see who can create the deadliest, the fastest, or even the largest arsenal."

Fitzwilliam's expression was tight. "With such dreadful happenings, I cannot understand why you would want to return."

"Because it is what she has known all her life." Mr. Bennet's tone wasn't harsh but firm.

"That is true, though I do think I could be happy here. I could see so many works of art when they are first shown and perhaps even meet some of the artists—like you met Gainsborough, Mr. Darcy. He is studied in art history classes and considered one of the great portraitists. To watch him work would be incredible."

"You could simply surround yourself with those who value your opinions and do not object to your intelligence. My aunt holds such salons. She cannot abide those who are insipid." Fitzwilliam cleared his throat and turned to watch the scenery pass as they continued along while Mr. Bennet shrugged to her. They had discussed Fitzwilliam's new reticence since learning of Ellie's true identity. How could they not? They'd spent the past two days with the man, who had been terse and mostly quiet. Mr. Bennet, in the meantime, was thankful Fitzwilliam had not shamed her or made her plight public knowledge.

"We have reached the gates of the estate."

Much as she did the first time she saw Pemberley, Ellie pressed her face close to the glass. "They are much the same." Fitzwilliam's shoulders rose as he inhaled. Had her comment bothered him? *I would think that would give him some satisfaction. Lord, she missed his usual open manner with her.*

"What is the estate like in the future, Ellie?"

She peeked at Fitzwilliam before turning to Mr. Bennet. "In disrepair. The east wing has partially collapsed and is surrounded by scaffolding while it is reconstructed. The house has been vacant since the last owner died. Death taxes have made it impossible for many families to keep their estates, and many are owned by organisations that maintain them and open them to the public."

"And Pemberley is owned by one of those organisations?" Fitzwilliam's nostrils were flared. It couldn't have been easy hearing his estate was in tatters.

"Pemberley was purchased by an outside organisation."

"*Outside.*"

"Yes, they are Chinese. Much like the group who purchased Wentworth Woodhouse. I believe that is your uncle's estate, isn't it?"

"Good God," said Fitzwilliam. "My uncle would succumb to an apoplexy if he heard such shocking tidings. I must say, if true, I might just be tempted to finally wed Miss Bingley for lack of another solution."

Mr. Bennet snorted while Ellie gasped. "You must be joking. Do you think she would make a suitable wife?" she asked.

"I daresay she would be as easy to control as Mrs. Bennet and likely spend as freely," said Mr. Bennet. "My wife could not stop speaking of the lace on Miss Bingley's and Mrs. Hurst's gowns after the assembly. I have heard her price Mrs. Gardiner's gowns with an accuracy that is frightening. The ability is remarkable, I assure you."

Fitzwilliam gaped at them for a moment before he tugged on his coat and straightened. "Whatever she is would be wholly unconnected to you. If what you say is true, Miss Ellie, I must take measures, no matter how severe, to prevent the future of which you speak."

She levelled a hard stare at him while she stroked her kitten's soft fur. "The problem is death taxes, which make it impossible to hold so much land without the accessible funds to pay the debt when the master of the estate dies. Do you think marrying a spendthrift will be of aid to you? I think your predicament would be worse than if you don't marry at all."

"Ellie, look."

She returned her gaze to the view from the window, the familiar façade of Pemberley approaching, appearing strikingly different than the first time she saw the place. "Wow, getting this glimpse of Pemberley when it is whole and beautiful is worth the craziness of all that has occurred."

"Regardless of why you have complimented my home, I thank you for it," said Mr. Darcy.

"Even in its worn-down state, Pemberley is fantastic, but I cannot compare it to this. It's as though I've seen a brilliant work of art in its original glory." When the carriage drew before the steps and the door was opened, Mr. Darcy alighted, followed by Mr. Bennet, who handed Ellie down. A thin but formidable-looking woman stood before them.

"'Tis good to have you home, sir."

"Thank you, Mrs. Reynolds. I hope my express arrived with enough time to arrange matters?"

"Yes, sir. I have rooms prepared for you and your guests as well as water warming for you to wash away the dust from your journey. Tea and refreshments can be prepared at your request, and dinner will be at eight."

"Excellent, thank you," said Mr. Darcy to the servant.

Before they started up the stairs, Mr. Bennet offered her his arm to follow. Just before they stepped inside, Ellie pressed her hand to her chest to prepare for the blow of seeing those frescoes in the great hall.

Mr. Bennet gasped. "Splendid indeed."

"Isn't it?" Ellie gulped in an attempt to swallow that lump in her throat. As beautiful as the artwork was two-hundred years from now, it was nothing to how it appeared at this moment. "The first time I set foot in this room, I stood rooted to that spot there while I took it all in."

Mr. Darcy turned while Mrs. Reynolds bustled away. "Would you care to refresh yourself or would you prefer to see the ballroom first?"

Ellie held his eye without wavering. "The family wing is up the stairs to the left, the portrait gallery is in the east wing, which is to the right. You follow the hallway until it turns." She pointed to her left. "That is a drawing room. In my time, it's decorated in blues, the music room is down that passage and on the right, your study and the library are on the left across from the bust of Alexander the Great. To reach the ballroom, we need to walk around the staircase and take that route."

With a lifted eyebrow, Mr. Bennet had watched the two of them while Ellie had spoken. "I can assure you, Mr. Darcy, My Elizabeth has never been to Derbyshire, much less your estate."

Mr. Darcy held his arm out. "I would suspend no pleasure of yours, Miss Ellie. Pray, take us where you would like to go first."

Quick steps took Ellie on the path she'd mentioned and through the arched entryway under the stairs. "That is the Canova Oliver was working on when I left the future," she said of the statue of Venus in an alcove to one side.

"My father met Mr. Canova when he toured Italy and invited him to Pemberley. We have quite a few of his sculptures."

Her stomach was clenched when she reached the doors to the ballroom, and her fingers trembled uncontrollably as a footman stationed in the corridor opened the door for her. The room slowly came into view, and she did her best to take measured breaths so she didn't hyperventilate. She was here! Finally!

The fine crystal of the chandeliers glittered, and the mirrors scattered around the walls made the room seem larger than it was. Much like the Hall of Mirrors in the Paris Opera House, Palais Garnier, they gave the impression that the entertainment was all around them and not any one dance or event.

The largest mirror was in the same place, having pride of position across from two banks of windows which lead to the terraces overlooking the gardens. Her knees wobbled when she approached, but she stopped before taking that last step when her reflection would appear in the glass. She was such a coward! This entire time she'd been pushing to get to Pemberley—to see this very mirror again—and now that she was here, she couldn't bring herself to look.

"Are you well?" asked Mr. Bennet.

"No. I cannot stop shaking, my stomach is churning, and I feel quite sick."

"Thus far, you have not been one to let your nerves get the better of you. Do not let them do so now."

Mr. Darcy clasped his hands behind him while he waited. His reflection shone in the mirror, but nothing was off about it. She held her breath as she poked out her toe, finally taking the plunge. At a gasp from Mr. Darcy, she turned to the glass.

Her hands flew to cover her mouth. It was her! Elizabeth Bennet was nowhere to be seen, and the distinctive ginger hair, green eyes, and black and white checkerboard Vans of Ellie Gardiner looked back at her. She peered over her shoulder at Mr. Bennet, who shrugged.

"I see naught but what looks like my Lizzy and Mr. Darcy."

"That's not your daughter I see," said the weak voice of Mr. Darcy.

Ellie's head whipped around to the gentleman's pale visage. "What do you see?"

He gave an incredulous bark. "A thin lady with red hair, green eyes—not so dissimilar to yours—and dressed in an odd manner. She is wearing trousers."

"You see *me*. I just don't understand how or why. Oliver saw me and not Elizabeth when we looked into the mirror together." Once again, Ellie ran her hand down her pelisse to her skirt. Her reflection did the exact same.

"Mr. Darcy?" When they turned, Mrs. Reynolds stood in the entry.

"Forgive us, but I promised to show Miss Elizabeth this mirror, and she was too excited to wait. Pray, apologise to my valet and the maid tending the Bennets. We shall refresh ourselves soon."

"Of course, sir."

"Wait," said Ellie, hurrying towards the housekeeper. "Forgive me, but could someone put him in my bedchamber?" She held out Marlow with careful hands.

"Yes, of course, miss. I shall do so myself. One of the maids can bring him some food and water."

"Thank you."

Mrs. Reynolds's eyes flitted to each of them before she hurried out.

Ellie's gaze met Mr. Darcy's as she approached the mirror once more. It was now or never. Without hesitation, she lifted her arm and pressed her palm to her reflection. Something wrapped around her other wrist as the same tugging sensation occurred behind her belly button, and she was engulfed in darkness.

Chapter 25

Ellie coughed and spluttered as a painfully intense light forced her to cover her eyes with her hand. "Ugh, bloody hell. Why is it so bright? Turn off the bloody light."

"Miss Gardiner? Can you speak to me?" Another flash seared a path into her brain once again, making Ellie flinch back.

She frowned and tried to work her eyes further open. "Of course, I can speak. If you could just turn off the light. It's like an ice pick to my brain."

After a couple of blinks to rid herself of the white spot floating in her line of vision, she looked up at a middle-aged Indian woman with long, black, sleek hair and dark brown eyes who stood over her with what appeared to be a thick pen in her hand. "I am Dr. Singh. Do you remember what happened to you?"

Ellie glanced at the sterile white and ivory walls, then shifted in the bed, which crinkled as though it was made of plastic. "Where am I?" Her voice was scratchy and soft. Why couldn't she make it louder?

"You are at Chesterfield Royal Hospital."

The hospital? What the—? "How long have I been here?"

"You were brought in two months ago."

She gasped. Two months ago? If she'd truly been here for that long, that would mean her body was here for the same amount of time she was in 1811. Was that possible? She had been in Elizabeth's body, but now, it seemed Elizabeth hadn't come to the future, or if she had, she'd been stuck in the hospital.

"Miss Gardiner? Do you remember what happened?"

With a hand to her forehead, her eyes fluttered rapidly. Yes, she knew what happened. After touching the mirror in the ballroom, she'd woken up in Regency England and spent the last two months with the Bennets and Mr. Darcy. Hadn't she? She frowned and shook off some of the fog muddling her brain. Had her time with the Bennets and Fitzwilliam been real? Her eyes were heavy and her head ached some, as though she'd slept for too long. Well, if she'd been in the hospital for two months, she must've been sleeping since she didn't remember a bit of it. What if her entire time in 1811 had been some bizarre fever dream—sort of like *The Wizard of Oz*? What if it had all been in her mind? A warm, wet tear landed upon her cheek. Had she really never known Fitzwilliam—never stood face to face with him? He'd been so real. She'd touched him. "The last I recall I was looking at my reflection in the large mirror of the Pemberley ballroom. Do you know what happened to me?"

"You were brought in unconscious. You were determined to be in a coma, though we never discovered the cause, and you've been here ever since."

"What about my job? Has anyone come to see me—Oliver, Lewis, or Debbie?"

Dr. Singh held up a hand. "I know you've had two men and a lady coming to see you. I assume they're the friends or family you mentioned. Unfortunately, I do not know about your job. I usually work the night shift, so your visitors are never here long when I am. Visiting hours, you know? One of the nurses commented that she rang someone when you appeared to be waking. Maybe one of the friends you mentioned will be here soon."

Ellie pressed a hand against the bed in an effort to push herself up, but her arm gave way before she could sit up. "Why is this so hard?" The doctor pressed a red button on the side of the bed, which lifted her. Ellie managed to lean forward and support herself for a moment, even if she wobbled some.

"You haven't been using your muscles, so despite physio, they've atrophied some."

"In only two months?"

"It doesn't take long. The good news is we never found evidence of trauma and no brain damage was indicated on any of your scans, so you shouldn't have much difficulty regaining the muscle tone you lost. I do want to order more scans now that you're awake."

"No, no tests," said Ellie. She held up the arm with an I.V. and touched an itchy place on her face. Was that a tube taped to her cheek? "I want to go home."

"Miss Gardiner, you can't just leave. We need to do further testing. What if you walk out of the door and collapse again? We need to determine what caused you to somehow spontaneously fall into a coma in the first place. Fresh scans may make the differences between now and when you were in your coma more obvious. I don't know about you, but I'd like to make sure this was a one-time event."

"I said no!" Ellie grabbed the tube on her cheek and started to pull. That blasted tape had to go! Something shifted in her throat, making her gag. Ugh! The tube went up her nostril and down her throat? She squeezed her eyes closed while she continued to pull. She wanted it out now!

"Miss Gardiner!" said Dr. Singh lunging at her. "You need to stop. We'll take that out when we're sure you can eat on your own. Until then—"

Ellie pushed the doctor's grabby hands away, holding them at bay with one arm while she finished yanking out the last of the tube with the other, then grabbed at the I.V. "I said I want to go home!"

"Ellie!" The familiar voice made her stop. She drooped at the sight of Oliver in the doorway with Debbie directly behind him. He rushed to her bedside and took her hands, squeezing them. "What are you doing, love?"

"I want to go. I don't want to be in the hospital. Please help me get out of here. Take me home."

"I can't imagine waking up like this and discovering you're in the hospital with two months of your life gone," said Debbie, who sat on her opposite side. "But you need to let the doctors and nurses do what needs to be done before you're discharged. You frightened us terribly, and neither of us want a repeat of that day. When I found you on the floor in front of that mirror, looking so pale, I thought you were dead. Oliver, Lewis, and I have been coming for an hour each day during visiting hours so you had someone talking to you. We both read that it makes a difference with coma patients. I don't know if it helped, but what could it hurt, right?"

Oliver tucked her hair behind her ear. "Even in movies the coma patient can sometimes hear what's going on around them or it helps them come back. I didn't know what else to do. We all felt so helpless."

With a sob, Ellie covered her face with her hands. She'd spent all that time in 1811 hoping and wishing to get back to her life, and now that she was here, she wanted more than anything to get back to Fitzwilliam. To have Mr. Bennet as a kind of adopted father. How fucked up was that? For all she knew, that time was nothing more than her overactive imagination keeping her company while she had nothing else to occupy her mind.

A pair of strong arms pulled her into an embrace, and she relaxed against Oliver's shoulder. "I'm no expert, but I think you're supposed to do things slowly when you come out of a coma. As much as I'd love to put you in the car and get out of here, I don't think we can just bust you out of this place, even though I'd do it in a heartbeat if I thought we could." The last was whispered near her ear, making her almost smile.

She drew back and wiped her eyes. "They hired someone else to help you at Pemberley, didn't they?"

"Yes, but that doesn't mean I don't need *you*." Oliver rolled his eyes and gave a dismissive wave of his hand. "Girl, you should meet that mess of a thing they hired. She has no personality and hardly ever speaks. Her tattoos!" He shook his head. "She also hates most of the artwork and would prefer to work on modern art. Now I ask you, why would someone become an art restorer to work on modern art? The whole point is getting to work on the old masters, am I right?"

"Maybe she wanted to pay the bills while she creates her own work. Her tattoos can't be that bad, can they?" Blimey, her throat hurt.

Debbie laughed. "They look like something out of a horror movie. What did she say it was called? Horror realism? I had a nightmare featuring the one on her neck last week. It startled me awake at three in the morning. I couldn't go back to sleep after."

"That thing is not as terrifying as the one on her right forearm. She pushed up her sleeves the other day, and I caught a glimpse." Oliver shuddered. "If her forearms are exposed in front of you, don't look. Trust me. Compared to the one on her arm, the neck is like Peppa Pig."

"I suppose you don't need me at the moment," said the doctor, "so I'll just go and order the tests. I promise we'll get you out of here as soon as we can."

Once Dr. Singh had gone, Ellie shifted, making that horrid mattress squeak under the sheet.

"Here." Oliver adjusted the pillow and helped her get comfortable. "Lewis and I would sit you up while we visited. It was much easier to pretend you were awake and listening that way. Oh! They finally hired him to catalogue the library with the possibility of it being a permanent position—like a curator."

She shook her head and sniffled. "I'm thrilled to hear about Lewis, but I'm terribly sorry for frightening you so."

Debbie grabbed her hand and squeezed. "You couldn't control what happened. I just don't understand why there's no explanation for it. But, don't you worry about a thing. I gave the new girl a room down the corridor, and everything in your room is exactly how you left it."

"Now I just need a new job."

Oliver made an indignant sort of gasp. "Heaven forbid! You're coming right back to work with me. I'll make them hire you back if I have to. After all, they're not going to get that house finished for next Christmas without more people working on it. There's just too much, especially when you consider the Great Hall."

"As long as you don't lose your job for me. I can't have you do that."

He tapped a finger to the tip of her nose. "Don't you think on it another minute, love. I'll be fine. Soon, we'll get you back to Pemberley and all will be back the way it's supposed to be."

Oliver had no idea how that notion made her heart give a painful squeeze. "You don't know how much I want that." The first thing when she made it back to Pemberley was to check out that mirror in the ballroom. Would her reflection still be Elizabeth, or would it be her? She had to know if it was all a dream, and if the reflection was Elizabeth, that would mean her time in the past wasn't a dream after all, wouldn't it? The past two months had been far too real to be no more than a dream. Good Lord! Too many questions spun around her brain—and she couldn't answer a single one while sitting in this damn hospital bed!

She shoved that sharp pang in her chest down so she wouldn't drown on her own misery. She needed to fight and work to be discharged so she could check out that mirror and get her life back—whatever that life turned out to be.

Chapter 26

Air rushed back into Fitzwilliam's lungs, making him gasp and sputter before could finally heave in a massive breath. After one last wracking cough, he opened his eyes and panted, gulping in air in an attempt to relieve the ache of his lungs. What had happened? As Ellie had reached out to touch the mirror, he had grabbed her wrist, then after a shiver and a slight tug behind his navel, he was engulfed in darkness without any ability to breathe. The air seemed to be sucked from his chest until it pained him to a degree he had never experienced. Goodness knows he had tried to breathe but nothing could be inhaled until now.

As his vision cleared, he was on all fours upon what looked like the marble tile of the Pemberley ballroom—except this floor was scuffed and worn, not at all in the condition Mrs. Reynolds demanded of the maids at Pemberley.

Fitzwilliam rose to his feet, the air once again knocked out of him at the sight that accosted his eyes. This was indeed the Pemberley ballroom! But where were Mr. Bennet and Ellie?

His gaze roved the walls, and he pivoted in a circle to ensure he saw every single inch. His senses ached for denial of such a travesty—to scream that it was not possible, but somehow, someway, he was in the Pemberley ballroom, just not his Pemberley ballroom. How was this possible?

The mirrors in this room were cloudy in places and the frames in need of a thorough cleaning, with dust coating not only the gilt but also the glass. The white stone of the fireplace was blackened with soot, and a yellowish tinge marred certain places. Thank heavens Mrs. Reynolds was not with him to witness this. She would be appalled at its current state. Under her supervision, the maids kept the house meticulously clean. She would likely succumb to apoplexy should she be confronted with the state of this room.

When he turned, the mirror Ellie had sworn was responsible for transporting her to 1811 stood behind him, oddly in pristine condition when compared with the other mirrors lining the walls. "How bizarre," he said in a whisper. His fingers reached out, but he snatched them back before they touched the glass. Where was Ellie? He could not touch the mirror until he was certain of what would occur when he did. He could not depart this place without knowing Ellie was well.

Voices coming from the passage made him duck out to the terrace, closing the door and tiptoeing down to what should have been the rose garden, except no rose garden existed. Instead, empty beds inhabited the space with not even one rose sitting dormant and awaiting the spring. His stomach tightened as he took in the sight of his beloved home. Gone were the gardens his mother, grandmother, and even great-grandmother had painstakingly planned and oversaw, the greenhouses and orangery were in wretched condition, glass panes missing and the exteriors in need of a whitewashing, and the fountain his father had installed for his mother at the edge of the gardens was dry as a bone, with no water flowing to the small pool below, not even a dribble. Good God, could Ellie's claims actually be true? What other explanation could exist but hers? And after seeing this travesty, how was he to apologise for his disbelief?

His legs carried him around the corner where a massive scaffolding encased the south corner of the east wing. A few men were rebuilding the limestone exterior, though a gaping hole still allowed one to view what was once a large and elegant guest bedchamber, Lady Catherine's favourite.

His stomach twisted into knots and his eyes burned as he distanced himself from the wall, so he went unnoticed by the men working, his gaze fixed upon the damage to his once beautiful home. When he reached the front, he sank to his knees in the grass, gaping at the façade. Aside from the damage to the east wing, the limestone was streaked with black. Was it soot from a fire? The great house that had once gleamed in the sun was now downtrodden and dirty. The cold damp seeped through his breeches, stinging his knees, but the pain of seeing Pemberley in such a condition made that a trifling irritation. Good God, it was just as Ellie had described.

His chest pained him, his thoughts reeled, and his vision blurred. What had gone awry? Had his unwillingness to marry for rank and fortune brought about the demise of his family's legacy? He had been captured by Miss Elizabeth Bennet's fine eyes at the assembly, but when he first saw Ellie's, a hint of something more dwelled in their depths. Oh, to discover what was behind that change! Merely losing one's memory did not bring about such an alteration. In that time, she had become necessary for him to breathe. He would have been pleased to wed Ellie had she been at liberty to accept his hand. God help him, but he loved her, and he had discounted her reality when she had finally trusted him enough to share her tale. He had been an ass.

This was her time, though he could not remember the year. Heaven above had placed her in this time for a reason. No, no matter how much he would prefer it were otherwise, Ellie obviously belonged here, the Pemberley of the future. A tear rent through his heart at the thought of leaving her behind. Wait! If this was the future, the one Ellie spoke of, then where was she? He had grabbed her arm and followed her through the mirror, but when he found himself upon the floor of the ballroom, she was missing. She would have never left him on the floor as he was, coughing and struggling to breathe. Was she injured or hurt? Had she been lost in the darkness?

He swallowed down the terror in his chest, pushed to his feet, and strode towards the west side of the house, but when he drew closer, a door opened, making him take cover behind an overgrown hedge.

"What exactly did the nurse tell you?" said a tall Black man with no hair and wearing a bright floral shirt.

"I told you *exactly* what the nurse said," replied a woman with short grey hair as she hurried around an unusual thing that could only be a carriage. "They think Ellie is waking up."

"I still can't believe you told them she's your niece."

"Well, they wouldn't have kept us updated on her condition if I hadn't, and she has no family from what she's told us. Who's going to object?" The doors of the carriage closed, and Fitzwilliam jumped when the vehicle roared to life and began moving down the drive without aid.

"A horseless carriage? Ellie mentioned naught of that," he said softly as the curious vehicle disappeared over the bridge. He frowned as the import of what they had said struck him. *They think she's waking up.* He jolted and leaned against the wall of the house. Miss Elizabeth awoke claiming to be Ellie after an accident. What if while Ellie had been in 1811, her body had been in a similar coma-like state here? If so, was he thought to be ill in his own time? Hopefully no one would inform Georgiana. She would be beside herself with worry.

At least Colonel Forster had heeded Fitzwilliam's warnings. Wickham had been moved to a militia regiment in Northumberland. The colonel himself had also made a special trip to Netherfield to reassure Fitzwilliam of the blackguard's remote location and the strict nature of the officer in charge of that particular regiment. At least Georgiana was safe while he was away.

Fitzwilliam peered around the edge of the hedgerow. No one was about, so he hurried to what had been a servants' entrance in his time and entered. He peered down each possible route, ensuring no hint of a voice could be heard in the passages before he forged ahead. When he reached the kitchen, he paused. The room was exceedingly different and contained several unusual devices, but he gave no more than a glance before starting up the stairs.

Upon reaching the first floor, he peeked through the door before leaving the servants' domain and entering the family wing. He also ensured no one was in the master's chambers before slipping inside. His eyes bulged at the garish deep red wall coverings and gold draperies on the windows and the bed. The furniture had also been replaced at some point with the new pieces, which were ornate and more fitting of the overstated décor at Rosings Park than Pemberley.

He shook himself. He was not in this room to critique the last person who sought fit to decorate it. Ellie had said she lived here, had she not?

The room boasted of little he might associate with a lady, though he did find clothing and other belongings in what was once his dressing room. Inside the drawer of the bedside table was a book he had just recently used before arriving here. The cover was worn and the pages held the scent of dust. The condition of the book was as unsettling as that of the house. He had just written in the journal yesterday—his yesterday, that is.

With careful hands, he opened the cover. His bold writing jumped out from the page: *Fitzwilliam Alexander Darcy 14 December 1809 – 10 June 1812.* An odd sensation travelled through him. This was obviously the future. Why would seeing the final date on an old journal make the reality of the situation more tangible than before? He was still writing this journal in his time and had not yet completed it. Perhaps that was the reason for the near-constant tossing and turning of his stomach since he had found himself here.

He paused and lifted a framed painting of sorts that had been under the book. A man and a woman sat on a shale beach, the man's arm wrapped around the lady's shoulders while she held a child in her lap. The little girl's red hair stood out against the blue of the lady's gown, if you could call it a gown. The style was quite different, not covering the entirety of her legs or shoulders, and her long wheat blonde hair hung over her shoulder. The portrait was so lifelike! How was such a feat accomplished?

His gaze returned to the little girl, whose vivid green eyes fascinated him. She could be none other than Ellie when she was young. Although her hair was long in this image, she greatly resembled the reflection he had seen in the mirror.

He sat on the bed, removed a folio from the drawer, and opened it upon the coverlet. Documents for her mother's and father's deaths were inside, along with papers which listed her university accomplishments. She seemed to have few possessions—unless she had a home elsewhere and this situation was temporary.

After he returned all but his journal to the drawer, he crept over to a stretch of wall to the left side of the mantel. Had it been covered or was it still here? He felt along the edge of the fireplace until he found the hidden latch, releasing the door with a satisfying click. "Thankfully, some things remain unaltered," he said softly. From the contents, he would guess the room had remained hidden after his death. The books on the small shelf in one corner were his as were the miniatures of his mother and father that rested upon the top.

He wanted to see Ellie one more time before he returned to Pemberley—his Pemberley—and the secret room would give him the perfect place to hide until she returned.

But what if she was gone for too long, meaning he would be gone for too long? He released a low growl and tapped the journal against his other hand. "I suppose I must make a decision should she be away longer than expected."

What was he to do? It was important that he say farewell face to face. After all, remaining in this time was not an option. He would need to return and do his best to sire an heir. If he learnt anything from this experience and his acquaintance with Ellie, it would be that he could not, under any circumstances, leave Pemberley to Georgiana's son.

His father had taught him to be a careful steward so Pemberley would endure. The responsibility he had felt upon inheriting the estate had been overwhelming, yet it was nothing to the crushing weight upon his shoulders now. As much as he wanted to hide away, that same sense of duty must be instilled in the next generation and the generation following. He had to change lest the Darcy legacy falter, and if that meant he would have to rid himself of his feelings for Ellie, he would do so. After all, she belonged here. She could not return with him. She could not be the mother of his children, no matter how much he wished the circumstances were different.

The Darcy legacy could not be reduced to the skeleton of a once great home and the tale of a reclusive and eccentric owner. If his own reticence and disdain for society caused this future, he would endeavour to make amends and do what needed to be done for the sake of his family and the future of his estate. Whether he was successful or not, he had to try. He had no other choice.

Chapter 27

Ellie let out a long sigh as Pemberley drew closer through the car window. The last time she'd taken in this view, she'd been in the carriage with Mr. Bennet and Fitzwilliam—or had she? The house and gardens had been at their best, a far cry from how they appeared today.

The damage to the East wing seemed improved—the hole was smaller—and the façade was still dirty, and since nothing could be done about the gardens in the dead of winter, those had changed little in the last two months. Those were projects for the spring, when, no doubt, they'd also repair the cascade.

Despite the heaviness in her chest, she still couldn't complain much about finally returning to the only home she possessed at the moment. The last few days in the hospital had been interminable. Even if she'd been kept busy with physio appointments, tests, and other rehabilitation, she had wanted nothing more than to wallow in her bed and wish for Fitzwilliam, but her practical nature won over. She refused to remain in that place one second longer than necessary. The nurses that entered at all hours of the day and night to poke and prod her, the aseptic smell, and that ridiculous crinkly mattress made her count the minutes until Oliver and Debbie would bring her home. More than anything, she needed a full night's sleep and to regain the rest of her strength. Perhaps now, she'd manage both.

"Here we are," said Debbie when she pulled up beside the house. Oliver hopped out of the back seat, and after messing about in the boot, hurried to her door. She grimaced at the walker he'd unfolded and set in front of her. She despised the very sight of that contraption.

"Do I have to use that thing?"

"The physios got you back up and walking some, but you know you're still weak and unsteady on your feet. You're so independent that this has to be your own personal form of hell, but please humour us. We don't want to have to take you to the A&E again."

Ellie bit back a groan as Debbie put a hand to her back to help her to her feet. Whenever she rebelled against one of the doctor's decrees or her own physical limitations, Oliver always pushed her to see reason, but was it too much to ask for him to stop bringing up when they'd had to call 999 and rush her to the hospital? His guilt trip might be done out of love, but it still rankled.

"Aren't you a sight." When she looked up, Lewis stood at the top of the stairs. "Sorry for being scarce. That library is an unorganized mess, and for the past week, books seem to disappear as swiftly as I find them. I found a first edition set of Evelina three days ago—like all three books, and in pristine condition—then they disappeared without a trace. Between the books and the food that keeps turning up missing, I'm beginning to think this stately old pile is haunted."

Debbie rolled her eyes and laughed. "I'm certain the food is the workmen sneaking into the larder. The longer they're here, the more at home they become. If I ever catch them at it, I'll definitely be reporting it to the powers that be."

"But a ghost would explain Ellie's mysterious coma," said Oliver, putting an arm around her back while she took slow steps towards the stairs.

"I'm sorry, but how would that explain my coma?"

"Because you kept seeing a different reflection in the mirror. Perhaps a cheeky ghost was responsible for that as well as whatever made you ill." When everyone gave him a doubtful lift of their eyebrows, he shrugged. "Well, it's possible! I didn't say it was probable. The tests were inconclusive, weren't they?"

Lewis grabbed the walker when she reached the stairs. "Oh! Here, let me take that. The steps aren't big enough for it."

After Debbie and Oliver helped her navigate into the house, she hobbled to the foot of the servants' stairs and looked up. "That will take forever."

"Here, let me." Without warning, Lewis scooped her into his arms.

"He's like a knight in shining armour." Oliver's hand was pressed to his chest while he gushed. "Don't get any ideas, ladies. He's mine."

Ellie set her head on Lewis's shoulder. "Don't worry. He's a handsome bloke, but he's your handsome bloke." Lewis was kind and a friend, but he couldn't hold a candle to Fitzwilliam, who could reduce her to a puddle of goo with a look.

When they reached the top of the stairs, Lewis didn't set her back on her feet but brought her to her room, setting her on the bed instead.

"Are you hungry?" asked Debbie.

"No, I'm just tired. I can't remember the last time I slept for more than an hour or so at a time. There were just too many interruptions at the hospital." And she needed to be alone to wallow in her own misery.

"Then let Momma Oliver tuck you in." He helped her under the covers and arranged them just so before kissing her forehead. "Ring us if you need us. You have our numbers." After Lewis kissed her in the same way Oliver had and Debbie squeezed her hand, they filed out and closed the door behind them.

She melted into the mattress and closed her eyes. Alone at last! She appreciated their love and concern, but her heart hurt and all she wanted to do was have a good cry, which no one would understand but her. How could her time in 1811 have been nothing more than a coma dream? All of it seemed so real. She was able to touch and feel the keys of the pianoforte while Fitzwilliam faked her performance, she'd been able to taste and smell the delicious meals Hill set before them at Longbourn, and the experience didn't jump around as so many of her dreams often did. How could it all have been nothing more than a vivid story created in her mind?

A warm, wet tear tracked down her temple, and she stared without seeing at the canopy above her. Once she got this out of her system, she'd need to get back to normal, whatever that was. After all, who pined over a man who only existed in her dreams?

"And now, my good Sir, I almost blush to proceed;-but, tell me, may I ask-will you permit-that your child may accompany them? Do not think us unreasonable, but consider the many inducements which conspire to make London the happiest place..."[3]

She knew that voice! Her eyes attempted to open, but she forced them to remain tightly closed. In the hospital, if she dreamt of Fitzwilliam, he disappeared as soon as she woke. Now, she couldn't open her eyes, or Fitzwilliam's deep voice

---

[3] Burney, Fanny. Evelina. 1778.

would fade into nothingness, and she'd be without him once more. Her traitorous mind was evil do this to her. Why did she continue to dream of him?

"Ellie?"

Warm flesh encircled her hand, making her gasp and her eyes fly open. If she could've, she would've sat up straightaway and thrown her arms around him. "Fitzwilliam?" Lord, he was handsome. "I'm dreaming again, aren't I?"

His dark eyebrows drew together. "Dreaming? Why would you believe you are dreaming?"

"Well, I woke up in the hospital after being in a coma for the exact time I was in 1811 with you. While I was gone, I seem to have been in the hospital unconscious, so I assumed all that happened was a figment of my imagination during the time I was ill. Otherwise, wouldn't my body have disappeared, or if I returned to the time I'd left, wouldn't I still be in the ballroom? I have had no other way of explaining it." This was all making her mind spin.

"If you were dreaming, then I must be doing so now as I am very much a fish out of water here. I was worried when I found myself on this side of the mirror and you were missing. I happened to overhear someone mention you were waking up before they departed in some sort of horseless carriage. Without the knowledge of your being here somewhere, I likely would have returned through the mirror without delay, but I longed to see you one more time before I returned. I have waited to have one more moment with you."

He stayed for her. How could she not love him more for that? She had to work to sit up, and leaned against the pillows, reaching out and tipping the book he'd been reading so she could see the title.

"I found *Evelina* and have been reading it while I wait for you."

She couldn't help but laugh a little. "So, you're Lewis's ghost."

He frowned. "I beg your pardon?"

"Lewis was hired as a curator in the library a month ago. He commented that some books went missing as soon as he'd catalogued them. He mentioned *Evelina* specifically."

As he stared at her, she gave him a sideways look. "What is it?" Was there a smudge on her cheek? Something on her nose?

"You are different here. Your face…" he said as he sort of waved a hand over his own face. "I saw your reflection in the mirror, but seeing you here and knowing you are…well, you…but different is a bizarre experience. I cannot credit it. Forgive me if I stare."

Ellie relaxed and smiled. "I imagine it's a little like when I first saw you atop Oakham Mount. I'd only seen your portrait, and you lived two-hundred years ago. That day, I thought I had lost my mind."

He sighed in a weary sound. "I *have* to return soon, but a part of me wants to remain here with you." His hand reached out and traced the tips of his fingers from her temple to her chin, leaving a tingling behind as she gasped. "And as much as I wish you would return with me, I do understand why you cannot."

She grasped the hand at her chin and held it tight. How was she supposed to let him go? "Do not feel guilty for doing what you must. Georgiana will be beside herself if you're in the same state I was in here, and you have a responsibility to your tenants as well as your servants and future generations. You must return."

His tortured gaze held hers. "I do love you. No matter what happens; I want you to know that. My proposal was sincere, and I sincerely regret the hurtful way I behaved when you told me the truth of your situation."

With a hand on her chest, she nodded. "I understand your reaction. Suddenly hearing I wasn't Elizabeth Bennet with memory loss but a woman who lived in the future must've been disturbing to say the least. You must know I could never hold that against you. You were kind to me when most would've been cruel. As for your behaviour in London, I cannot fault you for reacting out of shock and disbelief to such an outlandish claim." She bit her cheek for a moment. Should she tell him what was in her heart? Confessing she shared his feelings wouldn't be fair to him, particularly when he had no choice but to return and marry another. After a peek at the clock over the mantel, she squeezed his hand. The gesture was as much for him as it was for her. "It's six in the evening. Debbie, Oliver, and Lewis should be in the kitchen making dinner. If you don't go now, you'll be forced to wait until everyone goes to sleep. You would be more likely to be discovered." He had to go before she began weeping like a child and begging him to stay. She refused to be weak.

"You are correct; I am sure." He lifted her hand to his lips, pressing them fervently to her knuckles. Without thought, she used all of her strength to lift herself from the pillows and put her arms around his neck. She took in a deep inhale of his cologne and buried her face in his shoulder, taking comfort in his embrace until she forced herself to release him. That one embrace would have to last her for the rest of her life. This wasn't fair! Why was it her lot to love people who couldn't stay?

"You should go." She wobbled when she straightened.

"Are you truly well?" he asked, his hand cradling her cheek.

"Yes. I am merely weak from being in bed for so long. Being unconscious for two months has some drawbacks, it seems."

"I should stay—"

She sucked in a breath as she prepared to cut out her own heart. "As much as I wish you could, you must return to Georgiana, and you need to leave now before Oliver comes to help me to dinner.

He gave a reluctant nod, kissed her cheek, hesitating for a moment before withdrawing, and took one last long look at her before disappearing through the door.

Chapter 28

Fitzwilliam crept quietly through the family wing until he reached a servants' passage, but before he could slip inside, voices startled him and made him hasten into the closest room, keeping the door just barely ajar as two men emerged and walked past. From what Ellie had said, they were, no doubt, Oliver and Lewis. Not that he knew who was whom.

"Ellie seems off, doesn't she?" said the Black gentleman.

"What do you mean? Considering she woke to find two months of her life gone, I'd say she's handling everything as well as can be expected."

"I suppose, but I feel like she's sad and a little lost."

The other gentleman paused and leaned against the wall. "But don't you think that can be explained by what's happened? She must be worried that the company will decide they don't need her after being gone for two months, and she has nowhere else to go. You said she has no family."

"That's what she said, but she never explained how or why."

"And you told the doctor about what happened with the mirror, so they checked her for brain tumours and a stroke."

"A seizure seems far-fetched, though, doesn't it?"

"I'm not a doctor, so I don't know. I honestly think it's the only explanation they have left."

The Black man sighed and shook his head. "We should get her downstairs before dinner gets cold. Debbie worked too hard on this meal for us to let that happen."

As soon as the two men entered Ellie's bedchamber, Fitzwilliam made his way through the door and down the servants' stairs. What a strange time this was? Was a lady's reputation so little valued that two men, wholly unrelated to her, could enter her bedchamber without a chaperon?

When he reached the ballroom, he glanced around to ensure he was not being observed before he entered. Ellie had been right to hurry him along. If he had delayed as he had wished, the two men would have surely walked in on him still sitting by her side.

He sighed and let his gaze follow the length of the mirror— the cause of all this mischief. The large framed piece stood tall on the far wall just as it had for centuries now. It was incredible that this particular relic had survived intact and in such pristine condition after all these years. How was that even possible? The object seemed to hold some sort of magic, though who knew the source? Before travelling so far into the future, Fitzwilliam would have denied the existence of magic or any sort of time travel, but now, those firm beliefs had undergone a drastic change. How could they not? He now possessed incontrovertible proof.

He took a few deep breaths. Hopefully, those would mitigate some of the discomfort of the experience. That sensation of having the air sucked from his lungs and the subsequent pain of there being nothing left to breathe was torturous; it must be how it felt to drown. After one last deep inhale, he reached out and pressed his palm against the cold surface of the glass. One blink passed, then two, then three. Why was nothing happening?

"Blasted device. Why are you not doing as you ought?"

With a shake of his head, he took a step back. What was amiss? Ellie had mentioned naught of a "magic word" or any special way of invoking the mirror's power. With a low growl, he heaved in another breath and set his hand against the surface. Nothing.

"I must return. I cannot remain here! My sister will be worried sick. Why will you not transport me back?"

He scrubbed his face and ran a hand through his hair. This was ludicrous! He was talking and raising his voice to a mirror—an inanimate object with no feelings on the matter whatsoever. The contrivance could not alter its opinion and suddenly allow him through, or could it? Good Lord! Ellie had fretted at being sent to Bedlam, yet here he was providing anyone during this time enough evidence to send him to the modern equivalent.

One more time. He would try once more. He steeled himself and placed both palms upon the mirror. When nothing happened, he slid them over every inch of the cold, hard surface in the event he needed to come in contact with a certain spot. When he reached the point where he began, he dropped his arms and backed away. Damn! He was trapped here? If Ellie had travelled to Pemberley upon first arriving in 1811, would she have been denied passage until a certain point or a certain event occurred? Who was controlling this...this waking nightmare?

With care, he made his way back to the family wing but followed the servants' passages until he reached the master's dressing room, which thankfully was not locked, and slipped inside. He peeked into the bedchamber, but Ellie had yet to return, so he stole across the room, and unlatched the secret panel so he could hide while he waited.

The state of the small hidden room when he had first opened it had been a surprise. No one had seemed to have found it after his death since the furniture and shelves held a generous layer of dust. After all, naught had been moved, all was still the same as in his own time—the same furniture, the same books, more of his journals, and miniatures of his parents and Georgiana that he had kept tucked away in a small case.

The book! He hastened to the bedside table and grabbed the copy of Evelina he had read to Ellie just this morning. Once he was back inside, he pulled the door behind him until it clicked. Even with it closed, he could hear voices inside the bedchamber, so he would simply read until Ellie returned. Perhaps she would know why the mirror was not cooperative. He needed to get back to Georgiana, so he had to hope. He had nothing else he could do but hope.

Two hours later, the male voices that had entered the bedchamber with Ellie faded some before the door closed. Fitzwilliam stood with his ear to the seam of the panel for any hint that Ellie still had company but, after the silence stretched for at least a minute or two, Fitzwilliam emerged with great care from his hiding place.

Ellie turned and startled at the sight of him, her hand pressed against her chest with a gasp. "What are you doing here? I thought you had returned." Her red-rimmed eyes and the tears pouring down her cheeks tugged at his heart.

"I have tried, but to no avail. I pressed my palm to the mirror, but the device seems disinclined to transport me to Chesterfield, much less the past. Was there a particular method for travelling through the mirror?"

She frowned as her eyes widened. "I...I don't understand. I have only ever touched the surface for it to take me wherever it wants me to go."

He exhaled and shook his head. What was amiss? There had to be some reason he was still here. "I can only imagine, then, that you must be the missing factor since you were present on every occasion someone travelled through that monstrosity."

"That can't be," she said in a low voice. "If I am to return to 1811, I could and would change the past. I have already altered the past simply by going in the first place and telling you and Mr. Bennet who I truly am. Besides, I am certain Elizabeth will be thrilled to be back in control of her own body, and I refuse to live as a parasite."

"What if you can return me then journey back?"

Ellie bit her lip. Lord, she was adorable when she did so. He gently touched her chin, freeing her plump lip from her teeth. Before he gave in to temptation and kissed her, he stood and began pacing at the bedside. "I know it is a great deal to ask of you. After all, you are weakened from your first journey through, and you would, no doubt, be incapacitated again for the length of time you would be gone."

"I don't know. I do wish to help you, but I'm too exhausted to do so this evening, and even if you carried me down, I'd be stuck downstairs if I returned straightaway. How would I explain that to Lewis, Oliver, and Debbie?" She pointed to the open panel. "Has that hideaway been there the entire time I've stayed in this room?"

"And long before. It appears not to have been touched after my death—Lord, but it is bizarre to speak in such a fashion. I have arranged my estate matters, but now, if I walked out to the small chapel near the river, I would, no doubt, find my gravestone. 'Tis unsettling, indeed."

She reached into the bedside table drawer and drew out one of his journals. "Perhaps this contains something that may help us. I was reading it before I touched the mirror." Her fingers flipped through pages until she paused. "You arrived at Netherfield, then you mention the ball and insulting Elizabeth Bennet."

"Have you never read this portion before?"

"No, when I first found it, I'd flipped it open and read one particular passage, then put it down until I decided to look at it again, starting at the beginning. I'd just reached the point where you'd resolved to visit Georgiana in Ramsgate."

"And now you know what occurred there."

"Yes, unfortunately, I do." She kept skimming through the precise and slightly slanted writing, turned the page, then inhaled sharply and flipped back. "Wait! This is the first part I'd read, but it's not the same."

"What do you mean?"

She held out the book so he could see the passage. "It's right here. When I first read it, it said a young lady of the neighbourhood took a bad fall and died. Today, it reads: *We received word late last night of a young lady who had been missing since early morning yesterday. While on a walk, she took a fall which resulted in what the apothecary, Mr. Jones, describes as a 'coma.' When Mrs. Nichols, the Netherfield housekeeper spoke to Mr. Jones, he expressed his shock at the lady's state since most who have taken such a severe blow to the back of the head do not survive.*"

"I remember writing that entry and no other of the accident."

Ellie stared at the page as though the words might change at any moment. "I promise you. Before I travelled back, it said the young lady had died."

His eyes widened. "That could only mean Elizabeth Bennet had died."

"Exactly," she said before gulping so hard it was audible. "Had my inhabiting Elizabeth's body prevented her from passing as she had originally?"

Dear God, that could not be right. If what Ellie remembered was true, and Ellie's body had been in a coma while she was in 1811, and Miss Elizabeth had not been roaming around this time and place, then only one explanation could exist. Elizabeth Bennet was dead.

Chapter 29

Ellie woke with a start and jolted up in bed. Had the house just shaken, or had she been dreaming? No memory of a dream existed, but that didn't mean anything. People forgot their dreams all the time, didn't they?

Without warning, Fitzwilliam burst from the secret chamber, his hair dishevelled and wearing only his shirt and breeches. "What has happened?"

"You heard it too?" What a relief? She'd questioned enough about her sanity in the last couple of months without adding one more thing to the list. Earthquakes weren't exactly common in England.

"I felt the house quake too."

Doors slammed nearby, so Fitzwilliam ducked back inside the small room and closed the panel right before Oliver knocked and rushed into the room. "Ellie, love, are you okay?"

"Yes, I'm fine. What was that?"

"I don't know, but Lewis is investigating. Debbie messaged me from her rooms. She's on her way up." The new girl, Fiona, was spending the night in London to attend a friend's art opening.

Lewis hurried in from the hall door. "There's a cloud of dust in the Great Hall that's coming from the east wing. Unfortunately, we have no way of safely knowing what's going on until the sun comes up, which isn't for another two hours."

"Where is all that dust coming from? I started coughing when I reached the family wing." Debbie wore her robe and slippers as she closed the door behind her.

"I think part of the east wing has collapsed again," said Lewis. "We'll need to call the company, but their offices in

London won't open for a few hours. It would be best if we can assess the damage so we can let them know exactly what happened. I don't know about you, but I don't want to give them the wrong information."

"I agree," said Debbie. "In the meantime, the sun will not rise until after eight, so I'll make breakfast while we wait. We'll also be farther from all that dust in the kitchens."

"A cracking idea if you ask me." Oliver stood and looped an arm through Lewis's. "We'll get dressed, then help Ellie downstairs."

"I can manage." At their sudden doubtful expressions, she straightened as much as possible. "If I don't use my muscles, I'll never improve." Ellie tried to make her words upbeat. They were being so kind to her. She didn't want to be rude, but she didn't want to be treated like she was incapable either. Fitzwilliam was another problem. She couldn't abandon him up here, but she couldn't very well refuse to join them. They would find it suspicious.

"Ellie can walk down with me," said Debbie. "If worse comes to worse, she can scoot down the stairs on her bum like a child." Scoot? Ellie stifled a groan. Yeah, that sounded dignified.

As soon as the guys were gone, Debbie helped Ellie stand so she could use the loo and stuck close as they entered the hallway. Ellie immediately began blinking and coughed. "Blimey, you weren't joking about the dust out here."

"It's terrible, isn't it?"

Ellie managed until they entered the servants' stairwell where she sat on the top step. "Give me a moment. You know, you can always go down ahead of me. I don't expect you to wait."

"Like I'd leave you here to fend for yourself. Not on your life."

With a sigh, Ellie hauled herself up with the railing and picked her way, slow and steady, to the ground floor. She gave the ballroom doors a passing glance. What was Fitzwilliam going to do? She was stuck with Oliver, Lewis, and Debbie until she could claim with at least a modicum of credibility that she was fatigued and wanted to take a nap. After one last break in the stairwell to the kitchen, Ellie finished the trek and settled into a chair at the long table while Debbie started coffee and tea.

The next two hours were spent eating breakfast and half-listening to the conversation around her. As much as she tried, she couldn't get her mind off Fitzwilliam, who had to be sitting in the master's bedchamber twiddling his thumbs while he waited for her.

When the first rays of light peeked through the windows, Lewis and Oliver left to see what happened to the east wing, leaving Ellie to help Debbie clean up—not that she could do much. She wasn't walking at her usual pace, so Debbie lapped her more than once bringing dishes to the sink.

"Why don't you let me do this."

"I need to move around, Debbie. The physio said so. Remember?"

"Yes, I know, but I'd rather you saved your energy for something more fun than cleaning."

The door slammed to the side of the house and a moment later, Lewis rushed inside and grabbed Oliver's phone. "Almost the entire east wing collapsed. Can you Adam and Eve it? Oliver used my mobile to call the London office so they can get through to China before the close of business. I've got to email pictures." He was in and out before they could ask even one question.

"I don't understand it," said Debbie. "They had engineers and architects in this place before we came. The house was considered sound as was most of the east wing. It was just the areas around that hole that were of any concern, and they'd shored those up with supports until they could be fixed all proper."

At the ring of the bell at door, Debbie sighed and shuffled out. She returned with an unfamiliar silver-haired woman trailing behind. "I swear my house shook, and I told Geoff, 'Mark my words, the east wing has finally collapsed.' And lo and behold, it has."

"Ellie Gardiner, this is Barbara. I don't know if Oliver has ever mentioned her mother, Charlotte, but she owned the inn at Kympton once upon a time. Her family worked for the Darcys."

"From what I've been told, they were a part of the staff when this place was at its best, but nothing was the same after Fitzwilliam Darcy disappeared." Barbara wagged a finger with the last sentence.

Ellie frowned. "Disappeared? I thought he died and his sister's son inherited."

"Where'd you hear that?" asked Barbara. "No, from what my grandmother told me, he arrived back at Pemberley after staying with a friend in Hertfordshire and had brought two guests, strangers, with him: a young lady and her father. The housekeeper then, a Mrs. Reynolds, was certain he intended to propose or had proposed marriage to the girl. No sooner had they arrived than they disappeared into the ballroom. After a few hours had passed, the man was found cradling his unconscious daughter, and Mr. Darcy had disappeared. The man couldn't answer one word about where Mr. Darcy had gone. A week later, his daughter died, having never awakened, and Fitzwilliam Darcy was never heard from again. The entire mystery was a scandal that kept London talking for months."

Ellie's breathing was shallow and rapid. Oh, my God! "What happened to Georgiana?" She tried to keep her voice from cracking.

"Oh, you've heard of his younger sister?"

"Yes, I cleaned her portrait, and I found Fitzwilliam's journal from when she was about sixteen, which is how I know who she was."

Barbara leaned forward just a bit and set her hand on the table in the way someone would when gossiping. What tea did Barbara think she had? "Well, according to the will, the estate was put in trust for her eldest son, but when she turned nineteen, she married her cousin, a colonel in the regulars. He left the army and lived with her at Pemberley, managing the estate. He was said to be an excellent master and landlord, but they never had children. A distant cousin was found to claim the estate, but my grandmother said he was a degenerate who came from nothing. He moved in and spent what was in the Darcy coffers as though it were a never-ending source of wealth. He lived a posh and extravagant lifestyle until the drinking and his rich diet took its toll. It's said he left an heir, a son who he left behind in poverty when he inherited. The son, likely in revenge, left the estate to rot. The government used it as a hospital in the first and second world wars, but no Darcy or Darcy relation set foot here again. It was as if the place was cursed."

Until Fitzwilliam... Shit! She needed to return upstairs. She needed to tell him what'd changed. Wait! What if the reason the east wing fell during the night was the altered timeline—but wouldn't that happen without the commotion or anyone else noticing the change? Fitzwilliam following her through the portal—the mirror, whatever it was, hadn't seemed to make a difference, or much of one. Could this be from him not travelling back? But how would that matter? The mirror wouldn't work for him, and now the history was so dramatically different that the house was suddenly in a different state and more fragile. If his remaining had caused this, what else would and could happen before she could get him back through that mirror?

"Ellie?"

She startled.

"Are you all right?" asked Debbie with a frown.

"Oh, yes, I'm good. Just sad at how the house was treated for so long."

Barbara smiled and asked Debbie a question as Ellie began biting her lip. She needed to get upstairs and force Fitzwilliam back through that mirror if it killed her. The differences were her fault. The timeline was altered enough by her visit to the past, but he followed her here. The timeline had been changed irreparably by his absence.

"All this talk of the past has me fancying a cuppa," said Debbie, wiping her hands on her apron. "What about you, Barbara?"

"Tea would certainly hit the spot."

Debbie started the kettle and began gathering the supplies, but after a minute or so, nothing happened, the kettle hadn't started making the tell-tale gurgling noise it always did. She put her hand to the sides of the pot. "How bizarre. It's cold." She flipped the light switch, but nothing happened. "Do you know? I think we've lost power." They'd never used the lights much during the day as a row of windows along one wall provided ample light when the weather was nice so it wasn't unusual that no one noticed the difference.

With a frown, Barbara stood and flipped a switch near the table. "Maybe a breaker flipped. Do you know where the electrical panel is?"

"I think so, but I'm quite hopeless when it comes to this mess."

"I can go with you," said Barbara. "Ellie, will you be okay here by yourself?"

"You two go ahead. I want to go upstairs and get dressed."

The housekeeper put a hand on her hip. "You shouldn't be on the stairs by yourself."

"I'll take it slow and sit if I need to. I'll be fine, Mum."

"I'll check on you first chance I get." With a huff, Debbie hurried out with Barbara on her heels.

Ellie stood, grabbed an apple and a muffin from the counter for Fitzwilliam, then shuffled as quickly as her feet would carry her to the first flight of stairs. At the bottom, she looked up and bit back a groan. Why did they seem to go on forever? Oh well, no time to whinge about it. She couldn't muck about; she had to get to Fitzwilliam.

One step at a time, she tackled the first flight, then sat at the bottom of the next for a breather. "This is bollocks, this is." She couldn't sit there forever, so she hauled herself back up and tried to climb a bit faster, almost bear crawling to the top. When she opened the door to her room, she stumbled inside. "Fitzwilliam!"

He emerged from the ensuite, drying his face and looking adorably mussed, a frown upon his face as he helped her sit upon the bed. "You appear as though you ran here. What is amiss?"

"That sound last night was the east wing collapsing."

With a nod, he let the hand holding the towel fall to his side. "Yes, I am aware. I explored in the servants' passages and could tell a great deal has given way."

"The power is now out."

"I beg your pardon?"

"Power, electricity. We have lights and devices that are powered by electricity, like lightening but travelling through wires. You may have needed a candle in your hidden room, but we generally do not need candles unless we have an outage or just like them for the look. Anyway, something has made it go out."

"I do not understand what this has to do with the east wing."

"I suppose it could have been shut off because of the new damage. But Fitzwilliam, you changed the past when you didn't return."

"What do you mean?"

She told him what she'd learnt of the original history, then spelt out Barbara's updated story. "Don't you see? It's all different."

"Georgiana wed *Richard*?"

"It would seem so, but don't you see? We must try to get you back!"

He ran his fingers through this hair. "What if the mirror's capricious nature keeps you from returning to this time, and you're stranded in the 19th century?"

"Then I suppose I'm stuck. Everything is so nonsensical. For all I know, I'm supposed to go back. We know Elizabeth died in the original timeline, and my presence kept her body going. I can't explain how or why. All I can suppose is something beyond our understanding or control is happening."

Fitzwilliam set the towel on the bed and sat beside her. "If the mirror does not allow you to return, would you consider spending your life with me? My feelings for you have only grown since I first proposed. I cannot imagine spending my life with anyone else."

"That seems like such a long time ago."

He gave a crooked smile and shrugged. "It actually was if you think about it."

She laughed and nudged his shoulder with hers. "I do have feelings for you. When you proposed, I had to clench my hands into fists to keep from telling you I loved you. I didn't know what else to do. I thought it would be easier for you when Elizabeth returned and knew nothing of the time we'd spent together. I was broken hearted when I awoke in the hospital and thought you nothing but a wonderful dream."

His fingers laced with hers. "Do not trouble yourself over your refusal. Your reasoning makes sense, though I am pleased to know—no, more than pleased to know you love me as I love you." His eyes searched hers for a second before he leaned in and pressed his lips to hers. As his lips moved over hers, butterflies began fluttering and spinning in circles, and her body warmed. She'd always kept people at arm's length, yet Fitzwilliam had slipped through her defences. How had he managed it?

Before she was ready, he pulled away. "I should put my topcoat on if we are to return through the mirror. Should you change?"

"It won't matter. If I follow you, I'll return to Elizabeth's body. Remember?"

"Of course." He held out his arm. "Shall we?"

Chapter 30

When they exited the bedchamber, Fitzwilliam paused. "I smell smoke."

Ellie sniffed and scrunched up her nose. Was that smoke? She stepped towards the great hall, but the passageway became hazy, and by the time they reached the opulent staircase, a layer of thick grey smoke hovered near the ceiling. She inhaled sharply at the black cloud coming from the east wing. Pemberley was collapsing around them. "I think the house is on fire."

"Good God," he said, his face pale. "What am I to do? I know nothing of how to resolve this in this time."

She grasped him by the arms. "We can't do anything about it at this point. We fix it by returning you through the mirror. That's the only way to stop this. We must hurry."

Before she could pull him by his hand, he scooped her up into his arms. "Forgive me, but we must make haste, and you are in no state to run."

"I understand. I'm a regular tortoise."

"You must understand," said Fitzwilliam, his face tight. "My grandfather rebuilt Pemberley after a fire. When I was a child, my father mentioned often how swift the flames engulfed the house. He was a boy himself when the house was all but destroyed. The family was spared, but two servants, who had been in their chambers, perished. The blaze prevented their escape."

Ellie glanced over his shoulder as he carried her through the door to the servants' staircase. Flames licked up the wall, consuming a tapestry and began running along the carpet on the floor of the family wing. Her heart raced in her chest and a small cry escaped. "The fire's reached the corridor behind you."

He set her down. "Forgive me."

Before she could ask why, he lifted her over his shoulder, her bum awkwardly in the air.

"Are you serious?" This was a terribly undignified way to be carried.

"Very," he said. "I could not see my feet holding you as I was, which could prevent our escape. If I fall, you could be injured further."

When he set her upon her feet again, they were standing in front of the mirror. Smoke billowed in from the doors, making her cough.

"Ellie!"

"Ellie, where are you?"

She inhaled sharply. "That's Oliver and Lewis. I have to tell them the truth. I can't have them risking their lives for me."

"You know as well as I do that they won't believe you. Remember how I acted when you told me of the mirror and its powers. I overheard Oliver mention last night that you seeing Elizabeth in the mirror was a symptom of whatever happened to put you in the coma."

She gripped his sleeves to steady herself. "But I have you to convince them."

Fitzwilliam shook his head. "I understand how you must feel, but we need to go, Ellie."

A loud crack rent through the air, and when she looked up, the ceiling was covered in flames. They were out of time.

"Ellie!" Oliver stood at the door, his mouth wide open as he stared at Fitzwilliam.

"Get out of here," she yelled at him. As quickly as possible, she grasped Fitzwilliam's hand and pressed her palm to the mirror. The familiar tug came from behind her bellybutton, and suddenly, a bright white light was everywhere. What was this? This hadn't happened before. Before, everything that surrounded her had been pitch black, as if she couldn't open her eyes.

"Hello, Ellie."

When she spun around in the direction of the voice, her mother stood behind her. She looked over her shoulder, then at her hands. Where was Fitzwilliam? "Am I dead?"

Her mother wore a pale blue, filmy gown that draped around her perfectly. Her golden hair shone, and her complexion was healthy and held a hint of pink. How was this possible? Did heaven really exist?

"Despite how this may seem, you're still very much alive."

Ellie glanced around, but the impenetrable white light surrounded her. Nothing else was visible. "Then what is this place? Where is Fitzwilliam."

"Fitzwilliam is well. Do not worry about him. As for your other question, the answer is complicated. You see, this is sort of an in-between."

"I don't understand. You make it sound like Purgatory."

A slight curve quirked her mother's lips. "No, nothing like that. As I said, it's complicated. Even once I explain as best I can, you may still not fully grasp all I am to tell you."

"What you are to tell me?"

"Yes," said her mother simply. "As I said, this is sort of an in-between. You must understand that we live many lives, and this place is a small part of where we go to rest before we live our next incarnation."

"You mean a sort of after-life?"

She lifted an eyebrow and tilted her head. "Yes...and no. As I said—"

"It's complicated."

Her mother smiled. "Exactly. Each lifetime is a journey. We grow and we learn during each due to different experiences and what we study and accomplish. During each life, we surround ourselves with mostly the same souls and ultimately seek to be united with our soulmate, the person we are destined to spend an eternity with."

Ellie crossed her arms over her chest and kicked out a leg. "I don't mean to be rude, but that entire concept is a bit cheesy, isn't it? And how do you explain when a husband or wife die, and the spouse left behind remarries?"

She shrugged. "I suppose it may seem overly sentimental, but it's how things work unless a soul opts to live a short life while waiting for their mate to join them in the realm of living again. As for your second question, one of the spouses, whether it is the first or the second, is likely meant to be a part of the other's life but not necessarily that soul they search for. Your attraction to them would be different, and your feelings unlike those for your soulmate. Think of how easy it was to let Fitzwilliam into your heart. You've known him for centuries. You've searched for him in each life lived, and his love fulfils you in a way nothing else does."

"So, Fitzwilliam is my soulmate, and I'm meant to return with him to 1811?"

"That's complicated."

Ellie rolled her eyes and barked a slight laugh. "So you've said. Is there anything that's not complicated?"

Her mother watched her for a moment, then stepped closer. "I'm afraid not. This has all occurred due to an anomaly in the timeline. No one knows how it happened, but Elizabeth Bennet was not supposed to die when she hit her head on that rock. She wasn't even supposed to fall."

"And no one knows how it happened?"

"No. You see, she was meant to marry Fitzwilliam and live a long life—you were meant to marry Fitzwilliam and live a long life—but somehow the unthinkable occurred and you died. Before the problem could be remedied, your body was dead and buried, and your soul had been reborn into another life. Fitzwilliam, unsure of what he was missing, became a recluse, and the timeline was altered. Fitzwilliam's soul became lost. He has not left the in-between since that lifetime."

With a flinch, Ellie dropped her arms and stared at her mother. "You're saying that in a past life, I was Elizabeth Bennet? Wouldn't I somehow know that?" This had to be a ridiculous dream. She was conjuring this up for some explanation to appease her mind. Too many contradictions came with her mother's version of the situation. Maybe all of this, including being back in the future, was a dream. This was getting to be too much.

Her mother took her hands. "Yes, you were Elizabeth, and no, you wouldn't know. We never remember our past journeys when we're on Earth, only in the in-between, and at the moment, your focus is still more on your earthly journey than here."

This was preposterous! She'd officially gone insane! "If you can live life after life and arrange for me to go back in time into one of my old bodies, then why couldn't you fix Elizabeth's death sooner?"

"We had our reasons at the time. This was the first viable opportunity."

"And why is that?"

"Because when all of the possibilities of the future were calculated, all eventualities showed Ellie having an early death. Fitzwilliam's soul is still lost and not living in 202_. You were supposed to take that job at Pemberley, you were supposed to travel through the mirror, and you're supposed to die in that fire."

Ellie rubbed her temples with her fingers. "This is too much to take in at once." Was it just her or did the explanation only go in circles?

"I understand. You and I are not speaking between lives, so you have no current memory of all that has happened. You would understand if the situation was different."

"But Fitzwilliam said my eyes, though the same colour, were different than Elizabeth's. It was how he could tell I wasn't her. How is that possible?"

Her mother cradled Ellie's cheeks in her hand. "Don't you see? You have experienced several lives since you were Elizabeth Bennet. You aren't quite the same as you were when he first met you in that life. Just as I am not the same as when I was Jane Bennet."

Ellie inhaled sharply. "You're Jane?"

"Yes, and I was your mother in the future. We spend almost every life related somehow. We always overlap. It's why I was chosen to speak with you."

She stared at the woman in front of her, then shook her head. "Then who is your soulmate in 1811?" She gave her mother a side-long stare. "And don't say Mr. Bingley. That would make him my father."

Her mother laughed and shrugged.

"No, no way." She shook her head. "I just don't buy this. For one thing, Elizabeth and I are nothing alike. I'm an artist when she couldn't draw a stick figure, I can't play the pianoforte and she could, and I adore coffee and she despised it."

"And if we had the same abilities and likes in every life, we'd have been bored by our second lifetime," said her mother. "No one wants to live the same life and experiences over and over again. Having different abilities and preferences helps us learn and keeps us content."

"For what? What is the point of all this?"

"That is an answer I am not at liberty to provide."

With a sigh, Ellie pinched the bridge of her nose. This was going to give her a headache...or could you get a headache here? "Of course, you aren't. Why even bring me here or tell me this much?"

"Because we didn't want you questioning if you were supposed to one day return to the future. Once you finish this journey through the mirror, the portal will be sealed and never used again."

"That would create a paradox, wouldn't it?" said Ellie. "The entire timeline will be changed again if I don't travel back again in the future?"

"Let those who engineered this solution worry about that. Somehow, I believe they have it covered. It's exceedingly rare that they don't."

"Obviously they failed when Elizabeth died hitting her head on that rock."

"With as many souls as they keep track of, I think they can be excused the one slip. Besides, not all souls are good. If you remember meeting Wickham in 1811, he has been a thorn in yours and Fitzwilliam's sides for a few centuries."

"Are you saying he caused this?"

Her mother lifted a shoulder. "We are limited in our abilities, especially when we are a part of the living world, so I'm not sure how he could have managed it. Some do manage to cause mayhem and destruction beyond what we can imagine. History books are filled with the tales."

Ellie exhaled noisily. "I feel like I have more questions than I do answers."

"That's to be expected. The mortal mind can only comprehend so much, and life is...well, complicated."

"There's that word again."

Her mother chuckled and shrugged one shoulder. "You can't expect me to stand here and tell you every secret of life and the universe."

"But why tell me this much?"

"As I said, I've told you so you wouldn't question your journey or purpose."

"What would stop me from telling those in the living world what you've told me?"

Her mother laughed. "You could announce it to everyone, but you were terrified of being sent to Bedlam for being Ellie Gardiner when you first travelled back to Elizabeth's lifetime. Could you imagine how many people would ostracise you if you began speaking of souls living multiple lives and time travel? Somehow, I don't think you would do that." She took Ellie's hands in hers once again. "Now, I hope you have the answers you need because it's time to wake up."

"So, this is a dream. It's all happening in my mind?"

"Ellie, you adored Harry Potter when you were little. Do you remember what Dumbledore told Harry in the seventh book?"

"You mean after Voldemort used the Avada Kadavra curse on him?"

"Yes."

"He said, 'Of course it is happening inside your head, Harry, but why on earth should that mean that it is not real?'[4]"

Her mother squeezed her hands. "Exactly."

---

[4] Rowling, J.K. Harry Potter and the Deathly Hallows. July 14, 2007.

Chapter 31

Ellie blinked, exhaled in a whoosh, and jolted up in bed. Where was she or should she ask *when* was she?

The fine cotton muslin of the nightgown was soft under her fingers and the warm coverlet upon the bed was a soothing blend of ivory and Spanish green. A fire crackled and burned in the fireplace. She glanced up at the ornate canopy over her head. Pemberley. She was definitely at Pemberley—the Pemberley of 1811—just as her mother had said. At a sharp poke to her big toe, she laughed. Her kitten had pounced upon her foot moving under the bed linens and was doing his best to wrestle it into submission.

"Lizzy?" Her head jerked to the window where Mr. Bennet regarded her with wary eyes. "Are you Lizzy or Ellie?"

"You ask an exceedingly complicated question," said Ellie, lifting an eyebrow.

"Do I?" The tone of his voice was one she'd heard before. He was more than a little intrigued. "I do hope you will share with me how."

"Well, because it seems I'm both." She glanced around the room. Based on his question of who she was, she should've known they were alone...well, except for Marlow. Even so, she still checked. "But, before I explain, where is Fitzwilliam?"

"Fitzwilliam?"

She rolled her eyes at Mr. Bennet's crooked grin and tilted chin. She would need to accustom herself to Regency England and their propriety and manners—for good this time. Her life was here now, so there was no time like the present to start. "Pardon me, but where is *Mr. Darcy?*"

"To be honest, I am at a loss as to how to answer your question. You see, when you touched the mirror, Mr. Darcy grabbed your wrist."

"I know."

His eyebrows lifted. "You do? So, you know he vanished before my eyes as you collapsed to the floor."

"I admit I didn't know that part. You see, I awoke in 202_ in a similar state to how I awakened here that first day. The first time I touched the mirror, my friends found me collapsed on the floor of the ballroom and rushed me to the hospital. For the two months I was here, my body was being tended to by the doctors and nurses in the future. The day I was brought home to Pemberley, Mr. Darcy, who had been hiding while he waited for me, emerged and told me how he had simply appeared in the ballroom after journeying through the mirror. We'd wondered what had happened when he followed me through. The logical assumption was that while I was travelling from lifetime to lifetime, he travelled body and all."

Mr. Bennet's forehead furrowed. "Explain what you mean by lifetime to lifetime. You say you are both Ellie Gardiner and my Lizzy? How is what you claim possible?"

Ellie did her best to explain her mother's revelations, not that she understood them all perfectly herself. Meanwhile, Mr. Bennet sat upon the edge of the bed and listened, his eyebrows lifting, his eyes widening at some places, and even nodding in others.

"I suppose that is why some people are more familiar at a first acquaintance than others, as if we have known them forever. I do wonder though..."

"What is that?"

"I was married to a young lady before I married Mrs. Bennet. From the moment we met, Beth consumed my thoughts. My heart was full of her, and she was all I ever hoped for in a wife. I was five and twenty when I made her the offer of my hand. She accepted without hesitation. The expression of heartfelt joy upon her countenance that day, well, I shall never forget our happiness. I rejoiced when she told me I was to be a father a mere seven months after we wed. About a month before she would have her confinement, she became severely ill. The babe came early. He did not survive. My Beth came down with a childbed fever. One day she was smiling and happy and planning for the birth of our heir, and four days later, she was gone. I mourned her for over two years. Many thought me eccentric, but I cared not for their lack of understanding.

"Mrs. Bennet came out around the time I re-joined society. She wasn't as silly or vain when she was young, and she was quite pretty. I danced with her at the assemblies and found her agreeable enough, so three years after my Beth died, I asked Mrs. Bennet to marry me. I was lonely and did not wish to spend my life in utter solitude. I also required an heir." He gave an awkward laugh. "Obviously, all did not happen as I planned. An heir never came, and with the birth of each girl-child, my wife became sillier and more frantic about her future when I die.

"To this day, I miss Beth. I still love her as much as I did when I asked her to marry me. From what you have said, I must assume Beth was my soulmate. You were named for her. As you can guess, her name was Elizabeth, though I always called you Lizzy."

"How sad," said Ellie. "I'm so sorry. I'm amazed Mrs. Bennet allowed the name."

"She was sixteen when Beth died, and Beth was six years her senior. I do not believe they were much acquainted, so I doubt she considered the connection. Her grandmother's name was Elizabeth, so when I suggested it, she likely assumed I was honouring her relation and not my beloved." He inhaled a large breath and shook his head. "I suppose your revelation gives me much to anticipate when I die, that I may live again and be reunited with my Beth just as you are reunited with your Mr. Darcy in each and every lifetime. I thank you for that."

She squeezed his hand. "Perhaps you should thank Jane. After all, she is my mother in the future."

"I shall do so, even if she will be exceedingly puzzled by the gesture," he said with a light chuckle. "I had a letter from her while you were asleep. Mr. Bingley called upon her before his sisters even returned her call. Your Mr. Darcy notified him of her presence in London, it seems."

"How very like him," she said. Ellie bit her cheek and jiggled her foot under the covers, prompting her little black and white furball to pounce and go on the attack once more. "I am worried about Mr. Darcy. He should have appeared in the ballroom by now. I am sure he was holding my hand when I was pulled through the mirror, but we were so rushed. I also don't know if speaking to my mother slowed my awakening. It almost seems like Mr. Darcy should've been here when I woke. What if—?"

"How were you rushed?"

"His following me to the future had repercussions. The evening I came home from the hospital, Mr. Darcy attempted to return through the mirror alone. At the time, we thought that the right thing, but the mirror wouldn't work. He returned and explained, but I wasn't quite convinced I was supposed to return with him. While we were sleeping, the east wing collapsed, then the electricity stopped working. The house was falling apart around us all of a sudden. When I realised the house was crumbling due to Mr. Darcy remaining in the future, we rushed to escape back through the mirror as the house was engulfed in flames. I pressed my hand to the glass as the fire tore a giant hole in the ceiling of the ballroom." Ellie blinked back tears and sniffed. "It's gone. All of it is gone."

Mr. Bennet took her in his arms and rubbed her back. "But you are here, and alive. Your mother said you were sent back to right a wrong in the timeline. Your lifetime with Mr. Darcy should mean this estate is well and prosperous for many generations into the future. Think of what you know that the rest of us do not."

"That advantage seems rather unfair, doesn't it?" she asked, drawing back and wiping her damp eyes. "If I tell him where to invest his money and what artwork to purchase—"

"What if you were meant to be a wealthy family? What if the Darcy legacy—the one that died with Lizzy when she hit her head—is important, which is why you were returned to her life with all of your knowledge of the future intact? Otherwise, why would they not have removed your memories? If these people can make you travel through time, why can they not replace your memories with Lizzy's?"

"How could they have not known Lizzy died until it was too late?"

He gave a crooked grin. "Apparently, we are as fallible in death as we are in life. I am certain I am committing blasphemy by saying so, but I believe I prefer matters that way."

"Where is she?" came a loud voice from the hallway. "When she took ill, you surely gave her a room and sent for the physician. You would never turn any friend or acquaintance of mine from the house when they were in such grave need, Mrs. Reynolds. I know you well enough to be certain you would remain a consummate hostess with or without the presence of me or my sister."

"Yes, of course, Mr. Darcy. You know I would. As soon as she took ill, I placed Miss Bennet in that room. The physician was called, but he said naught could be done. He has examined her each morning since, but to no avail—"

No more than a second later the door burst open, and Fitzwilliam stood in the entrance, breathing hard and his cheeks slightly pink. Had he run up the stairs from the ballroom? "Thank you, Mrs. Reynolds. I apologise for the fright I must have given you when I departed without word and with such haste. I assure you; it will not happen again. If you could have a tray sent up, I am certain Miss Bennet is famished after sleeping for as long as she has."

The housekeeper, who had been gaping at Ellie with wide eyes, turned her stare to Fitzwilliam as though he'd gone barmy. "Of course, sir. I shall send for the physician now the young lady has awakened."

"I am certain there is no need for him to be bothered," said Ellie, her tone light. "I am quite well."

The housekeeper's wide eyes remained large while she nodded. After a distracted curtsey, she departed the room, closing the door behind her.

Fitzwilliam stepped forward three paces and almost leaned in her direction. "When I found myself in the ballroom, I had to remember that you would not have been there with me." Almost as an afterthought, he gave a small bow. "Mr. Bennet, I am pleased to see you well. I hope you have been made comfortable in my absence."

After Mr. Bennet stood, he returned the bow. "Your servants were initially very confused about your disappearance, but they have been excellent, thank you. I greatly appreciate their care of Lizzy. They have been solicitous indeed."

"Excellent," said Fitzwilliam. "Miss Ellie, when you feel well enough, I should like you to look at the mirror. I cannot explain why, but it has blackened in places, as though it is much older than its actual years."

"I cannot say I am surprised. I was told the portal would seal itself after we returned, and I am certain that is the explanation."

Fitzwilliam's head tilted ever so slightly. "You were told?"

"Yes, the moment I was pulled into the mirror I found myself in a bright white room, though you could not see the walls. They were like light. My mother was there. She told me much of why all this has happened, even if it's more confusing than not, and she indicated the mirror would never transport anyone again."

"Then, you are to remain." His hands clenched into fists then released.

"Yes, I shall tell you the story in full, but since I just related it to my father, I would prefer to wait until later, if you do not mind."

He blinked and his chin gave an odd twitch. "Of course. Perhaps at that time, we may speak more of my offer."

Mr. Bennet burst into laughter. "Oh, good Lord. I can only assume you wish to propose to my daughter. You did so in London, and she could not in good faith accept due to her predicament. Now that she is free to say yes, you wish to strike while the iron is hot, so to speak. I believe a room adjoins this one through that door. I shall view the prospect from the window until you are ready to speak to me, young man."

The door was left barely ajar, but Fitzwilliam still hastened forward and grasped her hand while he kneeled by the side of the bed. "Ellie Gardiner, I admire you, I ardently love you, and I want to spend my life with you. Your life will be drastically changed from what it once was, but I want to be that constant that will never alter. I want to discuss books with you and have you paint portraits of our children. You can restore any of the artwork in this house that you desire," he said with a slight chuckle. "I only want you to say 'yes' and promise to be my wife."

Ellie couldn't help the smile that grew as he spoke. "When did you first know you loved me?"

"Probably when I first found you on Oakham Mount, and you finished my entire flask of brandy."

"That? That is the memory you choose? Pathetic." She smiled to ensure he knew she was teasing.

He flinched back a little. "Should I have chosen a memory more suited to flattering your vanity?"

She pressed a hand to her chest and gasped. "Vanity? Me?"

In a swift movement, he lifted himself to sit upon the edge of the mattress and cupped her cheeks in his palms. "Enough. I shall stop thy mouth." His lips pressed to hers, much as they had before, setting off a torrent of butterflies in her stomach. They twisted and flipped around despite the kiss being quite innocent. "So," he said when he drew back. "Will you marry me? Will you spend your life with me?"

"No, I shall spend forever with you. What do you think?"

He grinned. "Even better." His lips claimed hers, and she lost all sense of time and where she was until a determined clearing of the throat made them jump apart.

"I hope you have a question to ask of me, Mr. Darcy."

Chapter 32

Pemberley glowed in the morning sun, and the chill of the breeze off the high ridges of the Peak caused Fitzwilliam's cheeks to smart. He glanced at Ellie, who strolled by his side, her small, gloved hand in the crook of his arm as they walked along the river's edge. A slight pink graced her cheeks, giving her a healthy complexion. He anticipated a lifetime of walks such as this, his heart content and Ellie by his side.

Much to the shock and consternation of Mrs. Reynolds and the physician, his betrothed declared herself well this morning, risen from bed, dressed, and appeared in the breakfast parlour. Mr. Graham, in particular, had shown his frustration, insisting Ellie remain abed for a fortnight at least. The man had also approved of Cook's insistence of broths and teas for Ellie since the lady had not eaten for the time she was abed and had only awakened the day prior. Ellie had scoffed at the notion, yet for breakfast, she was served a hearty broth, a small piece of bread, and tea. Mr. Bennet laughed under his breath while his shoulders shook from his mirth at her expression. Without delay, the footman who served her food hurried back to the kitchens, his tail between his legs.

His beloved pressed a little against his arm with an impish smile. "Do you think we could persuade Mrs. Reynolds to sneak some biscuits from the kitchens? I am hungry."

"They are concerned and do not wish you to relapse," he said. "We returned yesterday, and your body has been without food for the entire time we were away. Mr. Graham does not understand how you survived without nourishment, while I attribute it to the force or forces who sought to reunite us. Mr. Graham has chosen to be cautious, and my servants' excitement at finally having a mistress must be their excuse. As we cannot tell them the truth of the circumstances, we can only allow them to care for you as they see fit. Was your broth and bread so terrible?"

She gave a low growl. "They were delicious but not filling. Perhaps I should give you a lesson on the backwards ideas of Georgian medicine? I poured the linctus Mr. Jones gave Jane into the chamber pot. Do not get me started on the use of mercury, lead, and arsenic during this time. And bleeding! How many people has that 'treatment' killed off? Not to mention, the liberal use of laudanum, which is highly addictive, for pain and mental infirmities."

He smiled and covered her hand with his. "I foresee you questioning the physician and eventually the midwife over your care—as well as mine and Georgiana's treatments. You will be delivering our children and treating the servants before long as you will have driven away any and all apothecaries, physicians, midwifes, and the like. We will all be irrevocably in your hands."

Ellie shook her head with a laugh. "Oh, no. I do not want that responsibility, and I'll have you know husbands in the future can be with their wives for the happy event of childbirth. By living in this time, I shall have no epidural or form of pain relief. You will simply have to suffer through it with me. You should know what you have wrought."

He gulped. While he wanted nothing more than her round with his child, he could not say he desired to see her in so much pain. He could still remember his mother screaming when Georgiana was born. The memory brought a shudder. "We shall see if the midwife allows it."

"Am I not to be mistress of Pemberley?" she said, straightening her shoulders and levelling an arch look.

"Yes, you will be, and I am quite eager for you to assume the role. Should you enjoy living with me in this hovel for the rest of your days?"

She laughed. "I *should like* it very well indeed."

He grinned at her response. She was trying, though she often slipped back into her usual speech patterns. A part of him hoped those would never fully disappear. She would not be *his* Ellie without them.

"I shall confess that I'm not sure of how well I shall tolerate being dismissed for nothing more than the sin of being a woman. That sort of discrimination still happens in the future, but we've progressed loads. If you remember, we vote and have jobs. We've even had female prime ministers. With the obstacles in place today, I'm in awe of the female artists who've persevered to be a part of the Royal Academy or even just had careers."

He frowned, and his hand tightened around hers. "I can only imagine how frustrating it will be but know I shall never belittle your opinions or your knowledge. I shall never treat you as less than a rational creature. We shall be partners." Perhaps his reassurance would set her mind at ease. He had not witnessed a great deal of day-to-day life during Ellie's time, yet he had found several current newspapers in the master's sitting room. Much of what they contained was quite shocking.

"I appreciate that, and I shall scold you if you don't."

"I should expect no less." He paused and turned to her, taking both her hands in his. "When should you like to wed? Your father sent for your family to join us, and Bingley will arrive with Jane and the Gardiners two days hence. I could have the banns read, and we could marry in three weeks, or I could purchase a common license and we could wed almost any time. I thought you would prefer the chapel here over that in Kympton." He pointed to the stone building on the opposite bank. The very place his parents and grandparents had married.

She gazed up at him, her head slightly tilted. "You have not said much since I told you about what happened in the portal."

That conversation had been their first discussion when they had removed themselves so they were distant enough from the house so as not to be overheard. He had let her tell the story without interruption, then one conversation led to another. His opinion had somehow been neglected. Now that she requested his view, how was he to describe his feelings on the matter? He blinked a few times and opened and closed his mouth. "I suppose I am at a loss for words. Your explanation is beyond any I could have imagined and much like when you confessed your true origin, I can hardly credit the possibility, though after travelling through the mirror myself and witnessing the truth, I know what happened and what was said must be accurate...so I am at a loss. How am I supposed to look at those around me and not wonder how they influenced me or how we were related in a prior lifetime? To know you and I shall be together forever is more than I could have hoped. The circumstances are all so extraordinary, but since I shall spend an eternity with you, I find I cannot repine."

She stepped closer—much closer—and slid her hand up his lapel. "Therefore, I shall marry you as soon as may be."

"That was a *very* appropriate answer, my love." His heart was so full. He had never imagined such felicity existed.

"If you mean my speaking, I am trying. After twenty-five years, changing those habits will take time. Do not expect miracles."

He laughed. "You are my miracle. I require nothing more."

"What a lovely thing to say. Will you always speak to me so sweetly?"

"I shall." He kissed her temple, relishing in his ability to do so. Securing time alone had not been as difficult as he would have imagined. Fitzwilliam merely offered Mr. Bennet the use of the Pemberley library, and the gentleman gave them leave to walk without him. Ellie would not have considered a chaperon, and he intentionally forgot to enquire of Mrs. Reynolds or request a maid. He sighed. "I am too happy to hide my feelings for you, Ellie. I am certain I appear a lovesick fool to the servants, but I care not. They must accustom themselves to the sight for I cannot disguise my affection for you, nor do I want to." His arm slipped around her waist. "What of you? Do you mind if I whisper sweet nothings in your ear and shower you with affection?"

"Not at the moment, but I suppose as long as you are not hovering over me every minute of every day, I could survive it for an extended length of time." One side of her lips was curved. She was teasing him, and he loved every moment. She squeezed his arm. "I must thank you again for the necklace."

"You need not thank me for what I am happy to bestow. My mother had commissioned the piece as a gift for my future wife, which is why I suppose you found it hidden away in the attics in the future." The emeralds and pearls fashioned to resemble a choker of grapes was unusual and a fitting piece, indeed, for Ellie, since she was as unique as the jewellery. "I am only sorry my mother is not here to give it to you herself."

Ellie hugged his arm closer to her side. "As am I."

"Your mother and sisters will be here by the end of the week. Would Saturday be agreeable for the wedding? I shall need to pen a request to the rector at Kympton as soon as we return to the house if you agree."

"Saturday sounds as good a day as any." Before he could respond, she rose on her tiptoes and kissed him, brushing his top and bottom lip with hers before deepening the kiss. Her lips moved confidently while her fingers wove through the hair at his nape. He could not resist her charms and soon lost himself the sweetness of her; her soft form pressed against him.

When she drew back, she began to pull him back towards the house, but he tugged her back into his arms. "Have you ever done that before?"

Her chin hitched back a little. "What?"

"Kiss a man," he said.

Her cheeks reddened, and she stepped back again. "I doubt this body has kissed a man if that's what you're worried about, but yes, in the future, as Ellie, I have kissed a man. We kissed if you remember. Why?"

His arms ached to draw her back against him and soothe her. "You were rather bold just now, and I happened to read a few newspapers while I awaited your return from the hospital. It made mention of weddings and births. I noticed not all ladies are wed when they have children in the future."

"No, not all couples are wed or even in a relationship when they have children or have sex."

"Have sex?"

"Intercourse?" The red of her face had spread down her neck and to her chest.

"Ah, in this time, sex means male or female. You are saying it means the act?"

"It can mean both, depending upon how it's used." She let out a long exhale. "Look, twenty-five-year-old virgins are far from common in 202_. Yes, I have been with a few men, but before you say anything, I never had deep feelings for any of them. After my parents were killed in a car wreck, I tended to push people away. I never let myself get too close to anyone until I came to this time. Since I am certain Elizabeth has never…well, I'm not particularly excited about losing my virginity again if you must know. That's usually a one-time event. Since we're on the subject, maybe I should ask you your history. Most men of society were not celibate in the early 1800s, and ladies became pregnant without being married only it was hushed up and the children often given to tenants or foundling homes. Because I have had those experiences, albeit in a different body, are you going to be a hypocrite and change your mind about marrying me?

He flinched and lunged forward, taking her hands before she could retreat further. "No, I have no wish to change my mind. Forgive me. I should not have given in to my curiosity, I suppose, though I never considered you would endure losing your maidenhead twice. I apologise for that."

"I have only ever loved you," she said softly.

"Like you, I have never loved another. I believe I was waiting for you, whether you were called Elizabeth Bennet or Ellie Gardiner, to make my life whole. I am all anticipation to live this and all my lives with you. Good fortune, it seems, is mine for an eternity."

"You may be speaking differently in a few years." Her lively laughter washed over him and soothed him.

"Impossible, as my love for you will only grow. I can have naught but praise for the beautiful yet rational creature who is my wife." As he drew her into his arms once more, a loud rumbling made her giggle and cover her stomach. "We should return to the house. Mayhap we can persuade Mrs. Reynolds that the chill of the day necessitates some tea and biscuits."

"Fitzwilliam, I believe if you can persuade Mrs. Reynolds to our cause, you will be the best betrothed in the world."

The End

Epilogue

Lord Fitzwilliam Alexander Darcy V, the Earl of Holderness, or William to his friends and family, closed the journal before him and stroked the cover. Part of a series of journals, the book, passed down from father to son, was written by the first Fitzwilliam Darcy and his wife Elizabeth during the 1800s and had become a long-held secret amongst the first sons of the Darcy family since the death of that first Fitzwilliam in 1856.

The coveted advice and tips the books contained had ensured the continued prosperity of the Darcy family for over two hundred years through sound investments that still benefitted the family to this day. Cotton mills, the railway, and vast swaths of property in London and the surrounding areas that were once slums and cheaply purchased in the early 1800s became a virtual goldmine worth an enormous amount of money. After the institution of the death tax, the sons who followed continued as their predecessors had before them, investing and squirreling away funds for the next heir. Those gentlemen strategically sold no more property than necessary to forge ahead without harming their overall wealth and developed other assets to become long-term sources of income for the next generation. It was said that the Holderness Earldom had been gifted to them by George V due to their fortune as well as a singular financial tip that had increased the monarch's personal wealth substantially, not to mention their philanthropy for those in need, giving large sums of money to benefit the latest medical research, the homeless, and the hungry. William's own brother Henry was a researcher at Oxford and making substantial progress with his experimental treatment for lung cancer.

To the public, the source of their success remained a well-guarded mystery. None of William's predecessors could explain the knowledge or foretelling of what was said in the book; however, during a recent repair of the master's chambers, a secret room was unearthed. While searching its contents, William had stumbled upon the journals of Elizabeth Darcy, or "Ellie" as his ancestor, her husband, had called her. The secret chamber appeared to have been abandoned with Fitzwilliam's and Elizabeth's deaths. His mind was still reeling at the revelations they contained. They were too fantastical to be believed—time travel and reincarnation? Had Elizabeth some mental illness Fitzwilliam had successfully kept hidden from the world? Nothing indicated she'd ever been locked away. Her husband wrote of her with so much affection, the reader of his words was left in no doubt that his "Ellie" was the love of his life. So, how to explain Elizabeth's writings? While the rational part of his brain rejected her claims, how could he ignore the accuracy of the information left for the Darcy heirs?

His head jolted up at a knock. "Yes?"

"Sir," said Geoffrey, his secretary. "Miss Gardiner has arrived. I put her in the blue drawing room to wait."

"Thank you."

As soon as Geoffrey closed the door, William pulled over Elizabeth's journal and flipped to a sketch, one that he'd stared at often since he'd found it six months ago. One that Elizabeth had drawn of her appearance before she'd supposedly travelled back to 1811. What was he doing? This was impossible, wasn't it? He should've hired an investigator. They could've sorted this in a matter of days—tracked her down, taken a few covert photos, conducted a background check, and the entire thing could've been over and done with no more than a small pay-out and very little time and effort on his side. Instead, he'd located this Ellie person on his own—stumbled across her name was more like it—and summoned her to Pemberley under the pretence of some job. This was mental, it was!

He blew out a breath, scrubbed his face with his hands, then stood and headed towards the answer to his family's legacy. When he reached the drawing room, he paused with his hand on the doorknob and steadied himself. He needed to be unflappable when he entered. No matter what or whom this young woman was, she couldn't be what the journal claimed.

When he stepped inside, an average-height, thin woman stood in front of the mantel, gazing at the painting above, her ginger-hair shiny and falling almost to her shoulders.

"That's probably my favourite Constable."

Miss Gardiner whirled around. "I'm sorry. I didn't hear you come in."

William stared and had to give his head a slight shake. Dear God! From the style of her hair to the small mole above her lip, she was the drawing in the journal to a "T." How was this possible?

"Lord Holderness?"

He startled and straightened. "Forgive me. You seem young for the experience contained in your CV."

She smiled and turned to face him. "No worries. You wouldn't believe how often I've been told that. My supervisor at the National Gallery, Oliver, said the same when I started my internship. I've simply been fascinated by art my entire life and knew what I wanted. It made my uni and career decisions easy and made me determined to achieve my goals straightaway. That said, I could also make a similar statement about you. You appear rather young for an earl. I had an image in my mind of a stodgy old man." She stepped forward and offered her hand, which he shook, receiving a bizarre jolt. What was that?

He glanced down at his palm as he chuckled, then rubbed his hands together to try and rid of himself of that buzz. "I'm surprised you didn't Google me."

"No," she said, then arched one eyebrow. "Though now that I'm here, I guess it may have been a good idea. She glanced over her shoulder at the Constable and back to him. "I can't tell you how excited I am by the possibility of curating and restoring your family's artwork. I saw several of your family's collection when they were on loan to the National Gallery for the special exhibition on British landscape. The entire Darcy catalogue is rumoured to be incredible. People have often questioned how one family amassed such an influential collection."

He nodded. "I suppose we possess an eye for art. One of my ancestors, Elizabeth Darcy, adored art. She painted and selected many of the works that were purchased during her lifetime— Constable, Turner, Angelica Kauffman, Elisabeth Vigee-LeBrun—"

"I hope to see them one day. The art world did so much to exclude female artists at that time. I admire greatly those who lived their dreams. Kauffman and Vigee-LeBrun are two of my favourites."

Her vivid green eyes glowed and a quality in their depths pulled at something inside him. He couldn't help but study every nuance from the slight tilt of her head when she spoke of her love of art to how she now ran her teeth lightly over her bottom lip.

"Sir?"

He jumped and shook his head. "Forgive me. Perhaps I need some tea to fortify me for the rest of the afternoon. Would you care for some?"

She smiled and nodded. "Tea sounds lovely. I always have a cup in the afternoon for the same reason."

With a wave for her to follow, he led her down the old servants' staircase to the kitchen. "Debbie?" he said as he stepped inside.

The housekeeper stepped out of the pantry and wiped her hands on a towel. "Yes, sir?"

"My guest and I would like some tea."

"Of course. I'll have a tray ready in ten minutes. Would you like it in the library as usual?"

"Yes, thank you."

He attempted a smile, but he'd always been somewhat awkward, particularly with people he didn't know. "If you like, I can give you a sort of tour while we wait. You can see some of that artwork you've heard so much about."

"That would be brilliant." Her smile could've lit his stately old pile, it was so bright.

He led her up to the Great Hall where she stood in one place and turned in circles, examining the frescoes on the walls and ceiling. When they entered his study, she stopped and studied the landscape of Pemberley. "I do not believe I know this artist."

"That is Elizabeth Darcy's. She painted several landscapes of Pemberley as well as portraits of the family, many of which still hang in the house and dower cottage to this day."

Miss Gardiner tilted her head and stared at the piece a little longer. "I like her use of colour and how she captured the glow of the sunlight on the limestone of the house. It's an excellent representation."

"She had some relations by the name of Gardiner. Could you somehow be related? I believe they lived on Gracechurch Street."

The lady's eyebrows lifted. "What a bizarre coincidence. I suppose it is possible, though not by blood. My father was adopted as an infant. I have my family tree tucked away somewhere. I can check if you like."

"No need to go to that trouble. I was merely curious is all."

"If you're ever in search of a curator for your collection of books, Oliver's partner, Lewis, would be excellent. He currently works at the British Museum but has been hoping for a position in an old house for some time."

"Did Lewis ask that you put him forward?" he asked with one side of his lips tugging upward.

"Sorry, but yes."

He chuckled. "My current curator is nearing retirement. Have your friend email me his CV, and I'll certainly consider him if he's qualified for the post."

She startled a bit then grinned. "Oh, he'll be chuffed to bits. Thank you."

After a nod, Darcy held out his arm towards the door. "Our tea should be ready."

On their way to the library, Ellie pointed to a set of doors. "What is that?"

"That is the ballroom." He opened the doors and walked inside with her right behind him. He didn't have to look to know she was there. His upper back prickled at her nearness. "The idea behind the decoration—"

"Reminds me of the Paris Opera House, where the architect intended to make the patron feel as much a part of a show as the actual performance."

"That was precisely the same intention here, though started earlier. The large mirror has been on that far wall since the 1760s, and the rest were added over time."

"The age must be why it has blackened some."

"That's the general theory." Though not the reason Elizabeth Darcy gave in her journals.

Miss Gardiner stepped directly in front of it, making William hold his breath and the hair on his arms stand on end. Despite the claims in the journal, her reflection didn't change to that of Elizabeth nor were her clothes the empire waisted gowns of the early 1800s.

"My lord?"

Again, his head jerked so their gazes met in the mirror. "If you would prefer, you may call me William like my friends and family. Fitzwilliam is much too formal for my tastes, and the title is somewhat..."

"Weighty?"

He laughed. "That's a good way to describe it. Lord Holderness was my father, so when I took on the title, I always felt like a bit of an imposter." Good Lord, William, stop talking! Why was he telling her this?

Miss Gardiner looked over her shoulder. "I think I can understand. My parents were killed in a car accident when I was young. I've been called Ms. Gardiner by strangers since, and it always seems off. Not quite Mrs. Gardiner, but close enough to make me uncomfortable. I hope I am not rude to ask, but would you mind if I touch the mirror? I promise to clean it if your housekeeper objects."

Was that a good idea? Her gaze remained on him while her hand reached out towards the shiny surface. His heart pounded against his ribs, and his hand clenched. Finally, at the last moment, just as her palm made contact, he grabbed the wrist that still hung by her side. "Ellie, no!"

Acknowledgements

Plot ideas can come at the most arbitrary of moments, and this one certainly appeared out of nowhere. My husband was returning from Texas after airline cancellations stranded my daughter in Maryland with us. I was cleaning or working around the house. I remember the story in my head started with Ellie touching the mirror. Usually, I lose interest if I know an entire story from the beginning, but I knew the basic outline of this one in my head before I called my husband and gave him the entire plot while he drove. We've always been big sci-fi/fantasy fans and date nights have often included Star Trek, Star Wars, and others. We talked about all of the possibilities of the plot as well as the possible paradox. I couldn't resist giving a little nod to Harry Potter with the quote and the tug behind the bellybutton even though the mirror wasn't a portkey.

So, first and foremost, I have to thank my husband, who patiently listened. JAFF really isn't his thing, but I think he was a bit excited for me to put a time travel spin on the story.

To Brenna, who has become my sensitivity reader over the past couple of years, I thank you for taking that first read through. Sometimes you've caught things I need to resolve, and you ensure my LGBTQ characters are real.

Next is Carol for her mad editing skills. She pushes for me to not be lazy and to always keep the vocabulary time appropriate. This book was a challenge because you always had to look at who was talking before calling out a word. Can't blame her. Even when writing, I had to keep straight which POV I was writing and which character was speaking, or I'd have totally lost it.

My proofreaders save me a great deal of stress and keep me from going bald before release. Thank you, Marie, Debbie, and Patty. I appreciate your skills immensely!!

Thank you to my children. B who still calls home even if it's to chit chat for an hour while we watch her cook or cuddle with #TheRealGrunt. E and J still live at home and will completely ignore that I'm typing away when they plonk down on the sofa and turn on the TV. It's still nice when I talk to a teacher or one of their friends' moms and my kids have told them I write. When adults ask what I do, that's what my children tell them, even when I was teaching fitness classes.

And lastly, thank you to everyone who bought the book. Without you, I wouldn't have an excuse to type out whatever is in my head. I've had scenes and stories in my head for years that are now in print, which makes room for new ones. I love that, so thank you from the bottom of my heart.

About the Author

L.L. Diamond is more commonly known as Leslie to her friends and Mom to her three kids. A native of Louisiana, she spent the majority of her life living within an hour of New Orleans before following her husband all over as a military wife. Louisiana, Mississippi, California, Texas, New Mexico, Nebraska, England, Missouri, and now Maryland have all been called home along the way.

Aside from mother and writer, Leslie considers herself a perpetual student. She has degrees in biology and studio art but will devour any subject of interest simply for the knowledge. Her most recent endeavors have included certifications to coach swimming and a number of fitness certifications. As an artist, her concentration is in graphic design, but watercolor is her medium of choice with one of her watercolors featured on the cover of her second book, *A Matter of Chance*. She is also a member of the Jane Austen Society of North America. Leslie also plays flute and piano, but much like *Pride and Prejudice's*

Elizabeth Bennet, she is always in need of practice! She also adores travel.

www.ingramcontent.com/pod-product-compliance
Lightning Source LLC
Chambersburg PA
CBHW022020240626
47154CB00007B/2187